I0600368

THE DAGGER'S TIDE

THE FATED PATHS DUOLOGY

MACAYLA DAWN

Copyright © 2025 by Macayla Dawn

All rights reserved.

No part of this book may be reproduced in any form or by any electronic or mechanical means, including information storage and retrieval systems, without written permission from the author, except for the use of brief quotations in a book review.

Without in any way limiting the author's exclusive rights under copyright, any use of this publication to "train" generative artificial intelligence (AI) technologies to generate text is expressly prohibited. The author reserves all rights to license uses of this work for generative AI training and development of machine learning language models.

ISBN: 979-8-9931390-0-5 (Paperback)

ISBN: 979-8-9931390-1-2 (E-Book)

The story, all names, characters, and incidents portrayed in this production are fictitious. No identification with actual persons (living or deceased), places, buildings, and products is intended or should be inferred.

This book was written entirely by a human author. No generative AI was used in creating this work during any step of the conception process.

Cover Image by Getcovers.

For those unsure of which path to take.
Why not both?

BEFORE YOU READ

The idea behind The Fated Paths Duology came to me in a dream.

Growing up, I was a big fan of 'choose your own adventure' books. I began thinking of my favorite fantasy series—how they follow the main character making a hard decision after hard decision. I thought, 'What would have happened if they had chosen a different path?'.

The Fated Paths Duology follows Penelope Frey, underestimated seventh heir of Paralia, faced with a choice. Will she travel to Oresteia, her family's opposing Kingdom, and help them find what they claim she stole? Or will she follow her best friend to war, fighting for Paralia's army when that same artifact isn't found? Each book in this duology gives the reader a chance to explore what 'could have been' had Penelope picked the other option. Rather than being left with a "what if", we can experience each life Penelope might have gotten to live.

I believe we are all left with choices, and those choices make us who we are. In the end, who will Penelope become?

This isn't a duology like you've ever read before. I hope you enjoy.

Love,
Macayla

ORESTEIA

PARALIA

THE
KHIONEAN SEA

COPOLIS

ESCAEUS

THE STRONGHOLD

THE JANUS TREE

ORESTEIAN
GATE

THE EREMOS COTTAGE

THE
STENOS ISTHMUS

THE JANUS TREE

PARALIAN
GATE

KOMEUS

THE PALACE

THE
NERONIAN SEA

PROLOGUE

TO WATCH HER EXIST WAS TO WATCH THE SUN RISE upon the waves.

She was my constant, as certain as the tide. The warmth of her embrace eased my mind in a way only years together could. Her brown eyes held mine with trust, with understanding. Sunlight clung to her skin, as if it knew it belonged there. Her dark curls danced in the salty breeze—untamed, just like her very soul. Her laugh was the sound of the sea meeting the shore: familiar, endless.

But she never saw herself this way.

Not the way I did.

CHAPTER ONE

To be drawn to light is to feel alive.

To bask in the warmth of the sun is to feel at home.

Unfortunately for me, Paralia has not felt like home in a long time. Ever since my teenage years, I have longed to experience something new. I have begged the sun to hide, so that I may experience the touch of rain on my skin, or the bite of cold air upon my nose.

And yet, the sun does not give in. Day after day, my bright star shows up and asks me to drown in its rays. My only reprieve is the night sky and the coolness that evening brings.

So here I am, stuck lying on these sandy shores of Paralia, recharging my soul the only way I know how—allowing the sun to soak into my heart and skin.

* * *

"P! I've been looking everywhere for you."

Squinting my eyes open, I turn my head toward the voice coming to sit next to me.

"Cal, don't act like you didn't know I was here." I resume lying on my back with my face toward the sun. Callious and I just chatted not even an hour ago about where I would be spending the day. Truthfully, he purposefully likes to push my buttons.

All of a sudden, the feel of sand coats my body as he throws mounds onto me.

"Cal!" I giggle and rush upright, trying to spit the sand out of my mouth and brush it off my face. "What has gotten into you?"

"Oh no, I can't believe I got sand on you! I suppose that means we need to take a swim to get it off?" He lifts an eyebrow at me and pastes a smirk on that stupid tan face of his.

Now that I'm sitting up and able to look him in his sea-green eyes, I see that he has shown up to *my* spot in shorts made for swimming.

"We have dinner tonight—I can't swim today, and you know that!" I laugh and smack his arm. Cal stands and offers me a hand, but as I gain my footing and take it, he tackles me to the ground and shoves sand in my dark hair. "Callious!"

"Now you've ruined it, Nelly. I wasn't going to, but I am now required to insist that you go for a swim with me. You wouldn't want to head back home plastered with sand, would you?"

Scowling, I push out of his grasp.

"I assume you're expecting me to jump in with my dress on? I'll drown if that's what you want."

"You should know me better than that by now."

Cal grabs his messenger bag slung around his shoulder and whips out a deep green two-piece tank and shorts set. "Tailored just for you for these warm waters. You ran out of the Palace before I could give it to you."

"This is stunning—you shouldn't have!" I squeal as I hold the piece up to me. This may be the most beautiful thing I own, with gold detailing on the seams. "Where did you find this?"

"It was Eva's from years ago. She told me she knew of a seamstress who could give it a new life. I just got it back from her this morning."

Grasping the fabric, my smile drops with that declaration. Such a precious gift, and of course, it had to come secondhand through my sister first. I shouldn't be upset, it's still the prettiest set I've ever seen.

"So, does this mean a swim is in order?" He wags his eyebrows at me. Huffing, I roll my eyes in response.

"Give me five minutes to change, and we will race to the waters. And I will not be going easy on you this time."

❉ ❉ ❉

Five minutes later, give or take a few, we are shoulder to shoulder facing the Neronian Sea. Even though the name of our sea means cruel or barbarous, it's anything but. I have never experienced warmer, calmer waters than those to the west of Paralia.

I look over my shoulder at my oldest friend. Callious and I have been out here more times than I can count, but for some reason, this time feels different.

Maybe it's the way his eyes are shining brighter than normal, or the way he stands so confidently next to me, but I can feel an energy radiating off him that is addicting.

"Ready?" I ask.

"Ready!" He whips his eyes to meet mine. Years of friendship and a mutual understanding reflect in his sea-green eyes. I suppose that could be why looking at the Neronian is one of my favorite views—it reminds me of my best friend.

Deviously, we smile at each other. My heart is pounding out of my chest as I make sure my feet are planted firm in the shifting sand.

"GO!"

We run toward the coastline, elbowing and pushing our way past each other. Years of racing the other means that we have become equal in almost every way, knowing just how fast our opponent is and where they may fall.

My bare feet pound against the soft sand, kicking up small mounds behind us. I surge forward with a burst of energy, my long strides eating up the distance left. Callious matches my pace, determination evident as he pushes himself harder and harder.

My right foot careens into a divot in the sand and I stumble, but Cal is right there to grab my arm and make sure I'm able to keep going. Even though we are competing, he will never let me fall too far behind.

I steal a glance to my right. His athletic build cuts through the air, pouring every ounce of muscle into his stride.

Our feet meet the cerulean waters as we splash past

the shallow part and start swimming toward the waist-deep current. Laughing, he tries to push my head under, but I grab his wrist and attempt to push him over instead.

My body is exhausted, but the race was exhilarating. I pant, my lungs gasping for air. The warm sea caresses my lean figure as I lie back to wash the sand off. Somehow, Cal always knows exactly what I need.

He dunks his head below the surface and flings his dark hair around as he comes back up, coating me in the salty sea. Laughing, I push him further away from me.

"I absolutely won that race. What will I get for being first?"

"You're delusional if you believe you won that. But I suppose that's something I already knew since you still choose to be friends with me after all this time." He winks and dives under as he starts to swim toward me. Suddenly, there are hands around my waist.

I screech as he begins to throw me over his shoulder. "Callious! Put me down!"

"If you insist, Princess." He throws me away from him as if I'm only a sack of vegetables, and into the surf beneath us. I hit the bottom of the sea and rush back up for a breath, only to find him doubled over laughing so hard he can't keep his eyes open.

"I'm not sure why I allow myself to be treated like this by you. Maybe I've had enough!" I shove him with my elbow while wringing out my dripping wet hair. This is going to take forever to dry now before dinner tonight.

"The day you've had enough of me will be the day

I die, Penelope." He smiles as he shoves me back. "Thank you for allowing me to be here today with you, P. I hope I made it worth your while."

I shrug as I say, "I suppose the swim wasn't the most terrible idea you've ever had." Winking at him, I begin to swim back toward the shore where my clothes and responsibilities await. "This has been a fantastic day. Thank you for coming out here."

Halting me, he grabs my ankles and pulls me back in to spin around and face him. Lifting my eyes, I give him a questioning look. "What?"

He sheepishly smiles as he runs a hand through his hair. "Happy birthday, Nelly. I hope I can make twenty-one as special for you as you are to me."

My hand finds my heart, and I give him a sad smile back. "You're the only one who has remembered. Thank you."

He pulls me in for a hug. As we turn back to make our way back to the beach, he flings his arm around my shoulder and kisses the top of my head.

"I know," he murmurs into my hair.

Yes, better than anyone in my life, he knows.

CHAPTER TWO

WE HURRY BACK TO THE PALACE, NOTING THE HIGH tide beginning to rise and fall beneath the brick columns that hold my home high above sea level.

One gated wall and fifty-two stairs later, my legs are burning as I rush into my bedroom.

Grabbing a tan-colored towel, I begin wringing my wet strands through the coarse fabric. I put heat on my hair this morning for the first time in a year, but the saltwater always brings out my natural curls.

Huffing in annoyance, I finish drying my long locks as best as possible. If I hurry, I'll have just enough time to change and make it back down to the dining room on time.

My hair may still be dripping as I enter the dining room.

Scouring my wardrobe for something simple to slip on, I quickly find my favorite dress. I'm aware that tonight is important, but I truthfully have no idea what is being announced or what might be going on. The only information I received was second-hand at best through my brother, stating there would be a 'mystery guest'.

I can't help but twirl in the mirror and admire the light pink sheer layer that adorns the maroon skirt. My sleeves are billowed toward the middle but fit tight at my wrists, and my neckline hearts over my chest. I cannot believe my sister, Ana, tired of the dress so quickly. I was ecstatic to take it off her hands.

Slipping into pink flats, I head down the hall to our dining room with just a few minutes to spare.

✳ ✳ ✳

I place my hands in my lap as I sit and take a deep breath. It's not easy being without Callious in situations like this, where he cannot be the calm to the storm raging inside of me. Regardless of whether or not anyone else here actually sees me, I know he always does.

My siblings chatter as I look around our dining room. It's not often that we eat in this space together. More often than not, I tend to take my meals to my room for a moment of silence and solitude.

The room is a perfect testament to the natural beauty of our coastal kingdom. It's nestled within the heart of our Palace, overlooking the dark waters of the sea through grand windows adorned with transparent curtains that sway with the bustle of servants moving in and out.

The walls are painted sea-foam green, with white trim as an accent. Seashell chandeliers hang from the high ceilings, casting a soft, warm glow over the polished wooden floors below. Each chandelier is intricately crafted, using seashells from our shore alone.

The focal point of the room is the grand dining table carved from driftwood; its surface polished to a smooth finish that reflects the light. The table is decorated with a pale blue table runner, our plates and utensils coated in gold.

Tapping on a glass, my father rises and begins dinner, capturing my attention.

"Frey, please join me in standing as I introduce our guest for the evening."

Following my family to their feet, my gaze catches on the wide wooden doors that align the wall to our backs. Opening, they present a man with an aura of cool arrogance walking toward us with purpose. His head is held high, and the silver crown atop his head gives off an edge of bitter cold.

This man smiles as he reaches his place next to my father at the end of our table. Looking toward us with ice-blue eyes, I begin to notice many of my siblings' jaws have dropped. It appears the only one holding himself together is Everett, though that is no surprise.

"Thank you for welcoming me into Paralia. It's an honor to set foot once again on your warm coast. Though I do prefer my air with a subtle chill to it," he chuckles.

"You are always welcome here. It has been many years since we last saw each other, so allow me to reintroduce the Frey to you. First, my Queen, Briar." Father takes mother's hand and presents it to this man. His name is on the tip of my tongue, but I cannot seem to place him as my siblings have. There's something in his sharp features that is making me feel as though I've been here before.

"Next, my heir. Prince Everett, please present yourself and be seated."

Everett faces our guest and bows deeply. After carefully finding his seat, he brings his eyes back to our father's.

"The twins, Ana and Eva, please present yourselves and be seated."

They do the same, as is custom. Down the line, my father goes to Finneus, Leila, and Carter, until he reaches me.

"And my youngest, Pen. Please present yourself and be seated."

Trying not to huff in annoyance at the nickname, I follow in my family's steps and make eye contact with our guest, curtsying low to the ground. Bowing my head, I rise and find my seat. Once my eyes are back on my father, all nine of us raise our drinking glasses toward the ceiling in tandem.

"I am the Frey," my father states, still standing.

"And we are the Frey," we respond, taking a sip out of our glasses and placing them back on the table in unison.

"Well, that was a very cute show you put on there, Zannan. Your family has certainly grown in the years we've spent in strife."

I cannot help myself—my eyes grow wide. I have never heard someone speak so casually to my father. Even my mother would not dare use such a tone.

Who is this man?

Father only laughs back as he sits and replies, "Surely you are not still in denial that it was your Kingdom that caused this rift between us in the first place, Kori."

Kingdom.

Kori.

Strife.

Curse the sun above—this is Oresteia's King.

"It's very unfortunate that you do not know how to take responsibility for your actions. I do hope that Prince Everett can steer from your direction in that area should he go on to become King." Kori makes a pointed look toward my brother while taking a drink from his glass. Somehow, he looks as if he is at home here at our table. He lounges back on his seat as if it's his own throne.

Everett clears his throat and looks toward our father for permission to speak. With a subtle nod of his head, Everett declares:

"It would be an honor to take after my King in every aspect once I'm able to receive a crown of my own."

Kori waves his hand in the air and brings it down hard on our table, making me jump.

"Let's cut to the chase, Zannan. I would prefer not to have to stay for dinner if I can help it. Your seafood is…" He pauses to think. "Lusterless, to say the least. Now, give me what has been taken, or give me the girl."

All seven of our heads whip toward my father. My mother sits at his right, and she is the only one who does not look surprised at what is conspiring between these two. Silence overwhelms our space as my father and King Kori stare daggers at each other.

Ana is the one who chooses to break the silence. "My King, if I may, I believe we are all a bit lost regarding what King Kori just proclaimed to us."

My father looks toward her with softer eyes.

"Thank you for asking, Ana. Attendants, please clear the room for the rest of the evening."

Feet scurry as our servers and workers race out of the doors as fast as possible. Unfortunately, it does not appear as if we will be eating dinner anytime soon. As if on cue, my stomach lets out an embarrassing growl.

Carter kicks my foot from under the table and sneaks me a pointed smirk. Blushing, I grab my glass and take a slow sip of the fizzy drink, hoping it will curb my appetite for the time being.

Once the doors have sealed and the room consists of only the ten of us, my father stands once more. There's power and authority in his voice and his stance —we cannot help but lean in and listen when he addresses the room.

"King Kori Pan of Oresteia has declared his intentions to go to war on Paralia. He is under the impression that the Frey stole something of extreme value to their Kingdom. Should we not return the item tonight, which I have assured King Kori that we do not have," a pointed look passes between them, "we will then be forfeiting our rights to decline this looming war."

Before any of us can chime in, my mother adds, "Zannan, you must also tell them of the other condition."

My father's shoulders droop ever so slightly as he sighs and continues.

"Because I cannot convince Oresteia's King to reverse his declaration of war, I have negotiated to send an ambassador of Paralia to Oresteia until the season's change to give us time to look for this stolen item.

"This ambassador will give Oresteia insight into Paralia and our systems to help heal the rift that began between our Kingdoms long ago. Should this item not be found at the end of this season, war will begin."

The air is thick with shock as we process the words my father just spoke. Six weeks feels like such a short time in hindsight.

How are we supposed to look for this stolen item when it's clear we don't know what the artifact is?

Kori smirks from his seat. "Don't leave out the best part, Zannan. Tell them who's going back with me."

Our gazes snap back to my father's.

His old, stubborn eyes meet my own while his hand finds my mother's.

"Penelope."

CHAPTER THREE

THE DINING ROOM ERUPTS IN CHAOS AS MY SIBLINGS GO from outraged at finding out I will be living in Oresteia for the next few weeks, to relief in realizing that they do not have to. My father holds up his hand to regain control of the room.

Like dogs heeling to their master, they silence at once.

"Penelope will embark at dawn. The deal is done." He looks from us to Kori. "If you do not want the meal that has been prepared, I can arrange to have something else sent up to your room for you."

"That will be sufficient." Kori holds a hand out to my father. As he releases their handshake, he looks toward me, surveying me from head to toe. I shiver under his cold glare. "You might want to pack a coat."

Turning on his heel, Kori storms out of the room and lets the door slam behind him, knowing full well the level of uncertainty that he left behind.

My father is weary as he sits back down.

"Let's eat."

My stomach churns throughout dinner as my family tries to make small talk regarding anything other than the issue at hand.

Barely able to taste the food before me, I ask to retire to my room much earlier than anyone else. My mother shoots me an apprehensive look, but my father approves my request.

❊ ❊ ❊

Back in my room, I collapse on my bed in a fit of disbelief.

I'm traveling to Oresteia.

I leave in the morning.

It's my birthday.

I don't own a coat.

A single knock at my door interrupts my thoughts. Rubbing my face with my hands, I sit back up and face my bedroom door.

The bedroom door I will not see again for weeks.

My father's face enters my line of sight as the door opens. My mood sours more than it was just a minute ago. My arms cross over my chest defensively as I roll my eyes.

"Pen, I know this was shocking to you, but we need to speak regarding expectations I have for you for this brief stint away." He moves forward to my desk in the corner. Tugging at the chair, he brings it to the center of my room to sit in front of me.

"Forgive me for speaking out of anger, King, but I

am not in the mood to discuss the expectations you have for me when my entire world is going to change in less than a day," I snap.

"Penelope, you will hold your tongue. I will empathize knowing this was abrupt to you, but we had no other choice but to send you. You are the only Frey who has no other prior obligations here in Paralia. You know just enough of our systems to lend helpful insight to Oresteia without risking the potential of overstepping in your role."

"Go ahead and say what you truly mean. I have nothing to offer here, and because I know the least of the seven of us, there will be no chance I accidentally say something that could put you or Paralia in jeopardy." I shoot up from my bed and half-curtsy to him sarcastically. "I am so grateful to know that you believe in me and my abilities as a Princess, my King."

Spinning around, I race toward my bathroom, hoping he will take the hint and leave me be so I might process the change before me.

Faster than I've ever seen him move, father leaps from the chair and snatches my arm to hold me firm. I glance sharply at him while I struggle to shake my elbow out of his grip.

Removing his hand, he looks down his nose at me.

Ever the king, rarely my father.

"These next few weeks, you will let nothing stop you from searching for whatever it is that is lost. Here, we will do our part in looking as we are able. The only way to prevent this war is to find what was taken. Should you fail, we all fail. Watch your tongue and watch your back. There's a reason that things have been strained between us and Oresteia for over ten years. If you need anything, find anything, or hear anything, you will write immediately."

Shaking his head, he starts to walk back toward the door. "We are counting on you to do your part. Do not make me regret choosing you."

As he goes to grab the handle, I begin to panic. This may be the last time I speak to him before I am sent off.

"Callious!" I gasp.

He turns around, a questioning look on his face.

"Pardon?"

I attempt to regain my composure. "If I may, I would like to request an opportunity to say goodbye to Callious."

My father pinches his forehead between his two fingers in annoyance.

"I will have someone send for him. Is there anything else you would like to *request*, Penelope?" His tone has an edge of bitterness to it, coating the air between us in disappointment.

I allow my steely gaze to look toward him, knowing my father is gone and the King is fully present.

"I'm going to need a coat."

CHAPTER FOUR

ONCE I AM LEFT TO MY OWN THOUGHTS AND DEVICES again, I realize I don't have any clue how I'm traveling to Oresteia. Other than my apparent need for a coat, I don't know what to pack and what to leave behind.

I stand in the center of my room, the evening sun streaming through the windows. Everything lies in organized chaos as I grab the biggest bag I own and start throwing things in. I begin with practicality in mind, selecting clothing items that are breathable and fit for travel.

I carefully fold and place a long-sleeve gown of deep blue, adding in a pair of matching flats as well. Next, I grab my favorite leather-bound journal and throw from my bed, knowing I will seek both comfort and familiarity in my new space.

Lastly, I place my dagger on top. I'm not entirely sure I'll be able to carry this bag on my own.

Defeated once again, I sit on the edge of my bed. *How did today turn into this?*

✳ ✳ ✳

As I carefully comb through the rest of my room for necessities—despite the minimal space left in my bag to add anything else—the door opens with no warning.

There's no privacy in this Palace.

Callious looks sheepish as he enters, a hand on the back of his neck.

"Hi," he smiles.

"Hey," I sigh. Just like that, the constant noise in my head empties to nothingness as he comes to sit next to me.

"So, I hear you're leaving?"

"First thing tomorrow. It was news to me, or I would have told you this morning," I grumble.

"What a birthday, huh?" he chuckles, attempting to lighten the mood.

"What a birthday, indeed." Against my wishes, tears begin to form against my lower lashes. Leaning my head on his shoulder, I try to wipe my tears against his rough shirt. "Did you have to wear something so uncomfortable? I can hardly bear to have my head here!"

Laughing, he pushes me off. "No one asked you to lay your head on me, Nel. That's *my* shirt you're sacrificing."

Shoving him back, I begin to laugh. Leave it to him to find ways to reverse the tears that were streaming down my face.

Suddenly, the room quiets. As the minutes tick by, I don't know what to say to him. How do you say a temporary goodbye to a forever friend when you don't know what the outcome will be in just a matter of weeks? Anxiety gnaws at my stomach like the sea to the shoreline.

"Cal, I don't have any special words of parting to offer you. The best I can give is the promise to write if I am able, and my lasting loyalty as your friend."

"If you do not have anything to give, let me give enough for both of us. I have a proposal to make." He leaps off the bed, takes both of my hands in his, and kneels before me on the cold, hard floor.

"Callious, be serious!" I gasp. My wide eyes take in his nervous and sincere demeanor.

My family would never allow such a thing.

He laughs at me. "Not that kind of proposal, P. Although, I cannot help but add that I would give my life to have yours be tethered to mine for the rest of our days. I have loved you since the day you walked into my father's shop with Everett. It has been you and me in my mind ever since."

I smile at this, reminiscing on better days.

It truly has always been him and me.

"I want our hearts to beat in tandem until we die together. I want you next to my side during this looming war, where I can watch your back and you can watch mine. You are the only person I trust with my complete mind and soul. You are the moon to my tide, effortlessly pulling me back into your calm embrace. And so, I ask you this:

"Will you go to war with me?" He pleads, grasping my hands with fervency. "Will you give up your crown to fight by my side?"

The weight of that question does not hit me right away. As it sinks in, I weigh out my two possibilities.

Even though leaving is something I was unable to decide for myself, it's thrilling to think of the new atmosphere waiting for me in Oresteia. All of it is unknown, and that delights me.

But, I swallow. *By going with Callious, I could make this decision for myself. I could have new experiences and still be with someone I know and love, without the burden of being a royal any longer.*

All of a sudden, I am filled with blind rage.

Does he believe running is the only option I have?

"Are you referring to the war I'm attempting to prevent by *going* to Oresteia? If I do not go, war will come immediately. We will not have months to plan, a season to prepare, or days to stand in waiting.

"I am doing something to keep our people and lands safe. You know I love you," I pause, my heart caught in my throat. "But I cannot be whisked away to fight when I can do my best to make sure it doesn't happen in the first place!" I attempt to part my hands from his, but his grasp holds firm.

"Nelly, that's not what I'm saying. Paralia and Oresteia have been at each other's throats since we were nine years old. *Twelve years* we've been in constant strife with them. War is inevitable, whether you find this item or not. You know I believe in you, but to be parted from you would be to sever a limb from my body, *and I cannot go with you.* So please, come with *me.*"

"I cannot just sit back and attempt to believe that. If I leave and abandon my duties, who will go in my stead? Who will go and bid peace between the two Kingdoms, hoping to twine our futures together?

Father already made it clear that I am the *only* Frey who can travel to Oresteia for this long. If I don't go, no one goes."

"But you don't know anything about them!" The strain on his face mirrors the rise in his voice. I have never seen Callious so angry, and his anger has never been directed toward me.

"Just because I was not allowed to be involved does not mean I am of no use!" I scream at him, utterly appalled. "You sound *just* like my father. I may have to take it from him, but I will not take it from you!"

He stands in shock, regret forming on his face. Abruptly, he releases my hands and walks to the edge of the room where my desk sits. Callious runs one hand through his shaggy hair, while the other runs lightly along the notes thrown haphazardly on my desk. Wishes and dreams outline those pages—thoughts I will never speak aloud.

Facing me once more, his breathing calms. "Pen, I'm sorry. I know you aren't allowed in the royal council, and I know it eats you alive to know so little of this Kingdom and the next. I never meant to downplay your ability to do anything that I *know* you are capable of. The thought of you leaving is truly ripping me in half, and I didn't handle it the way I planned when I walked in here. I made you something." He reaches into his pocket and walks back toward me.

"Let me start over. Can we pretend the words that were just exchanged hold no weight over the two of us?" he asks.

I reach for him, nodding and pulling him closer in

front of where I sit on my bed. All anger is forgotten, and I appreciate just how easy it is to be next to him.

"Nelly, I plan to enlist for our Kingdom's army in the morning. I would give anything to have you come with me. You don't need to give me an answer tonight. I would prefer it if you took the time to mull over your options and do what is best in your eyes. I'll be at the Paralian Gate at dawn. If you show up, I will happily twine my arm with yours and never leave your side."

He pauses and cocks his head to the right, pondering. "If you do not, my heart, and this necklace, will be with you wherever you may go."

He pulls his fist out of his pocket and presents a pastel yellow necklace to me, adorned with a beaded chain and a cream-colored seashell.

"Callious... it's... beautiful!" I fluster as he moves behind me.

He turns to place the necklace and clasps it around my neck, and I can feel his hands shaking as the weight of his words sinks into my skull.

A life with him, permanently.

A life apart from him, temporarily.

A new world for me either way.

Once the necklace is secure, I lightly touch the scalloped edge, admiring its soft shell. I stand and spin around to hug him so fiercely that it feels as though my heart and soul are joined with his.

"I will *never* take this off, Callious, no matter what. My soul is so full of you that I could hardly call it my own." I look up at him, meeting his sparkling gaze.

Releasing me with a reluctant smile, he begins to walk out of my room, and my heart pains. I want so badly to call for him to stay with me. I fear that if I did, I would give him false hope as to what we are and what we could be. Regardless, he requires an answer, and I'm the only one who can give that to him.

"Callious," I call, as he reaches for the doorknob. He turns and looks at me expectantly.

"Wait for me."

CHAPTER FIVE

Dawn breaks hastily as if to quicken my departure.

I jump out of bed, my bare feet surprised by the coldness of the hard floor beneath me.

As if it's grounding me, reminding me that even in times of hurry, I must pause—if only for a moment—to remember where I stand.

Not wanting to waste a minute in order to avoid running into Kori—and whomever else might witness me sneaking off in a direction that isn't toward Oresteia—I quickly change and grab my belongings. I survey my room, wasting a moment to look at myself in the mirror, taking care to remember this version of myself.

One that I will never have again.

My last morning as a royal. I cannot say that I will mourn that title, and yet, it still stings to relinquish your grip on something that has always been part of your identity.

My curls are pinned up, drawing attention to my dark eyes. My dress is of the deepest color that I own, so that I might not draw too much attention to myself —a blue that rivals the color of the night sky.

I tiptoe through the halls, my heavy bag holding tight to my shoulder, the marble floors swept clean of all sand and grime. A gentle breeze flows through sheer curtains, reminding me that day is quickly approaching.

And with it, my deadline for meeting King Kori.

Callious left at once last night after receiving his answer, needing time himself to pack and make arrangements.

And to tell his father.

But there's no doubt in my mind that his father would be excited for Callious, if not *proud* that he's enlisting.

Hopefully, he does not let slip that I am coming with him.

Though I'm sure everyone will find out soon enough.

There's a slight warmth to the air as I enter the open Palace grounds, the morning's rays finding my skin. I still for a moment, soaking it in, listening to the world I know. My head tilts back, my eyes shut of their own volition. I imagine for a moment traveling to Oresteia, finding whatever has been stolen, and becoming the person my family wishes that I am.

Steps sound behind me, drawing me out of my trance.

Spinning to face them, my skirt tangles on my leg, and I trip over myself, losing my grip on my bag. It hits the sand next to me as I land on my hands and knees with a *thud.*

I flinch as I look up, expecting Callious, even though he said we would meet at the Paralian Gate at dawn.

And I am already late.

A shiver runs down my spine as my eyes meet those of a cold, calculating King.

Kori.

His gaze sparkles with amusement. "It appears you've found where you belong."

I jump up, brushing the grains off my dress and hands. As I slowly grab my bag and hoist it back up over my shoulder, I question what my next move should be.

Do I pretend to go with him, then try to sneak off to meet Callious?

Should I say I forgot something and try to leave another way?

Before I can come up with an inkling of an excuse, he says, "You're late."

I gulp, feeling as though I've been found out. "I needed a moment to say goodbye to my family."

He raises an eyebrow at me. "Right."

I shift back and forth on my feet, my eyes looking everywhere but him as I try to come up with something —anything—to say.

Kori breaks the silence once again. "For someone who was hoping not to be followed, you are very heavy on your feet."

My breath is stolen from my lungs, fear taking hold of my heart.

This is it. He's going to tell my father and declare war on us, anyway.

Or he will steal me away against my will, and I will never return.

I prepare to bolt, knuckles white on my bag strap. If I must, I'm willing to leave it behind in order to get away faster.

He steps closer, his powerful figure towering over my frame.

"Where were you going, girl?"

I shake my head, trying to mutter the lie that I wasn't going anywhere, that he's mistaken.

All that comes out are gasps of air.

He pinches the skin between his eyebrows in frustration, grumbling under his breath.

"Go," he says, surprising me. I stay rooted where I am, expecting this to be a test of sorts.

He crouches down to match my height. "You have two days. Two days to get to where you are going before I message your father our official declaration of war." He nearly spits these words in my face. "I hope what you are running off to deems itself worthy of the deaths of many, lamb."

I stare wide-eyed into his ice-tipped gaze, nodding along as those words drill into my skull.

"Go!" he says forcefully, waving me away as he turns on his heel and stalks off towards our golden Palace gate.

I stand there, clutching my bag, breathing heavily as I wait.

For him to leave my line of sight. For it to be a trick...

What in the sun's name just happened?

When he does not return, and when my family does not show, I slowly begin to follow the sandy path beyond our Palace gate, where the Paralian Gate lies.

And where Callious awaits.

❆ ❆ ❆

My feet ache.

I do not make it a habit to walk these worn paths. There has never been any need for it.

Until today.

The ground is hard, surely worn down by shoes more suited for this journey. The rolling hills are filled with paspalos grass—tall stalks that grow stubbornly in our dry, sandy plains. A cool wind is rare, but when it drifts through, I love watching the grass sway—like it's asking me to dance along.

And when those days come, Cal and I do. We race barefoot through the fields surrounding the Palace, just to feel a glimpse of the wind at our backs, propelling us forward.

The thought of him is the only thing keeping me going right now.

I'm beginning to regret not asking Callious to meet me at the Palace gate. My feet quicken, my shoulders weary from carrying this sun-forsaken bag for most of the morning. The sun is directly above me now, and my stomach growls in recognition that I haven't eaten anything since last night.

A figure stands in my way, coming toward me as

quickly as I walk toward them. Blinded by the sun's rays, I shield my eyes so I might see more clearly. The moment I do, I ease, recognition flooding through me.

"Callious!" I call, stopping where I am and allowing him to meet me.

I am so very tired.

Panic momentarily floods my body. *I am not meant for a life in the army. I am going to be eaten alive.*

Before I can go further down that rabbit trail, Cal reaches me and pulls me into a hug, holding me so tightly that my feet lift off the ground. I melt into his embrace.

"I was just going to find you. I started to worry that you had changed your mind." He hesitates, setting me down and pulling back to search my face. "Or that Kori had forced you to go with him anyway."

I back out of his grasp, my hands on his arms.

"Kori did find me this morning," I say. "He let me go, though. I thought it was a trap, but he did not come back for me." My feet shift, not wanting to look him in the eye as I tell him the rest. It feels as though I've failed already, somehow. That he will regret asking me to come along. "He said he will declare war in two days."

Callious blinks, stunned. "Two days is generous. From what I've heard already today, the Paralian army was assuming this afternoon we would get word."

I tilt my head, confused.

Surely it's not in Kori's nature to be generous.

Cal notes the change in my face and lays a hand on my lower back, steering me toward the Paralian Gate.

"Nothing to worry about. Regardless of when, we will be ready." His eyes crinkle as he looks down at me, just a head taller. His voice lowers as he says, "I am so glad you are here, Pen."

I smile back, relief flooding my system. How could I ever question that he would regret me coming? He is my oldest, dearest friend. We do everything together.

As we walk, our companionable silence stretches along the plains. I do not mind it at all—he's always known when I need space to think and when I don't.

But I do find myself wishing I knew what he was thinking right now.

The Paralian Gate looms in front of us, so close that I can see the guards stationed around it.

Nerves start to get the better of me. "Have they set up camp yet? What should I expect to find?"

He chuckles at me. Not meanly, but amused. "They've had a camp set up for twelve years, Nel."

I blush, ducking my head. I glance sideways at him, watching as light catches his dark hair, highlighting the lighter streaks the sun has left over the years.

Fondness pierces my heart, tightening my chest.

"I'm so glad you're my best friend," I whisper, not able to hold those words in.

His eyes meet mine, sparkling at me as they always do. As they always have.

"I couldn't have asked the sun above for a better one," he declares, his arm wrapping around my waist, squeezing gently.

We come to a standstill, now in a line of people awaiting entry to the Gate.

Butterflies float violently in my stomach.

"They'll be expecting someone better," I mumble, uncertainty coating my tongue.

Callious raises an eyebrow at me. "Someone not in a dress?" he jokes, attempting to lighten my mood.

"A person with authority or knowledge to offer," I start. "Like one of my siblings."

He doesn't respond to me right away, the line continuously moving forward. Closer and closer we grow to the Gate, its presence large and intimidating. Cal walks beside me, hands now in his pockets, scanning the crowd. It's then that I register the uniform he's wearing, the branding of our Kingdom on his beige, linen shirt.

"What if they turn me away?" I ask. I do not say what I'm really thinking. *What if they take you and not me? What will be left for me then?*

I feel the weight of his gaze on mine, assessing how to best comfort and encourage me.

"Only you get to decide who you are now, Nelly," he urges. "They will see who that is. They won't turn you away."

A small breeze stirs my skirts as we arrive at the Gate, next in line. The world around me feels as if it's suffocating, the heaviness in the air weighing me down in tandem with my bag. A golden fence closes us off from the rest of the people, two guards in similar, dark outfits stand with clipboards in their hands and swords strapped to their backs.

My legs shake as I stand, watching as they assess me from head to toe.

A watchtower stands behind the fence, guards

looming there as well. I gulp, trying to cover my unease with false confidence.

"Name?" the guard on the left states, not even taking a moment to look up.

I glance at Callious, and he nods at me, motioning for me to speak.

"Penelope." I nearly swallow my tongue, the word like clay in my mouth.

He looks up then. "Surname?"

"Uh…" I pause, trying to speak quietly enough that I will not catch the attention of those around me. "Frey."

The other guard looks up then too, whispers murmuring from those within earshot. It's punishable by death to lie about your identity when enlisting. I was hoping they would only ask for my first name…

"And does your father know you are here, Penelope?"

My knees nearly buckle.

Here we go.

"He is my King, and I wish to serve him in this way."

I look to Cal for support, hoping what I said did not sound stupid, but he is already leaning toward the guard next to him, saying something in his ear.

The guard nods, taking note of something on his clipboard.

"Welcome to the Paralian Army, Frey."

The fence's gate opens before me, beckoning me to this new world and life I would have never sought for myself.

Cal walks with me, nodding to those we pass. The whispers begin to spread like wildfire.

Was this a mistake? I am so out of place here.

I can feel their stares permeating, awareness raising the hair on the back of my neck.

"It's his youngest, I think. Don't really remember their names."

"What is she doing here? Could the King have sent her here with a hidden purpose?"

"If so, I wish he had sent one of the boys. At least they're trained."

"She's just going to slow us down. I hear she doesn't know anything about the strife with Oresteia."

My shoulders tense, embarrassment coloring my cheeks as I realize that any hope I had at making my own name here was futile. Callious will not want to be seen with me, so that his own advancement isn't hindered.

Cal places an arm around my shoulders, as if hearing my thoughts. He steers me toward the back of the camp, where cream tents are erected.

We pass a group in brown uniforms like those at the front gate. They murmur to each other, but it still reaches my ears.

"She walked away from a life of luxury to hinder us here. She doesn't know what's at stake."

Cal glares at them, stepping closer, as if shielding me from their sharp words.

"You don't owe them *anything,*" he says quietly.

I nod at him, but my stomach is in knots all the same.

At the back of the camp, it's quieter. People mill

about, entering and exiting tents. They sharpen weapons and sit around the smoke of campfires.

We reach a large tent, full of tan uniforms meant for those enlisting.

Meant for me.

I take a breath, steadying myself.

And I step inside.

CHAPTER SIX

I CHANGE QUICKLY, SLIPPING ON THE LIGHT PANTS AND shirt, realizing that I will not need any of the clothes I packed.

I carried my heavy bag all this way for nothing.

Though the shirt is long-sleeved, it's extremely breathable. I suppose that it would have to be, with the weather of our nature. The sun has reached its full peak, and it's *hot* and *dry*. Dehydration coats my mouth.

I lace up my new boots, grateful for something sturdy on my feet, and exit the changing tent. Callious waits for me, my bag at his feet.

"I hadn't realized you packed your whole room, or I would have carried this for you."

Smirking, I pick it up, hoisting it over my shoulder with a groan. "I tried to come prepared."

"Let's go find your tent so you can unpack and leave all your preparation behind."

I roll my eyes at his wink, following after him like a wounded dog.

By the time we find my tent, I'm convinced I'm one step away from collapsing. My shoulders burn, and my boots have collected half the Kingdom's sand. Everything here looks the same—rows and rows of cream canvas.

Hopelessness grabs my heart.

How am I meant to know my way around? I'm a lost cause.

There are no signs pointing the way, no helpful people waiting to guide us in the right direction. How Callious was able to pick up on all the locations and whereabouts of things in the short time he's already been here, I have no idea. He is clearly more meant for this than I am.

My tent is at the far edge of camp, wedged between one that smells of fish and another where someone snores loud enough to shake the stakes holding it up. I look at Cal, helpless and unimpressed. He giggles a bit, earning a smile from me.

Before we know it, we are laughing together so hard that tears start to stream down our cheeks. We do not register that the snoring stopped, nor do we see the person groggily step out into the sun until they are in our faces.

"Keep it down, kids. I need some shut-eye," he yells, stumbling back into his tent.

We pause, trying to keep our laughter contained. Cal mocks the man, and we erupt once again.

I hope it's always like this.

We enter my assigned tent, not chancing being scolded again. I survey the small space as my pack drops to the ground. There are four narrow cots, with just enough room to walk between them. The only one with no belongings under it is the one furthest to the left—the one closest to the fish tent.

Great.

My cot is barely wider than my shoulders, and I cannot imagine someone of Callious's stature sleeping on something this small. There's a blanket folded neatly on top, scratchy and brown.

Is everything here void of color?

Worshipping the sun comes with a commitment to vibrant hues and warmth. My closet is filled to the brim with lively shades.

I suppose that, being part of an army, you would want to blend into your surroundings for the battles you fight in.

And I guess that means sand-tinted *everything.*

That's fine.

I sit on my cot, legs creaking under my weight, as if it's convinced that I do not belong here.

That would make two of us.

Cal plops my bag next to me with ease, his work with his father as a bladesmith honing his strength and abilities.

I should have made him carry it sooner. Pride is a color I do not need to wear around him.

Unzipping it, I pull out my few belongings. I bring my throw blanket up to my chest, hugging it like it's my best friend. I'm *so* thankful I brought this.

I grab my journal and my dagger already in its belt. I place the journal under my blanket, realizing that I forgot to pack a pen.

Perhaps Callious could find me one, since he already knows where everything is.

I look up at where he stands, watching me. "Do you think they would mind if I keep my dagger strapped to me while wandering camp? Or are there rules against weapons?"

He raises an eyebrow. "It's war, Pen. They actually *encourage* you to keep a weapon on you at all times."

Right. That was stupid.

Before I can respond, a voice booms outside. I startle. "Head to orientation at the mess tent. Ten minutes!"

Immediately, everyone around us begins moving. I scramble to my feet, careful to secure my dagger's leather belt around my waist. The dark green color doesn't exactly blend in, but maybe that will be okay. The gold of the hilt catches the sun as I exit my tent, blinding me.

My heart thuds. I'm not sure where the mess tent is, but I make sure to follow the flow of uniforms, keeping my head down.

Everything within me wishes I could simply disappear.

The mess tent is a massive canvas structure, so much larger than those we are sleeping in. It's bound by thick ropes with heavy wooden stakes driven into the ground.

I wince at the volume inside as a guard hands me a parchment scribbled with a schedule of sorts. Mine is barely legible, times and places merging as if they are one.

A smell wafts through the sticky air toward me, making my stomach growl. I can't place the smell exactly—something warm and unseasoned—but I still want it desperately all the same.

I've lost sight of Callious in the shuffle; everyone around me is a sea of beige.

"Order!" someone calls from the front of the tent. I watch as a guard, a few feet taller than most, stands on top of one of the worn, wooden tables. He is built like the cliffs near our Palace, and I worry that the table will not support his weight.

I wonder if the darker your uniform is, the higher your rank might be. If that is the case, he must be well within his ranks.

Everyone stops what they are doing, quiet as his clear voice rings out.

In a blur, he walks us through the basics of what we need to know. What time we eat, where we can relieve ourselves, when lights-out will be, and what happens if we miss roll call at dawn. None of his information sticks, though I try. My mind is the tide, information coming and going with each wave.

Just as quickly as this meeting started, it's over. I stumble around, hoping to find something to eat. or at the very least, water.

"First day?" an older man asks, smirking at me. He's covered in grime, his gray apron enveloped in a variety of stains.

I nod, heat crawling up my neck.

He grumbles something about the army's desperation for recruits. "The name's Mastris, but call me Mas. I'm this army's cook and the best one you're gonna get, so no complaining. There's no rule saying I have to feed you."

Wide-eyed, I nod, my eyes caught on his white beard. It's unruly, as if it hasn't been properly managed in years.

My father would be appalled.

I mean... the King would be.

I shake off the thought as Mas holds something out to me, wiggling it in front of my eyes as I come back to reality. A couple of... crackers?

He sees the confusion on my face, clearly unamused. "It's hardtack, darlin'. Eat it before you pass out on me."

With that, he slaps the hardtack in my hand and leaves.

I take a tentative bite, expecting terrible things. I'm so hungry that I would eat *anything* right now. It does curb my appetite, but the texture dries out my mouth even more.

Cal finds me as I leave the tent.

"Come on! We don't want to be late." He grabs my arm, pulling me toward an empty space in the middle of chaos.

"Where are we going now?" I'm not trying to, but my voice has a whine to it. I'm tired, and hot, and thirsty. Right now, all I want to do is go back and sleep on my hard cot and snore as loudly as my neighbor did earlier.

"You have to go through the training ritual so they can place you within your rank."

I stop in my tracks, nearly pulling him down with me at the abrupt change of pace.

"What?" I cry. "In front of people? Can't they just put me at the bottom and call it good?"

He steers me once again, his voice lowering as we make our way through yet another crowd. "They have to know what you can do, Nel."

I whisper back, an urgency in my tone. "You and I both know I can't do *anything*, Callious."

There's no time to keep arguing, as it appears training has already started.

An instructor blows a horn, capturing our attention. A woman, one of the few that I've seen so far since being here, stands at the front of the group. Her chin is pointed, looking down at all of us.

"Backs straight!" she yells. All of us immediately fix our postures, righting them in unison.

She begins to call out names from a clipboard in alphabetical order.

It's not long before my name is called.

"Frey!"

I walk to the middle of the circle, as I've seen the others do. All eyes are on me, watching my every move. She asks me to run to a large wooden pole and back as fast as I'm able, timing me. Gasping, I put my hands on my knees as she makes note of it on her clipboard.

Then, she has me grab a practice wooden sword and go through a series of strikes and counters, moves and blocks. The sword is heavy in my hand, my arms shaking.

"Strengthen your grip!" someone calls. My lungs are burning. She has me hold certain stances for what seems like forever, so long that my arms and legs start to shake.

I falter, over and over, my shirt clinging to me with

moisture. The crowd around me is a blur through the sweat dripping into my eyes.

Finally, my time is over. As I return the sword, I see her shake her head, clearly disappointed.

You and I both.

Callious hands me a water skin as I walk back to my place beside him. I drink greedily, gulping, then wiping my mouth on my sleeve.

Soon enough, it's his turn. He flies through the running portion faster than anyone else. He's a natural with a sword in his hand, blocking and striking as if he's practiced this exact sequence in his sleep.

Maybe he has.

By the time the sun starts to dip behind the hills, my body has momentarily stopped screaming. We are dismissed, having been reminded that lights-out and roll call are not negotiable. I limp back to my tent with trembling legs, unsure if I'll be able to get back up in the morning.

Cal parts ways with me, his tent just a few down from my own. I mumble a goodnight, hardly able to speak through the tightness in my chest.

Inside, the glow of a lantern calls to me, my cot waiting.

I collapse onto it, face-first, noticing that none of my tent mates have made it back yet.

I've never shared a room before. I wonder what that will be like. Will we stay up and talk? Will they look at me once and see right through me?

Will they see that I'm a fraud?

No one warned me that this would be so hard. It's

as if I am being made new—scraped raw and molded into some *person* that the army requires me to be.

I don't know how to be that person.

I lie there, my scratchy blanket behind my head in a makeshift pillow, my throw covering me in the scent of home. My clothes cling to my sticky skin. Though the air is warm and musty as the night grows closer, my sweat cools me down.

Maybe tomorrow I will do better. Perhaps I will wake up a different person, the exact type of person that they need me to be.

Or, I'll break and leave from here with my tail tucked between my legs, with nowhere else to go.

I've given up everything.

My breath hitches, tears beginning to well.

I cannot give this moment more than it's already trying to take. Morning is coming regardless of how I feel, and either way, I will still be here.

My eyes shut, growing weary.

A little sleep might be all I need.

CHAPTER SEVEN

A HIGH AND UNYIELDING WHISTLE TRILLS THROUGH THE air. I jolt upright, rubbing my head at the sound, hoping the ache in my ears does not last long. My dreams begin to slip through my memory like silk. Pieces of ocean waves, Palace walls, and green eyes drift away like smoke.

Groaning, I swing my legs over the edge of my cot, my blanket askew behind me. My tent mates have already departed, though it's possible they did not sleep in here last night—I fell asleep so fast I wouldn't have noticed them coming or going.

My cot creaks as I lace my boots back on my feet and gather my unruly hair in a quick ponytail.

Outside the tent, others are already moving.

My uniform is stiff on my body, smelling of yesterday's sweat. I would absolutely kill for a hot bath right now, or at least for a dip into the Neronian. I can hear the waves crashing against this side of Paralia, as if calling to me—asking me to return to what I've always known.

To be who my family wants me to be.

I shake that thought away. I chose this. For myself, but also for Callious. No one made me run from what was being asked of me. No one forced me to abandon my crown.

But they would have forced you to leave for Oresteia and undertake a seemingly impossible duty.

Dawn is on the horizon as I exit my tent, allowing me to see a few steps ahead of me. Camp is a busy hum of movement, forcing me to follow the crowd and hope they are taking me to where I need to go.

Tendrils of smoke curl up from fires in different spots, snitching on those who stayed up all night talking. My boots hold steady in the shifting sand, giving me balance I did not have yesterday.

I arrive at the mess tent, looking for Callious in every face I pass. A sea of brown is all I see.

I would know it's him, I convince myself. *I know him better than anyone. Surely he is here already.*

Joining the line for breakfast, I swallow the nausea building in my stomach. I'm not hungry, but I can't predict when my next meal will be, and I don't know what we will be doing today. Sun-forbid I ask someone and get laughed at.

If Cal were here, he would tell me. He was supposed to be next to me in all things—guiding me through this. I did not sign up to do this on my own.

I steady myself, my thoughts turning frantic. Taking a deep breath, I focus on what is around me.

The smell of... porridge?

The sound of metal striking metal.

The feel of my linen shirt against my fingertips.

My heartbeat turning steady in my chest.

I hold up my bowl to those serving us behind the cook line, the shiny white clay chipped and cracked in multiple spots. A ladle full of something hot gets poured into it, the heaviness of the meal weighing down my arms. I smile at my server, an older woman with a permanent scowl, and try to thank her for my food.

I get shoved from behind, the line hurriedly moving behind me so that everyone has time to eat. She waves me on with her spoon, flicking it in my direction. Sludge flies off, hitting me in the cheek.

I grab a utensil and a water skin from the table next to us. I look around, trying to find an empty seat or a space of solitude, when I spot Mas coming in from the back flap of the tent.

Relieved to see a familiar face, I try to head his direction, wondering if he would know Callious's name and maybe point me in his direction.

He spots me, eyebrow raised.

"You're headed the wrong direction, darlin'. Tables that way," he points behind me, his other hand on his hip. Before I'm able to respond, to ask him if he's seen my friend, he turns on his heel and jumps right into the cook line.

I humph. Turning around, I find a small spot available to sit between two other beige-colored uniforms. Hanging half off the seat, I try to eat my meal politely, careful to keep my manners intact.

I burn my tongue with my first bite, so I gulp down

a cool drink from my water skin. Breakfast tastes like salt and sand in my mouth, and the water, surely filtered from the sea itself, does little to wash away the taste.

The boy beside me, not too much older than Cal and me, wipes his mouth with the back of his hand, eyeing me. "You really a Princess?"

I look at him, caught off guard. "No. Not anymore, I guess."

He shrugs. "I wouldn't have left all that," he waves his fork in the air. "For anything. But that's just me."

I blink, stunned as he gets up and leaves. I finish my meal, if you could call it that, and head outside where recruits have started to line up. My head swivels, still searching for Callious.

Where could he be?

The guard from yesterday begins, telling us to step forward when our name is called. I follow suit, back straight.

When it's all said and done, I have not heard Cal's name.

We are split into groups, assigned different duties. We are told this is part of the structure here—helping make sure that camp runs smoothly and within operation at all times.

As they speak, addressing us all, the sun continuously rises. I begin to beg it for some reprieve, wishing for just a moment that we could have a break from hot, scorching weather for once in my life.

I would not miss the sun's embrace if it were to forsake me.

By mid-morning, I am elbow-deep in a wooden barrel of muddy water, scrubbing dishes from breakfast. Sweat drips down my forehead as the sun beats down on me.

The skin on my hands feels raw, the water just as hot as this morning's food was. I have my sleeves rolled up, but it's of no use—the water soaks the fabric all the same.

My arms ache, having not been given a chance to rest and recuperate from yesterday's ranking session. My back is sore, my knees are numb from being on the hard, packed ground.

Still, I do not stop, just as those in my group keep going too. I am meant to be here; I have the ability to be *great* here. I only need to rise above my own expectations for myself.

Which, unfortunately, are very low.

Just when I've begun to appreciate the rhythm of the work I'm doing, I feel the ground start to rumble. Murmurs ripple across camp like waves cresting the shore. Soldiers gather in formation, recruits following their leads. I drop what I'm doing in the sand, wiping my forehead and rolling my sleeves back down.

A carriage rolls in through camp, its gold-rimmed wheels grinding over sand easily. The body of the carriage, fashioned with wood and gold detailing, is flanked and pulled by armored guards. Their chest plates are adorned with the King's branding over their hearts.

I squint, recognizing the picture at once for what it is. Paralia's coast is prevalent, showing off the cliff's edges and the sea's waves hitting the shore. The Palace is in the background of those details, overlooking it all, a sun behind it that you can hardly see, even when up close.

The guards are in perfect formation, showing us what we *should* look like when all is said and done. My heart stops as I find myself pressed between a sea of bodies, none of which seem as nervous as me.

What could someone in my family be doing here, if not to bring me back?

I gulp, immediately looking for a place to hide.

When the carriage finally stops, I've found a space near the mess tent at the back of the hoard of people, trying my best not to draw attention to myself. I slouch behind two taller men, hoping they are too busy jostling each other to notice that I'm using them as a shield.

Then, the carriage door opens.

I watch, hoping for Everett—someone who might be persuaded to listen to my reasonings and hear my side of things.

But I am nothing if not unlucky.

Because he steps down.

The King.

My heart clenches.

No one says anything, no one dares to move a muscle.

He is dressed in a burning shade of orange, trimmed with yellows and reds. His boots are polished to shine, even though they will become covered in sand regardless. His hair is lightening at the temples, age showing.

Still, his eyes haven't aged a day; their dark color is just as calculating and intelligent as always.

The King does not look around, as if none of us are truly worth seeing. He looks straight ahead, not glancing in any one direction.

His voice carries, powerful and sure. The voice of a King.

"I am the Frey," he begins. "And we are at war." He pauses then, surely enjoying the panic that begins to cross everyone's faces at that realization.

I guess my two days are up.

He continues. "The youngest of the Frey was charged to travel to enemy land and aid our Kingdom. She abandoned her duties, forsaking the royal name, surely standing in your midst. Her actions have jeopardized the truce between us and Oresteia, and they have declared war."

I gulp, my palms sweating.

"If you know her whereabouts, you are bound to report it immediately. She will be dealt with—she will be *punished.*"

He does not mention my name, as if ridding myself of an identity *and* a title all at once. One of his guards comes forward, pinning a notice to a wooden post in the middle of all of us with a hammer and nail. The parchment flutters, ever so slightly.

A hefty reward is displayed.

A chance to change someone's life.

An ink-filled stroke of a pen is all that it takes to condemn me and remind me that I am not cut out for this life; that this must have been a mistake.

No one moves, no one speaks.

The King searches the crowd then, looking for someone ready to speak up. Still, no one does.

Movement catches my eye, a hand lightly touching my elbow. I spin around, ready to run, when I see the boy from breakfast this morning. His hair is shorn to his scalp, a scar running from eyebrow to eyebrow that I did not notice earlier.

He leans in to whisper in my ear, trying not to be obvious. "You'll be safe here."

Taken aback, I pull away a bit, unsure. "How can you say that?"

"It doesn't matter to us where you come from," he continues. "We've all got reasons for wanting to leave home. You're fighting with us. That's enough."

I shake my head. "I doubt that will be enough for *everyone*."

He nods. "It is. You'll see."

I face toward the King once more and watch as he turns back to enter the carriage. The door shuts with a *bang*.

They ride away without looking back.

As soon as he's gone, voices begin to ripple through the group.

"Can't believe he showed his face here."

"What kind of father puts a price on his daughter?"

"If I were that girl, I wouldn't do what he says either."

I wander from behind the tent, heart hammering, listening to what they're saying. Are they not loyal to the King? What actions of his do I know nothing about because I was cooped up in the Palace?

A voice speaks from my left. "That bounty isn't worth giving you up, darlin'."

I turn. Mas stands there, watching me.

Before I can cut in, prove to him that he's wrong, a woman beside me speaks up.

"You're ours, girl. You're gonna sleep, eat, and fight like we do. And someday very soon, you'll bleed with us. You might just die as one of us, too."

"Why would you give up the chance to turn me in? To help your families?"

She snorts. "This *is* our family, girl. Welcome to it."

They go off, leaving me standing there astonished at their generosity and kindness.

Somewhere behind me, I hear orders being barked at the recruits, but my brain can't focus on the words being said.

All I can focus on is the small kernel of hope blossoming in my chest—a renewed sense of purpose beginning to take shape within me.

※ ※ ※

Later, as the sun sets, I'm sitting by a fire, staring into the flames and listening to stories being told. I feel stripped bare—vulnerable in the worst way. And yet somehow, shielded and cared for all the same.

Someone sits beside me without a word, close enough that our arms brush.

My heart recognizes the shape of his shoulders, the rhythm of his breathing.

"What a day we've had, huh?" Callious says.

"Where have you been?" I ask, still staring down

the flickering flame in front of me. Anger starts to seep into my tone at his absence. I feel exasperated.

"I had orders today. Nothing special, just new drills and lots of talks." He elbows me, leaning in, trying to catch my eye. It works, my gaze naturally finding his own. "I'm sorry I left you today. I'm sorry I didn't have a chance to tell you. I couldn't say no."

The sincerity in his voice breaks down the walls I built, my body leaning into his on its own. My head finds his shoulder as we look into the firelight.

"I missed you," I breathe.

He kisses the top of my head, the gesture natural. "If they tried to take you," he pauses, entire body coiled and ready to fight. "If they had laid a hand on you, I would have—"

"I know," I interrupt, panicking. He gets riled up so quickly. "I know."

A calloused, gentle hand finds my jaw and directs me to meet his eyes.

The fire's glow shines in his green irises, giving them a rich tint of gold.

My favorite colors, wrapped up together as one.

"You don't have to be who *they* wanted you to be," he says, searching my face.

"I know," I respond, trying to be convincing.

He sighs, relaxing against me. His tone is wistful. "Who do you want to be?"

I hesitate, thinking. "I want to be the type of person worth protecting. Worth choosing, worth trusting."

"You already are," he responds, certain.

My breath catches as he leans closer, his thumb brushing my jawline.

I don't pull away.

"I'm so glad you're here," he admits, barely a whisper. Just loud enough for me to hear it—for us to share this moment.

I give him a soft smile.

Before I can tell him the same—that I am so glad I came, even though it has been so hard and I have doubted myself already, a horn blows from the middle of camp.

I look at Callious for answers, but he jumps up faster than I can register.

His muscles coil, tense. Others follow, standing alert, freezing mid-conversations.

A recruit runs up to our fire, breathing heavily.

A muscle ticks in Cal's jaw. I stand next to him, steeling myself for whatever is to come.

"Scouts just came back," the recruit says in between gasps. "Oresteia is moving down the Isthmus. We march to meet them at dawn."

The fire flickers, but it has lost all its warmth.

Tomorrow, everything will change.

How could I ever be ready?

CHAPTER EIGHT

WE MARCH TOGETHER IN THE MORNING, WEARY AND warm.

Adrenaline fills our bodies, coating our skin with excitement. I'm not ready for this, for what may come, but how could I ever be? This is a new world I'm partaking in. There can be no hesitancy, they harp. We must move and breathe and live and fight as one.

Our company is two hundred people strong. Our Captain stands at the front, heavily armed. The rest of our army has stayed behind at the Gate, hoping that should we fall, they can keep them from entering Paralia.

Here on the Isthmus, our sands begin to merge into drifts of snow in the middle. We see Oresteia's army, dressed in menacing onyx, marching straight toward us as we are to them.

Our world seems as if it has split in two—Paralia's golden sands stretch behind us, calling us, reminding us of its heated embrace. But in front of us lies Oresteia and its frozen exterior.

Wind cuts through this part of the Isthmus, temperature differences intermixing to create a vortex of sorts. Grains of sand and snowflakes dance together, landing on our clothes, in our hair, in my eyes.

On this narrow strip of land between our Kingdoms, it's as if the ground cannot decide what it wants to be.

What if I can't either?

It feels as if the cool breeze coming from Oresteia calls my name, making me wonder what could have been if I had traveled there. Would I have been able to prevent all of this? Could I have protected my Kingdom, my friends?

My thoughts are short-lived. Here, in the midst of battle, there's no time to think.

My boots sink into slush where heat and cold join together, my own armor already slick with salty air and winter sleet. Somehow, we arrive at the middle of the Stenos Isthmus before Oresteia does.

Two days. It's been two days since I said 'yes' to Callious, forsaking my name and deciding to create one for myself, in my own way.

Kori gave me the liberty of knowing how long I had before war would be upon us. And whether that was a calculated move on his part, or pity taken upon me, I am grateful for it.

Near the back of the group, my eyes find the water to our left. Our sea meets theirs with a kiss—our dark current overtaking and overlapping their light waves.

The ice-filled, pale waters of the Khionean Sea

stretch as far as my eyes can see, coming from Oresteia's Kingdom. They reflect the graying of the sky above, the sun not able to reach this part of our world with its rays.

The rhythmic lapping lulls me, gifting me peace and an empty head, even in the midst of chaos and uncertainty. Cliffs rise from the waters on either side of the land, the power of the sea over the years cutting them into jagged edges. This bridge is both a blessing and a curse to our Kingdoms.

In a way, it's a way to keep us unified; connected. On the other hand, it's a constant reminder that we are bound together, our lands split apart for a reason.

And that we will never be the same.

But could those differences not be celebrated? Could they not bring us closer together?

Callious stands a few rows ahead of me, his silhouette sharp against the dreary horizon. He turns his head back, just far enough to glance my way. Our eyes meet easily, and he smiles—surely trying to reassure me and ease the panic beginning to make its way into my heart.

He is my steady anchor in a sea of unpredictability.

Our horn sounds, and I tune back into my surroundings. Oresteia's company is right in front of us now, staring us down. Our Captain is taking his place in the front line, as do they.

Were we trying to negotiate? I missed it.

Our horn goes off again, in tandem with theirs.

We surge forward as one, as best as we are able, with only two days of preparation under our belts. We brought a mix of recruits—some who have been here for just a few days, like myself, and others who have been training for years. With that, we are all unsteady in our trust in one another.

Boots slip against the mud and snow under our feet as we enter enemy territory. Our blue Paralian banner ripples in front of me, front lines colliding in a sea of colors.

Metal clashes, and it reminds me to take my dagger out of its belt before I'm too late. I rip it out, gripping its hilt tightly, knuckles white.

Oresteia's soldiers move quickly, efficiently—like shadows slipping through the wind.

The space between me and them vanishes too fast.

"Raise the shields!" someone shouts. Shields go up around me, but I do not have one of my own. Too heavy for me to carry, and there wasn't enough time to craft a lighter one.

A whisper cuts through the air to my right, something whizzing past my ear. I duck, hearing it hit the person behind me.

I look back, hoping to see that it was just a simple nick on the arm.

My eyes widen as I look upon their fallen form, now lying on the cold ground.

He fell without a sound.

I whip my head to the front, my breath coming in shallow.

I just watched someone die.

The sleet is unraveling my ponytail, pieces of curls sticking to my face and hindering my line of sight. My chest feels tight.

But there, in the front of Oresteia's line, I see a

figure in a deep shade of red, unlike the rest of them. She holds a bow high, with confidence, her eyes alert and ready. I freeze. It seems that she's looking right at me. Her arrow is back, the tip pointed in my direction.

The arrow is pointed at me.

It flies past me, cutting the skin of my cheek. I move nearly too late, stumbling backward into the space that is now empty behind me. Callious appears just as suddenly, his shield up, bracing both of us in the midst of all of this.

"You can stay close to me," he breathes. I nod, terrified. I look back up, looking for her, but she's disappeared, surely moving onto her next target.

How will we ever win something like this?

My fingers are locked around my hilt, the cold weather freezing them to the spot.

Chaos breaks loose.

We run past our soldiers, past theirs, past bodies lying wounded, or worse. Our line crashes completely with Oresteia's, voices raised together in battle cries and pain-filled shouts. I run because they are—because I might die if I don't.

Callious stays with me, making sure I do not fall behind. I know that if I did, he would stay with me—risk his life for me. I cannot let him do that.

I cannot be the reason he gets hurt.

My first strike is a wild swing. I nearly drop my dagger as someone barrels into me, my boots losing their grip on the terrain. One of their soldiers—barely older than I am—slams his own fighting knives against mine, his eyes wide with fear and determination.

I catch his strike easily somehow, adrenaline telling

my limbs what to do. At the force of our weapons meeting, he loses his grip on one of his knives, the blade falling onto the earth.

He's knocked onto his knees. I have the upper hand, my brain screaming at me to twist his knife from his hand and deal the final strike.

But I hesitate. So does he.

He could be just like me. Here to create a new name and a new future for himself.

How could I truly be against him?

He notes the pause on my face, taking that chance to catch me off guard. I hardly register him picking up his fallen blade, or him beginning to drive it upward toward my ribs…

But his lethal blow does not find its mark. Callious crashes into him from the side, shield-first, knocking him down. Callious hits him in the head once more with his shield, ensuring that he will stay down for a while.

If not forever.

Cal turns to me, breath ragged. "Are you okay?"

My chest hitches, embarrassment suffocating me.

"What was that?" he asks. "You can't freeze on me, Nelly. You *can't.*"

His eyes continue to scan the battlefield, but all the same, they are still too focused on me.

Just focused enough that he does not see the flash of black behind him.

I cannot warn him fast enough.

"No!" I yell, reaching to grab the closest thing to me—his armor's collar—just as he turns to see what I'm looking at.

I yank him forward as the soldier swipes, his sword grazing the side of Callious's neck.

The sound he makes is quick and short, like a breath caught in his throat.

Cal turns completely as he falls back into me, planting his back foot to drive his own sword into that soldier's stomach, finding a vulnerable place beneath his own armor.

He stumbles then as he removes his blade. He drops to one knee in the melted ice, his hand pressed to the wound.

I lunge for him, not paying attention to anything else around me. His blood soaks through the beige fabric of his collar. It's hot in my hands as I try to quench the bleeding.

"It's just a shallow wound, P." His teeth grit, breathing labored as he tries to reason with me. His eyes find mine. "Thanks to you, it's not as bad as it could have been."

"You're lying," I cry. My heart is pounding in my ears, the loudness of it drowning out the noise and screams of the battle beyond.

I see a flash of black charging toward us. Standing, I step between the soldier and Callious. I lift my dagger, squaring my feet. I'm *ready*. I will not hesitate this time.

I drive them back in a flash of strikes and blocks that surprise me. I don't look at their face, don't register their age or think about their life circumstances.

I don't want to know who they are, or what they've been through to get to this point.

My only goal is to get them away from Callious.

When they fall, just wounded enough that they cannot get back up, I walk back to my best friend. I stand above him as he rises from his knee, my lungs running out of oxygen.

My hands shake as Cal takes my dagger from me, using his pants to clean the blood off of it. I take it back from him, our fingers meeting, that small amount of contact enough to steady me once again.

We will not die today.

Maybe tomorrow. But not today.

The fighting slows, both of us back to back, not willing to leave the other. Oresteians begin to retreat, so we do too. Both of us have been hit by loss today.

We regroup as we make it back to the Gate, relaying our names to the General in charge so he might make a list of our lost and tell their families.

Cal leans on me, one hand holding a sleeve against the bleeding. His weight is welcomed by me, warm and heavy. Somehow, it's a comfort, reminding me that at least he is here, and that we are still together.

✳ ✳ ✳

We sit on the ground next to the campfire together that night, after he's been bandaged. It could have been much worse, the nurses said. He should be up and ready again tomorrow if he can rest tonight.

Just a shallow neck wound. But it will scar.

"They'll send scouts," he mutters to me, obviously still in pain. "They'll want to see how we're faring after our first battle, and start to plan their next steps. Overnight, if they haven't already."

"Why are you thinking about that right now?" I ask, my hand brushing sweaty hair off his forehead. I'm sitting cross-legged next to where he lies, propped up with an elbow. "You need to get some rest—you heard what the nurses said."

"Just because I'm bleeding does not mean they'll stop their plans." He looks up at me then, grinning mischievously. "Besides, I'm bored. Today was exhilarating."

I roll my eyes. "I'm glad one of us had a good time."

His fingers mess with the seam of my pant leg, silence ringing between us for a few minutes.

"I want to ambush them," he whispers to me, his voice serious. "I want to take one of their scouts alive. Prove myself."

I stare at him. "Surely you're not serious," I say. "You're *hurt.*"

He nods, as if he did not hear a word I said. "Tonight. When they're trying to gain an advantage against us, let's turn it against them. I know this camp like the back of my hand already. They'll think no one will be able to outwit them. You and me, Pen. We could turn the tide of this war. *Tonight.*"

I hesitate. "You wouldn't want me with you. I'm not good at all this." I motion around us, waving my hands in the air.

He catches my wrists, pulling me down to his level. There's no teasing in his gaze, only sincerity. "I trust you, P. I told you I wanted you by my side—to have your back and have you watch mine. We are better together, in all things, as it always has been."

His words fuel me.

I want to be the type of person worth his trust. Worth his love.

I nod. I always give in to his rash whims. I just can't seem to help it when it comes to him.

Cal smiles at me, the fire's light reflecting off his features.

Tonight, while everyone sleeps, we will set a trap.

Together.

CHAPTER NINE

ON THE FAR SIDE OF THE GATE, ON THE OUTSKIRTS OF camp and the part closest to the Isthmus, there's a gap in our gilded fence.

"They'll come in through here," Cal says, so certain of so many things.

He was made for this life. I can barely keep up.

"So are we going to just… wait here? And grab them?" I ask.

"Let's set a tripwire. We can hide in the shadows over there," he points. "Coming from the Isthmus, they won't be able to see us quite as easily if we lie down in the sand."

I follow his lead as he crouches near the gap, threading wire and light-colored rope between the two posts. His eyebrows furrow, but his hands are precise and steady.

He works quickly, tying it off and plucking it to make sure it's taut enough to quickly catch a boot or two.

The salty air is thick with night, the only sound the crash of the waves and the crackle of spent campfires. The sand is soft and cold underfoot. Moonlight filters toward us in chunks, just enough for us to see right in front of us.

I feel guilty, as if I'm doing something wrong. I trust Callious and that he wouldn't lead me astray. Ambushes aren't necessarily something they let recruits do.

We brought strips of cloth with us—one for a gag, one for around the scout's wrists.

It feels like Cal thought of everything.

I lay in the sand next to him, making sure to stick to the heavy shadows. I lean into the chill of the ground, the sun's rays having evaporated from it hours prior.

"They might see the wire if the moon's light catches it," I say, trying to be helpful.

"It's black wire. We'll be okay."

So sure.

As we lie there, I begin to nod off, the day's events catching up with my weary body. I lean my head on Callious's shoulder, careful to avoid brushing against his bandaged neck. The bleeding stopped a while ago, but he's keeping the wrapping on it just in case.

So much has happened today.

The sound of heavy footsteps jerks me awake. Coming from the tents, headed this direction, is a figure. As he gets closer, I see that it's the same recruit from breakfast—the one with the close-cropped hair.

The one who said I would be safe with them.

Cal tenses beside me, and we dig ourselves deeper into the sand, trying not to be seen.

What would happen should we be caught? Would he turn us in? Would there be punishment? Banishment?

I have nowhere else to go.

My hand finds my dagger, the rest of my body freezing in a fight-or-flight response as he grows closer.

He walks to the edge of camp, beginning to unbuckle his pants *right in front of us.*

I shriek. The boy stops what he's doing, squinting in our direction. I avert my gaze, quickly covering my eyes.

"I didn't know anyone was out here," he mutters, stumbling over his words. I hear his buckle, and I deem it safe to look back up. He's walking to where we lie, staring at us wide-eyed, his hands raised in surrender. "I was just trying to relieve myself. I've been holding it for hours."

He looks us up and down, eyes narrowing in suspicion. "What are you doing out here?"

I blink. "Uh… we've… also been holding it for hours?" I look at Callious, hoping for some help. He just grinds his jaw, surely assessing how this changes our plans.

He gets up then, brushing the sand off his body. "Are you alone?"

The boy seems taken aback, confused. "Yeah, I mean, they said I could go before lights-out. So my tent mates will be expecting me back, but…" he rambles. His eyes bounce back and forth between the two of us. "Wait. What are you guys *doing* out here?"

Before I can come up with another bad excuse, Cal grabs the boy by the collar and yanks him down with us in the shadows.

"Congrats, Alex. You just got yourself a spot on the ambush squad."

"What?" he yelps, but Callious wraps a hand around his mouth before he can say anything else or yell for help.

Cal lowers his voice. "We are trying to capture an Oresteian scout. If you mess this up for us, I'll throw you into the Neronian without a second thought."

"I can't swim," he mumbles, gulping.

Callious rolls his eyes as he releases his grip on him. "City kid."

We settle into our positions once again, our accidental teammate lying between us in case he tries to bolt back to camp.

"I don't have a weapon on me," Alex whispers to us.

I look at him, raising my eyebrows in disbelief. "Even I know you should carry a weapon everywhere you go."

He opens his mouth to talk back, but footsteps sound near us.

Coming from the Isthmus.

Our bodies tense, coiled and ready. I can hear my heart beating rapidly in my ears, the thud of my chest drowning out everything else.

The footsteps are soft, deliberate—as if someone is merely dancing upon the grains of sand.

Cal catches my eye, nodding to me. I breathe out, deeply and slowly, remembering the plan.

"When he trips, I'll run out and put him face first into the ground. I'll take care of his head and his arms—you need to grab his legs."

"What if I'm not strong enough to hold him?"

"Adrenaline will carry you through."

I come back to the present moment, watching the figure approach our fence's gap. He moves like a ghost. His face is covered in a hood, his apparel black like today's soldiers. Still, his clothes seem off for some reason. They hang off of him, as if they are a size too big.

Odd.

He begins to slip through the opening, one boot over the tripwire. His head is on a swivel as he moves, constantly searching his surroundings.

Then, his back foot catches the wire, the rope tightening as it's meant to.

The figure stumbles in the dark, and Callious shoots out of the trees, wrestling the scout to the ground. His legs fly out behind him, face pressed into the soft sand as his arms get pinned behind his body. He tries to roll, but I'm there with Alex in an instant, both of us holding a leg down.

Cal presses a blade to his throat.

"Don't move," Callious bites.

"Nice trick," the figure—a man—says, his voice low and far too calm. Perhaps that's just how Oresteians are.

"Give us your name and your rank," Cal barks.

"...cannot speak with my mouth full of sand," he mumbles. Cal eases on his grip, allowing him to lift his neck slightly. "I think you will find that my name would complicate matters more than any of you could likely handle."

I narrow my eyes. "Try us."

I feel him go rigid beneath our hold. He lies still, not struggling. He cranes his neck to look back at me and Alex. Moonlight glances off his cheek, a piece of it catching his eyes as they assess me.

The light brightens them, though I believe even in the dark I would be able to see their color clearly.

They are an icy-blue, the color of the Khionean Sea.

They pierce me, familiar, freezing me to the spot.

"Unfortunate," he whispers, so soft I can hardly hear it.

He averts his attention back to Callious, leaving me cold without his gaze.

"You do not understand what's happening here," he says. "But if you want, I can play along."

Alex cuts in, having apparently decided that this is his moment too. "You're Oresteian. That's all that matters to us, and the only thing that will matter to our Captains."

"I'm a lot of things," the scout retorts. "But you'll see that soon enough."

His gear is loose on his body, his features too clean.

I look at Cal. "I don't know about this anymore. He seems important."

"He's just trying to get us to let him go back to his camp," he responds. "It's what he *wants* us to think."

I doubt that, for some reason. The sincerity in the Oresteian's tone is something I believe.

The scout laughs, the sound catching me off guard.

Cal groans. "Get him up. I'll tie him off."

The three of us hoist him to his feet, his hood falling from his white-blonde hair. His skin is so pale, as if translucent in the moonlight.

The gag gets placed in his mouth, and the other strip of cloth around his wrists. The boys search him for weapons while I hold onto his arms, his hands cold under my touch.

"You seem out of place," he mutters to me through the gag. "This is new to you, too, isn't it?"

I peer at him, confused.

What am I supposed to say to that?

Before I can respond, Callious cuts in for me. "Don't speak to her."

The scout nods, grinning, as if confirming something he was questioning.

We march him back to the heart of camp with Alex trailing behind us, acting as our guard. The scout doesn't fight us, nor does he plead. He doesn't question our next moves or try to convince us to let him go. He just walks with us, casually, as if this is all going exactly how it's meant to.

He walks like a soldier, but he talks much more like someone with proper schooling.

Someone like me.

I glance at him from the side, my hands gripping his arm tightly just in case.

Something about him brings forth overwhelming curiosity. Perhaps it's just the wrongness I feel regarding this situation, or the weirdness of his earlier question.

We are at war, I remind myself. *These are the types of things you need to be ready to do.*

My skin itches, and I feel uneasy.

I don't know this scout's name, but I do believe I know this much:

This was not just a lucky ambush.

We've caught someone who *wanted* to be caught.

And we are leading him right where he wants to go.

CHAPTER TEN

WE WALK THROUGH CAMP, THE ORESTEIAN HELD tightly between us. Base is nearly silent, everyone having headed to their tents long ago, lights-out long passed. The air is thick with tension, with questions.

I'm not sure how our Sergeant will take this— Callious, Alex, and me. Since we actually caught a scout, surely we won't be punished...

Right?

I'm not expecting praise or a reward by any means. The sun knows that acceptance and applause are two things I've never asked for, because I knew that I would not receive them.

From my family, at least.

Callious is different.

He stands tall and proud as he walks, chest puffed and shoulders straight. Alex trails behind us, watching our backs. The scout moves his bound hands, shifting the way of his wrists. He is as calm as ever as we approach the middle of camp, which baffles me.

How could anyone be calm in such a circumstance? Even the constant rise of the sun is still met with changes as the seasons pass.

Callious and I exchange glances, his eyebrow raised at the turmoil written all over my face. The reality of our choices is sinking into my bones, weighing me down. I don't know what all of this means yet, but I feel as though it's going to change everything.

Suddenly, we are in the vast, empty space that our many tents surround. A bigger one—the strategy tent —lies in front of us. A lantern is on inside, hushed voices carrying on the slight evening breeze.

"Sergeant," Callious calls, his voice steady. Within moments, one of our leaders, a man of about middle age, stalks out of the tent flap. His eyes are sharp and alert. They flicker briefly over our prisoner before they settle on the three of us.

"And what," he asks evenly. "Is the meaning of this?"

"We've captured an Oresteian scout. He attempted to sneak in tonight, near the Isthmus, to spy on us and gather information."

As Callious talks, I catch movement out of the corner of my eye.

Did this scout just… roll his eyes at Cal?

I huff under my breath.

The Sergeant calls for two others to come assist, and we step aside so they can take this man with them. He stands without any sort of resistance, giving in freely and easily to their whims.

Maybe being handed over was all part of his plan.

"Take him to our holding tent," the Sergeant

orders. The scout does not flinch or waver. He nods slightly, moving with the other two. Our Sergeant stays behind.

I watch him disappear into the night, and the shadows overlaying camp. My heart beats hard, knowing that I have unwittingly put myself in the position to be punished.

This sense of dread overwhelms me, and I don't understand why. I knew what the consequences of this would be—it's not as if Callious forced my hand or my actions. I *chose* this.

"Follow me," Sergeant says, leading us toward the war tent. "I'll need a word with all three of you first."

I look to Callious, then to Alex. Alex is chewing on his fingers, eyes downcast. Cal, on the other hand, is *definitely* still feeling prideful regarding his choices and how this evening went.

Classic.

Sergeant leads us into the dimly lit tent, looking at a huge table in the middle layered with maps, weapons, location pins, and more. He nods his head towards the others in the space, and they leave us at once.

Once they've left, he leans against the table, arms crossed with one ankle over the other. "So," he starts. "Tell me why you decided that, as new recruits, it was a smart decision to move without orders."

Cal speaks for all of us. "It was necessary. I knew they would try to make a move on us tonight, assuming we were weak and recuperating from today's battle. And it paid off. We got him easily and—"

He's cut off. "You should have come to one of us, or to your Captain. What if your leadership had set up their own trap? You could have compromised a number of things because you are not privy to that information. Why? Because *you do not rank high enough.*" He sighs, shaking his head. "I will admit, you were successful, and because of that, we have an opportunity to gain more knowledge on Oresteia. But that is where my compliment will end. You've put us all at risk. Whose idea was this?"

I start to speak up, hoping to save Cal from harsh punishment. "Sir, if I may—"

Cal interrupts me. "It was mine, sir. Alex stumbled upon us during a, uh," he pauses. "A bathroom break, sir. And I forced Pen to come with me, selfishly."

A prickle of frustration rises within me, but I swallow it down. I don't want his protection. I knew the chances of punishment; I knew that there would be consequences. His shielding me feels like a punch to the gut, as if he does not believe that I would be able to handle the weight of what we've done and what that would lead to.

"Noted," Sergeant says. "Alex, you are dismissed. Do not let me find you involved with these two again."

Alex nods, mumbling under his breath as he shuffles out of the tent. I feel bad for him.

"You are both—"

Before he can dish out our punishment, one of the men that took the scout away interrupts.

"Sergeant," he begins. "The boy refuses to talk. Says he'll only talk to her." His head nods my way.

What?

I look wide-eyed at our Sergeant, scared he'll think I planned this as some elaborate ruse. He pinches the skin between his eyebrows, huffing. I'm about to say I have no idea why he'd want to talk to *me* when Callious speaks.

"We'll get answers, sir."

The Sergeant rolls his eyes and sighs, clearly not impressed or happy with having to deal with both of us. "If you make a move like that again, you're gone. Understood?"

I gulp. I have nowhere else to go. Callious, though, could go back home, or anywhere else if he truly wished.

We both nod, silent. There's nothing else to say. Nothing we can do to rebut or minimize his scrutiny.

The three of us leave the tent, the reprimand hanging tautly in the air. Cal's shoulders are stiff, and he refuses to look my way. He's silently fuming.

I know he's mad at the Sergeant, but surely he's not mad at me? We took this risk, and we did it together.

The tent has a deep chill to it as we enter. The scout is seated on a stool in the middle, his wrists still bound, but his gag has been removed. He seems to perk up at my entrance, looking me up and down with those familiar blue eyes. He settles after, seemingly breathing out in relief. He's still alert and relaxed, but there's something about him now—something different from when he was just with us.

Two guards whisper quick words to our Sergeant. Sergeant looks at us, arms crossed, as if debating whether leaving us alone with this Oresteian is a wise choice or not. I wither under his glare while I await direction.

"You have five minutes," he says, finally. Then, he turns on his heel and follows the other two outside.

I wait for Cal to take the lead. I can feel the weight of everyone's expectations against my chest, making it hard to breathe in this small space. Where do we begin? What do we even say? Will the scout even tell us the truth—or answer us at all?

As I spiral, Callious moves to stand in front of the boy. "Why are you here?" he asks.

The scout doesn't answer right away, nor does he spare a glance at Cal at all. Instead, his eyes peer into my own, making me nervous.

Callious notices, trying to step in front of me, relieving me of most of his gaze. "You've been sent to spy on us. *Why* are you *here*?"

The scout finally speaks, eyes still locked on me. "I'll only answer," he says. "To *her*."

I look at him, questioning. Callious glances at me, clearly hesitating. The boy's voice was calm and collected, but I can't help but wonder if there's some ulterior motive here.

Why me?

I step forward, tentative.

"Who are you?" I ask.

He smiles at me then, a radiant smile that is seemingly out of place for both the time and the space we are in.

"My name is William," he admits, his tone kind and warm.

I nod, chewing at the inside of my cheek while I look to Callious for guidance on what to ask next. He motions with his hands to just keep going, keep asking.

"What were you after today?"

He tilts his head, his pale hair falling across his forehead. "I was hoping for a glimpse of something."

I narrow my eyes at him, at his crypticness. "And did you find what you were looking for?" I ask incredulously.

William's grin widens. "I did."

Anger rises within me.

Why must interrogation be so complicated?

"What does that even mean?" I ask. "What are you trying to say? Or better yet, *not* trying to say?"

He doesn't so much as flinch at the frustration dripping from my tone. Unfazed, he just looks at me, his icy blue eyes sparkling with mischief and delight.

I'm glad someone here is having a good time.

"There's so much more to this war than all of you could ever understand. This is a mistake. Beg your King to meet with ours—find another way."

I throw my hands up. "What are you *talking* about? Oresteia declared war on *us*. You beg *your* King." I pause, thinking. "And we don't understand this war? But somehow *you* do? Then how about you enlighten us, scout?"

"I can't explain it to you. Not yet," he shakes his head. "War isn't the most dangerous thing arriving to our Kingdoms, Penelope."

Taken aback, my jaw drops. Before I can respond, Callious speaks up for me. "How do you know her name?"

"They whisper about you in my Kingdom," he admits to me, still not caring to look at Cal, "Of the girl who gave up her crown to fight instead. Word travels fast."

Stuttering, I try to find the words stuck in my throat, but our Sergeant moves back into the tent, then, the look on his face one of authority and power. My stomach is queasy.

There's something so unsettling about this boy, something I can't place. Looking at him makes me nervous.

Who is this William?

"Time's up," Sergeant says.

Cal begins to walk out, holding the tent flap open for me. I hesitate. I know this is our dismissal, but I don't feel ready to leave yet. There's so much left unsaid, so much that we don't understand.

What is he truly talking about? What is he really trying to say?

Still, I walk away, chancing one last glance back at William. He smiles again, as if we are old friends, and winks at me.

My eyebrows furrow at him, and I turn around to leave.

Callious walks me back to my tent in silence. When we arrive, I bury my head into his chest, relieved to have such a safe space after an evening of frustration and anger. He lets me, holding me tight, only letting go when I'm the first to do so.

After a quick goodnight, I sit on my cot in the quiet. My tent mates—whom I have still not met—lie asleep.

When I lie down a few hours later, I stare at the top of my tent, questioning everything.

What did he want from us? What was he hoping we knew more of?

I start to drift to sleep when suddenly, horns sound.

I jerk awake, sitting straight up.

The girl next to me barely sits up, groggily looking at me and around the tent. "Prisoner musta escaped," she mumbles. Then, as if she was never truly awake, passes out again.

I clutch my throw blanket to my chest.

He's gone.

Just like that, he's escaped and gone back to Oresteia to tell them everything.

I don't know why my heart feels pained at that, why my chest feels too tight all of a sudden.

Perhaps his only goal was to come and spread false information, to make us feel stupid and unready for our next battle.

I lay back down, resolve coating me.

"He'll regret that," I whisper into the night, the words bitter on my tongue.

But for some reason, I do not fully believe that it will be him who will regret this.

For some reason, I feel like it will be me.

CHAPTER ELEVEN

THE MESS TENT IS WARM THIS MORNING, SMELLING OF things I probably do not want to eat. The air is sticky, humid. My curls frizz at my scalp, even though I have them pulled back in a tight bun. I join the line, waiting for my turn to eat undistinguishable slop.

I never thought this day would come, but I miss the Palace's fish.

Mas doesn't look up when I arrive at his part of the line. Still, I know he sees me. He's not serving today. Instead, he's… kneading something? Probably more hardtack.

As if we don't have enough already. I can't get *away* from that stuff.

His calloused hands, caked in dirt and sand, press the dough flat, folding it repeatedly as if it's second nature.

I wonder what he did before this.

As I grab my tray and begin searching for a space

to sit among the recruits, his rough voice speaks out from behind me.

"Heard you got yourself in some hot water last night, darlin'."

I turn around, my cheeks warming. "People are… talking about it?"

He huffs. "There's not much that happens around here that I don't know about."

Sheepishly, I dance between the balls of my feet. "We caught a scout. He's already escaped, though."

"You caught yourself a Prince, darlin'," he says. Mas eyes me then, with something akin to suspicion. Maybe waiting to see what my reaction would be?

I'm shocked. Stunned. Appalled. Confused?

"What…" I nearly drop my tray. "No," I begin.

"Yup," he says matter-of-factly.

"Why would the Oresteian Prince be… here? Surely he's meant to be hidden away in their Palace, rather than out in this war."

Mas shakes his head at me. "Only the sun knows what he's doing milling about in the dark. Sounds like he gave the Sarge some good information," he pauses. "That is, if he can be trusted."

I step closer to him and lower my voice. "What did he say?"

My brain cannot help the curiosity that has gotten the better of me. At the Palace, we are taught not to gossip. But still, this feels like information that I *need* to have. He *knew* me.

Do I know him? Did he come here to warn *me* about something? What if I'm the only one who can figure out what is really going on?

I scoff under my breath. *As if.*

"Something about a jewel, a crown. Stolen, supposedly. You know anything about that?" Again, that dumb eyebrow raised in my direction. I'd cut it off if I could.

"I don't," I say. He doesn't look convinced. "I *don't!*" My voice rises on accident, people in line eyeing me now. I duck my head, trying to remain unnoticed.

"Well, that's a shame, darlin'. It's a good story."

I look at him, weighing my options. I don't have much time before morning chores and training, and I can't tell if Mas can be trusted completely. Do I ask him to tell me the story? Or do I cut my losses and hope that I can hear whispers of it later today?

Resigned, I sigh. This is the best chance I have to figure out what might really be happening in this war.

And between our two Kingdoms.

"Would you tell me? I ask, sweetly, trying to lay on the charm.

Mas snorts. "Took you long enough to ask."

He motions for me to follow him to the back of the tent, where the cooking equipment is. There's no one else back here—the others are busy serving everyone else.

He wipes flour from his hands onto his stained apron, and I follow his lead as he sits on a wooden barrel in the corner. It groans under his weight. I lay my tray in my lap, the food growing colder by the minute.

I suppose now is as good a time as any to eat.

"Before your time—before mine, even—our first King and Oresteia's met," he begins. "They were old enemies, lots of bad blood between the two of 'em. Had lost everything they ever loved and cared about."

It's as if the air in the room stands still as he tells this tale, his tone enchanting and the story pulling me in.

How was I never taught our own history?

"Our two Kingdoms are connected by the Stenos Isthmus, you know that much," he says. I nod. "Well, one evening, that Oresteian King was over on our shore, and Paralia's King took him to our cliffside, hoping to find some sort of truce between the two of 'em."

I tilt my head. "How do you know this story?"

The condescending look he gives me sends a shiver down my spine. "I've been around a long time, darlin'. Do you want to hear the rest of it or not?"

I give him a sheepish smile, a blush rising to my cheeks. He continues. "It's said they made a bargain. Cut up their hands and shook, their blood dripping down onto the sand. Right then and there, from the ground, grew what the storytellers call the Janus Tree. It's a closely guarded secret, so not many know its name or where it is. Supposedly, it's a door between the Kingdoms for your families."

I interrupt. "That doesn't make any sense."

"Don't have to make sense to be true, darlin'," he retorts. "That's not even half of it. There in the middle, a jewel was found. Called it the Queen's Heart. The Oresteian King claimed it as his own, said it was a gift he was owed. Our own King let him have it, said the peace between our Kingdoms was worth relinquishing it, even though it was found on our shores."

My grip on my utensil tightens.

He looks around, lowering his voice to a whisper and leans in. "I've heard whispers that the jewel funnels magic, that it stretches across their Kingdom. Without it, they lose access to their own abilities. Their Stronghold'll keep 'em going, but not forever. And now that jewel is gone, replaced with a fake a few months ago. They think your family did it, and now here we are fighting for our lives and eatin' cold food."

I furrow my eyebrows. "That cannot possibly be the whole reason why we are at war."

Mas's eyes lift from mine, looking behind me. I feel someone's hand brush across my back. Turning, I find Cal smiling down at me. "You don't have to sit and listen to whatever this old man is telling you, Nel."

Mas huffs, shifting his weight to stand. "Oh, but she should listen to you? That's rich coming from the boy who decided to go against orders."

Callious winks, still not taking that sparkling green gaze off of me. "I didn't mean to interrupt," he says. "I was just looking for my girl."

Our cook gags. Still, I blush and divert my eyes back to my empty tray. As Mas begins to leave, I ask, "Is that how the story ends?"

He turns back to me, grimly. "They're connected, darlin'. That Tree and that Heart. If one's gone, so is the other."

My heart drops into my stomach as he leaves, sweat coating my hands.

Surely that's not right.

Cal sits on the barrel where Mas was, taking my tray from me to place it in the sand. His hair is windswept and golden from the beating sun. His gaze flickers for a moment, concerned.

"Hey," he says, reaching for my chin. "What was he saying?"

My voice shakes. "I'm sure it's just a story."

He tilts his head, guiding my eyes to his. "Even the grandest stories have a thread of truth in them. And if what he claims is the truth, then we will figure it out together."

"Why wouldn't my family teach me these things? Our own history?"

Cal ponders this for a moment before speaking. "I didn't hear your whole conversation, but I've heard plenty of whispers this morning. If our King long ago gave up his claim to what rightfully should have belonged to both Kingdoms, it's possible your father," he pauses, realizing his mistake. "I mean, King Zannan might be embarrassed by the weakness of his own ancestor."

I scoff, mumbling. "That does sound like him."

He reaches over to take my hand, where my fingers pick at the fabric of my pants. Somehow, that feeling of our hands together is both nothing and everything all at once. All I've ever wished for, but never thought I would get to have.

Mas's voice booms from behind us, breaking our trance. "Get out of my kitchen, you two."

We laugh as we stand. I return my tray to the pile of dirty ones that will be cleaned by a recruit later, and follow Callious outside.

The sun blinds me immediately, its rays not covered by a single cloud.

I wonder, if the jewel truly once belonged to both of us, then how could we be in the wrong for taking it, if we did?

If it's truly shared, what are we even fighting for?

I think back to the fallen bodies from our battle. *Not everyone will see the end of this war,* I think. *Some of us won't make it back home.*

Cal notices me lingering behind and turns, scanning the crowd for me—a crowd oblivious to the *real* reason we're here.

He spots me, my best friend's eyes locking onto mine—as if he'd be able to find me anywhere.

Callious grins at me, beckoning me to follow him. I giggle, worry melting off my shoulders like ice in the sun.

The calm to my storm, the sea to my shore.

He's my constant, even when the world around me seemingly never is.

Even when I don't know what to believe anymore.

I walk toward him, joining him with the mass to await chore orders for today.

But deep down, my heart stirs.

War isn't something to be taken lightly.

It's something we'll never be able to undo.

CHAPTER TWELVE

THE REST OF MY DAY SPINS AROUND MY HEAD IN A BLUR of unanswered questions and half-whispered rumors coming from those around me. Everyone in camp knows that William is Oresteia's Prince and that he was captured last night before he ultimately escaped. It seems as though no one knows of our involvement.

Wouldn't want to encourage other recruits to make risky moves, I guess.

While heading to my training session, I see Alex. I try to make eye contact with him in passing. He ducks his head, clearly avoiding me.

I guess Sergeant scares him just enough to actually do what he says.

My body longs to feel focused and conditioned within the routine I'm slowly getting used to. Instead, the day drags me down like the Neronian tide.

Today's training session is especially brutal. Now that we are past our first battle and well beyond the lie that our lives are *not* at stake, our sergeants shout and push and pull at us for hours on end under the scorching sun.

I'm dripping in sweat already, my light clothing doing nothing but sticking to my skin as I block, strike, repeat. I haul buckets of our training weapons back to the tent where we store them so they will not rust under the salted air.

My arms hang limp at my sides, my back screaming at me to lie down in the sand. I sway, having trouble staying upright.

Callious and I are in separate groups, split up for different tasks and with different training schedules. I see him now across the way, finishing his own sparring. His face is set in concentration, sweat running down the sides of his neck as he blocks and strikes at his opponent. Cal overtakes the other boy, pinning him to the ground with seamless ease.

He helps him up, clapping him on his back, his smile a mile wide. I walk over to them as they rack their swords, clapping slowly in mock impression.

Cal sees me. "Have you come for your turn to fight against me, P?"

"You're delusional." I laugh, the act taking the rest of the energy I have left. "I came to tell you that I'm going to take a nap before dinner."

His face turns serious. "No, you are not."

My feet are dead under me. "If my body does not find my cot in the next five minutes, I fear I will find myself horizontal right here where I stand."

"It's a beautiful day!" he exclaims. "You can't waste a free afternoon with a *nap*."

Deadpan, I say, "The sun is melting the skin off my bones. I'm going to die."

"If I found you somewhere cool to rest," he begins, a smirk on his lips. "Would you consider going with me?"

"Such a place does not *exist* in Paralia."

"What if it did?" he asks, wiggling his eyebrows.

"Callious," I snort.

"Pen," he retorts. "*Come with me.*"

I roll my eyes. "Fine, but you *will* have to carry me."

At that, he whisks me up, wrapping an arm around my back and another around my legs. I sink into him, my body weightless in his embrace.

"It's unfair how convincing you are," I mumble, my eyes closing softly.

As I drift off while he carries me to who-knows-where, I hear him say, "It's unfair just how much I would do for you."

※ ※ ※

My stomach grumbles, waking me from the nap I still got to have, despite Callious's attempted intervention.

Groggily, I raise my head, noticing that we are coming up on the bottom of the cliffs that surround the east side of Paralia.

I wrap my arms around Cal's neck, looking around. "Where are we?"

He looks at me, surprised at my consciousness. "Secret spot," he says.

"Are we allowed to be outside of camp? Isn't it almost dinnertime?" I worry, my stomach noting that it's almost dinnertime and I don't have enough energy to skip a meal.

He shrugs, my body moving with the motion of his arms. "They never said we couldn't explore."

I have Cal set me down, choosing to walk the rest of the way as he shows me the path we are following. After a bit longer, we come across a rocky hole in the side of the cliffs. Neronian water rushes into it, creating a river of sorts that floods the mouth of the cave.

Callious jumps in, the water up to his quads. He offers me a hand, guiding me into the lapping waves, careful to make sure I don't slip on slick rocks.

"What is this place?" I ask.

He leads me further into the cave, the water warm against my lower body. In the back of it, the sea gathers into a pool of sorts, steam rising from it. Light floods in from the mouth of the cave, casting a golden glow on the spring.

Cal's grip is steady and familiar in mine, helping me up out of the water onto a small, smooth patch of rock not covered by the sea.

"I found it my first day here while I waited for you," he says, beginning to strip off his boots and socks. "I went fishing. Mas gave me a rod and some bait and pointed me in this direction. Found this instead."

Excitingly, I unlace my boots, following his direction. We take off our outer garments, leaving only the shorts and tanks that we wear underneath for extra skin protection from the sun.

I'm about to question whether or not Cal should get in because of his bandages, but he peels those off without a second thought. The skin is already healing nicely.

I dip my body into the pool slowly, letting the heat sink into the muscles that scream at me. It's perfect—so much warmer than I expected but not scalding. It softens the ache in my back, making my body feel weightless.

This is my favorite thing about the Neronian. It makes you feel as if you are flying.

Cal decides to jump in instead, the waters crashing at his arrival. He emerges from them with a rush, shaking off his hair. Salt water flies, hitting me in the eyes and mouth.

I grin, shoving him. "Warn me next time!"

"Rate that," he says, floating onto his back, eyes closed, mouth curved into an easy grin. "One of my best, surely."

"Seven," I remark, leaning against the cool rock at my back.

He looks up at me. "No way that was *just* a seven."

"You lost points because you're annoying," I joke.

"That's *it*," he says, and everything breaks loose. He splashes me, throwing water in my direction. I leap over there, trying to wrap my arms around his head to pull him under. He grabs hold of me instead, flinging me onto his back and diving *backwards* into the water so I'm pressed beneath him.

We come up for air, laughing relentlessly, shaking water out of our ears and our noses.

Eventually, a quiet calm finds both of us as the sun

begins to set. Tired and breathless, we watch as the golden sun lowers in the sky, casting this cave into a slow arrival of darkness.

I settle against him on the rock cropping as we dry out, him sitting perched up against the cave's wall, me lying with my head in his lap, looking up at the ceiling. Water drips from our bodies in a slow rhythm, drawing me deeper back into the sleep I still desire.

"No naps," he murmurs, his hand idly playing with my hair.

"Too late," I whisper. "Slept on the way here."

"Tell me something, then."

I look up at him, his green eyes locked on me. "Like what?"

"What are you thinking?"

I smile. "I don't know if I have the time or the energy to think anymore. Information gets thrown at us so quickly. Things change within moments. I'm barely hanging on."

Silence then, as he considers what I'm admitting. Somehow, I think he knows that's not all.

I sigh, turning on my side to face the mouth of the cavern. "What if Oresteia isn't truly our enemy? What if we *are* fighting a war built on lies? Or worse, what if Paralia is built on deceit? What if we've been dragged into something we'll regret in the years to come— something neither of us can take back?"

He shifts, his tone serious. "Is that how you feel?" I hear him swallow. "Did I drag you into this? Do you... regret... choosing this? Choosing *me*?"

I push up, spinning around to face him. I nestle myself between his legs, sitting cross-legged. My hand finds his chest as my voice takes on what I hope sounds like resolve and honesty. "You didn't drag me anywhere. I chose this. You. I chose *you,* Callious Spathe."

My heart hammers in my chest, but my tone is steady. My eyes search his, bouncing back and forth between them. I fight the urge to touch the scarring wound on his neck.

Please believe me. There's nowhere else I'd rather be.

He does. I can just tell somehow, the way you can when you've known someone nearly your whole life. The way you know the back of your hand, or what your favorite color is. It's deep within you—something woven so tightly into your very being that unraveling it would be to undo yourself.

To know him is to know my own soul. I cannot help but recognize his.

"I can't lose you," he says, tucking a wayward curl behind my ear.

"You won't," I urge. "We have each other. We trust each other. I have your back, and you have mine."

"If I had come here without you," he says, hesitating. "If you had gone to Oresteia instead, I fear I would have done anything to bring you back."

I smile gently, leaning into his touch. "I know."

"I love you, Pen," he admits. It should be a shocking revelation, but deep down, my heart already knew. "Even if this all ends badly, even if you hate me by the end of it. The second I fell for you, when you fell onto my father's shelf, it was over for me. I've always known it. I never thought..." he hesitates. "I never thought I would get to have you."

My mouth opens to speak, but it appears he isn't done.

When is he ever? I smile at him.

"Thank you. For choosing me. For giving up everything to be here. I—" he clamps his lips shut, seeing the amused look on my face. "What?"

"If you'd shut up," I start. "I'd be able to tell you that I love *you*, Callious. There's nowhere else I'd rather be."

He nuzzles his nose into mine. "Be mine?" he whispers.

My breath hitches. "I've always been yours."

I'm met with a smile as bright as the sun itself. He leans in to give me a quick kiss on the cheek. He is as constant as the tide, but still as reckless as the waves.

My best friend.

⁕ ⁕ ⁕

We return right before dinner's end, our clothes clinging to us in wet splotches, our hair still dripping despite doing our best to wring it out. No one asks where we were, not even bothering to spare us a second glance.

Perhaps we really are allowed to go wherever we want when things are over for the day. Maybe... Just maybe... We'll get to do that again.

The thought turns me giddy, my insides fluttering with unkept butterflies. Today was *perfect*. It's as if we have found our own secret hideaway, away from the rest of the world.

War doesn't exist in the cave. There are no lives at stake, and there's no Kingdom to be beaten. There, within the damp rock walls, we are just Penelope and Callious.

We sit together to eat, our legs touching, a newfound closeness between us that has ultimately been growing since the day I first met him.

Boldness gets the better of me as my free hand makes its way to his, my fingers itching to hold his, when silence overcomes the mess tent.

All heads turn, eyes whipping to peer and catch a glimpse as our General walks in.

Rarely seen out, he's one to marvel at. His stride is strong as he walks through our tables to the front of the tent. No one speaks, no one dares move a muscle. He towers over everyone, commanding authority.

He's dressed in the darkest shade of brown—so deep it's nearly as black as the night itself. His skin nearly blends in with his own uniform, so clearly beloved by the sun. His hair is just as dark, crafting a perfect picture of stealth and courage.

He's decorated with awards, medals and pins, showing that he is both qualified and capable to be in this position.

His voice booms out over the tent, tone echoing with power.

Tension fills the air.

"There have been rumors," he begins, his voice clear. "Among the lot of you, there have been concerns."

He pauses, eyes raking over our still forms. "Dismiss them," he says. "Paralia may be a Kingdom built on shifting sand, but *we* are not. This is our land, and our battle to fight. We may not have started this war, but we *will* finish it."

Clapping spreads like wildfire, cheering and whistling ensuing at his words. I feel hope rising from those around me as we stand, applauding his confidence in us.

I begin to nod, clapping along with my fellow recruits. He says something else, but I can't hear him over the roar of our crowd. As he leaves, and as others resume their meals or leave to do nightly duties, Callious elbows me in the side.

I glance at him, a questioning look on my face. "I don't trust Oresteia," he says, serious.

Snorting, I say, "I don't think anyone here does. That's the whole point of all of this." I wave my hand around.

He shakes his head at me, clearly not in the mood to joke. "None of it adds up, Nel. The Prince here? Caught by us? A jewel that somehow, *we* stole? Magical abilities? Come on. They're spreading lies, hoping to confuse us and keep us disoriented. They know we're stronger than them—know they don't stand a chance."

I search his face and the concentration there. He's so smart, so wired for this type of life and thinking. But still, deep inside me, I can't help the trickle of doubt that begins to bloom.

What if they're not lying?

Rather than admit this to Cal, who I know isn't in the right headspace to hear me out, I just say, "I hate all of this."

He smiles at me halfheartedly. "Who knew war would be so complicated, right?"

I huff a quick laugh. We finish our meal in a hurry, ready to wash up and go to bed after our long day of training and playing.

As we exit the tent, a fuss begins to break out in the middle of camp. Someone is shouting, looking for someone.

We glance at each other, then quickly start running to where all the commotion is.

My blood runs cold.

I cannot believe this.

A royal courier is here, yelling at anyone who will listen.

And the words he's saying?

They're about me.

CHAPTER THIRTEEN

"...Frey—TRAITOR! Penelope Frey—TRAITOR! There will be no leniency given for harboring a criminal. Turn her over or risk death!" the Courier shouts, waving that piece of paper that was pinned to our post. This one is young, perhaps no older than sixteen.

I shiver. *My father knows I'm here.*

Does he know what my father will do to me if I'm turned over? I fear that my chance to apologize and go to Oresteia instead is long gone.

I'm in the back with Callious, standing slightly behind him so that I'm not spotted by this boy. I'm sure all we are to him is a sea of tan, nameless faces.

But somehow, everyone knows me.

I find that to be ironic, seeing as though I felt like no one in the Palace truly *knew* me.

Callious being the exception.

The Courier shreds the paper with the reward on

it. There's no longer a monetary reason for someone to turn me over. Now, it's just life or death.

Perhaps the King does not truly care if I'm returned or not. To act as if he's forgotten about me would prove him weak.

And we can't have that.

So, he sent someone else to finish up his dirty work.

The Courier continues to yell. "You swore your loyalty to our sea and to the crown. Remember the oath you have taken. And know that if he could, King Zannan would be right beside you, fighting along with you."

I scoff at that unintentionally, muttering 'right' under my breath, which gains me looks of appreciation from those around me.

Oops.

As he makes his way back out of camp, I feel the weight of a hundred eyes set on me. I brace for impact.

Is this the part where I'm betrayed? Is this the day I have to own up to all the mistakes and choices I've made?

I look at Callious, searching, preparing to say goodbye and let his face be the last I see before I'm whisked away toward my grim fate.

But still, not one voice speaks up.

Instead, they all go back to their duties and chores. No one looks at me differently. No one says anything.

Relief floods my system as I breathe deeply once again, in and out.

※ ※ ※

Later that night, I sit at a different fire in a different part of camp. Others laugh and tell stories of their lives before being here.

Some have been preparing for this war for years, for as long as there's been any strife between us all. Some joined when I did, new recruits who didn't have any other future plans and did not mind joining ranks to fight for Paralia.

I sit silently near Cal on a log that makes my back feel numb.

He'll be back, I think. Just because the King's messenger was sent off without me does not mean he'll give up. *This won't be the last time my name and face are thrown around. It won't be the last time they call for my surrender.*

It won't be enough. I have to do something about that.

An idea begins to take spark, igniting in the back of my mind. It's not much, just a small change that won't make that much of a difference. But as I live and breathe and fight here, I'll naturally become more unrecognizable. And eventually, the war *will* end.

Will I be alive to see the conclusion? Only time will tell. But if I *am,* who do I want to be then, at the end of the day? The same girl I came in as? Or someone new entirely—someone *I* create for myself?

My thoughts are interrupted by the sound of a violin and of someone beating on a barrel with spoons. Singing breaks out, music bursting from all edges of camp. A chaotic symphony arises, causing people to lurch onto their feet and *dance.*

I laugh, clapping along. This is nothing like the balls I've been forced to attend. No, this is *fun*.

Firelight fills my vision as bodies dance around it in the dark, stomping and twirling and hollering. I squint as a figure stands before me, a hand outstretched.

Callious.

I take his calloused fingers, joining him in the dancing circle. He spins me under the night sky, the necklace he gave me all those nights ago slipping out from under my shirt at the movement.

He sees it, reaching toward it to hold it lightly.

"I've been wondering where this went," he says. He runs a thumb over the shell, then lays it back over my heart, front and center. "Don't hide this away. I like seeing it on you."

I blush. "I wasn't sure if wearing jewelry was allowed…"

He winks, giving me a knowing smile. From under his shirt, he pulls out a leather cord, a metal ring around the end of it. It's a dirty silver, clearly aged. Something is inscribed in the material, words or numbers that I can't make out in the dark.

"I've never seen this before." It's not really a question, but my voice pitches at the end all the same.

"Father gave it to me before I left. Said it was a Spathe heirloom, the only one I could take with me. Been passed down from the men for generations," he pauses. "He claimed it would give me strength, stealth, and security. But more than that, it would give me sight. Sight to see beneath the pretenses, sight to see what really matters."

He drops the ring back against his chest, grabbing

my hands and bringing them both up to his mouth. He kisses my knuckles lightly, one by one. My fresh cuts sting at the saltwater lingering on his lips, but I do not mind the pain that comes with his affection.

It's all I've ever wanted, after all.

"I just want you to know," he says, leaning in to rest his forehead against mine. "You're all that has ever really mattered to me."

Before I can reply, the music picks up, a ruckus breaking out as people quicken their steps. Cal and I are ripped apart, laughing, watching as everyone around us revels in the foolishness of this moment.

How can we dance and sing in the face of certain doom? It's as if light demands to be seen in the midst of darkness.

I spin, dancing on my own in the presence of those around me, kicking up sand and dust as I raise my hands above my head. I bound after everyone else, following their lead as we interlock arms. We travel in a circle around the fire, clapping and kicking and yelling with all our might.

Perhaps this is our reason for fighting in this war, I think. *So we are able to continue to have moments like this. With each other. With our families.*

I look at Callious from across the way, the fire glinting off his curly hair. *With those we love.*

✵ ✵ ✵

We walk back to my tent hours later, tired but exhilarated. I've been trying to muster up the courage to tell Callious of my earlier idea. In the silence, I realize I've been waiting to see if he will bring it up.

Sometimes I forget he can't read my mind.

"I need a change," I begin, gauging his reaction out of the corner of my eye. "The King is going to keep coming back for me. I need to be different—*look* different. I want people to forget my name, to not think of me as a Frey at all."

"What are you saying?" he asks, stopping us where we are.

"Will you cut my hair?"

Stunned, he looks at me, his eyes traveling from my scalp to where my curls rest around my waist. It's tangled and windswept, much like my heart. In my dancing, my hair came unraveled from the loose braid it was in after our swim.

My hair has been this length for as long as I can remember. It's a sign of wealth and beauty to have long hair. My curls have always made it impossible to look as kept as my sisters, but a part of me always loved that.

Still, I'm too easy to recognize. Even in an army of thousands.

Cal's voice is soft when he finally speaks, barely hearable over the sound of my heart beating in my ears. "Are you sure?"

I nod, pulling my dagger out of my belt. I hand it to him carefully, laying it over his outstretched hand.

"You don't want to do it yourself?"

I shake my head ever so slightly. "I can't," I admit. "It feels like… betrayal. Of my family. Of the life I knew," I laugh halfheartedly. "Which is crazy, right?

After all, I did forsake them to come here. Not that I regret that at all, I'm just saying—"

He cuts off my rambling, grabbing my frantic arm with his free hand to still me.

I pause.

When he sees that I've come down from my rise, he turns my dagger over in his hands, as if reminiscing on the day I received it.

Five years old, a birthday gift tradition. A small bladesmith shop in the city, my family's favorite one. Everett making the trip to take me, as everyone else was too busy, or perhaps they forgot it was my birthday altogether.

Wandering, looking at all the pretty weapons, wondering what my own will look like, when I trip on a loose tile near the front of the store.

Then, crashing, running into a shelf holding valuable, heavy tools. Everett coming to the rescue, holding the shelf upright so it did not fall on me. Then, yelling.

Not from my brother, no. He's never raised his voice at any of us like our father has. But a boy my age, stern and serious. When he looks at me, though, he stops, as if stunned.

"It's always been long," he murmurs, interrupting my inner memories. "Ever since I met you, when we were kids. I like it this way."

I gather it up, holding it at the base of my nape. "I know."

He steps behind me, and I close my eyes as his hand takes my curls.

Then, the soft shearing sound of hair being cut, a tug at my scalp as he cuts it nearly to my chin.

Hair falls like embers at my feet.

"I tried to make it even," he says, sheathing my dagger into my belt.

"My curls will cover it," I respond.

Reaching up, I still feel the phantom tickle of hair across my shoulders and down my arms. My head feels lighter, freer.

I don't look like a Princess anymore, I think. *I bet I look like someone who belongs here, in this war.*

Cal crouches at my feet, and I look down at him, watching him gather a wayward curl to tuck into his front shirt pocket. "In case you ever want it back some-day, you let me know."

I laugh, but it catches halfway up my throat, remembering that I still have yet to tell him the other part of my plan.

"Um…" I begin. "I need a new name."

"You've got enough names for the two of us, Nel. People here probably don't even know you as Penelope."

Warmth spreads in my chest at him saying my full name. He never does. *No one* ever does.

"Some do. What if I started going by a code name? A different type of nickname?" I think. "You could have one too."

"An interesting idea," he says, mulling it over. "What would mine be?"

I smile, having already thought this over. "Nightingale."

"Nightingale? Like the bird?"

I nod. "From the stories we were told as kids, the ones that would be found singing near the end of battles, to remind the soldiers that the end was near.

They made a big impact on our Kingdom's legacy. I think it's perfect for you."

He considers this. "Alright, Nightingale. I like it. Now we just need to figure out yours."

"You pick," I say.

We walk again as he's clearly deep in thought. I have no idea what awful idea is going to come out of his mouth.

Finally, he says, "Tidebreaker."

I raise an eyebrow at him. "Go on?"

He takes my hand in his, swinging it as we arrive at my tent, the lantern inside already blown out. "Tidebreak is where the Neronian's waves crash and reform. It's a name for something that has the capability to change everything. That's you."

"I haven't changed a single thing," I say.

"You've changed me. And I know you'll change this war's outcome."

Before I can rebut again, he stops me. "You can't change it—you told me to pick."

Rolling my eyes, I sigh, giving in. "It feels like we're kids again, sneaking around the Palace and relaying secret spy orders to each other."

That gets him to laugh, too, smiling brightly at me and the memories we share.

His face turns serious, catching me off guard. "I forgot to tell you—I got pulled into a meeting this morning during chores."

I lay a hand on his arm. "Is everything okay? Are you in trouble?"

He takes his free hand and ruffles his hair with it,

rubbing the back of his neck. "They want me to be a Captain. Or at least, begin training to become one."

I gasp. "That's... incredible!"

I hug him, quickly, squeezing him tightly as I try to calm my beating heart.

What does that mean for us? More chances of danger for him?

He releases me, rubbing my arms in comfort. "I guess they were secretly impressed by my gall at capturing the scout. Especially when it turned out to be the Prince. They've been watching me since ranking on day one, and they said I have a lot of potential."

Cal hesitates. "They assured me this wouldn't come between what you and I are. They don't care too much about intermixing relationships, so long as everyone fights and trains."

I muster a smile, hoping it looks sincere. "I'm so happy for you, Callious."

"That's not everything. While I was in the meeting, I heard the General talking with some of our Captains. We're marching again tomorrow. Half of us are relocating to Komeus to restock on supplies and see if anyone will join our company. You and I are going."

"I haven't been to the city in a while," I swallow. "I hardly know my way around anymore."

His shoulder connects with mine, giving me a gentle shove. "I know it well. Just stick with me. You'll be alright."

"Guess it's a good thing we cut my hair then, huh, Nightingale?"

"They won't lay a finger on you, Tidebreaker," he responds, playing along.

After a quick goodnight, I slip into my dark tent.

Perhaps tomorrow will be good. A chance to recoup. The beginning of the path to victory for Paralia.

As I drift off to sleep, I can't help but feel as though something is waiting for me in Komeus.

And I do not think it's going to be something I enjoy.

CHAPTER FOURTEEN

THE SALT IN THE AIR SEEMS TO BITE LESS THE FURTHER we walk from the Gate.

Komeus sprawls just ahead of us, perched on sandy dunes like a crest of waves overtaking a shoreline. There are no walls to separate it from the outside world. There's never been a need. It's simply a place to shop; to live.

My siblings and I rarely make the trek to Komeus. Everything we could ever need comes from within our Palace walls, or it's brought into it for us. It's where I met Callious for the first time, my birthday dagger reason enough to travel from our home to his.

Paralia's vast cliffs are close enough to Komeus that any attempt at a water invasion would be worthless, unless our intruders can climb steep rocks effortlessly. Though we do have a few guards stationed here to give the people peace of mind, the ocean does most of the city's defending.

The city rises in spiraling layers, buildings white and tan, orange colored roofs sun-bleached from the relentless sun.

We slow as we approach, our company still in battle-ready formation. Callious is beside me this time, near the back. I hope that, should we find ourselves with some free moments during this supply run, I might get to go say hello to his father, or delight in Cal's company at one of the many shops.

The air smells of smoked fish, lunchtime arriving all too soon.

Cal wipes the sweat from his brow, his dark curls now coated in the sand that covers his hand. He's grim, eyes alert. My shoulders are slumped, my feet tired already. I can feel the rattle in my lungs from the dust in the air.

Cal studies the buildings ahead, as if expecting them to combust spontaneously right before our eyes.

"I hope my father is doing fine," he says, low enough that only I can hear.

My chest tightens. "Why wouldn't he be?"

"He hurt his back," he admits. "Right before I left. He knew I wanted to enlist, but still I offered to stay behind. He's slowing down in his old age. I hope that business hasn't been taken from him in my absence."

My eyes flick to Komeus, as if searching on their own for his father. "Hopefully, we have time to go see him," I say. "Maybe that will ease your mind."

I wish fervently that I could give some sort of help, to have one of my siblings check in or have the Palace healer step in and look him over. But what does a forsaken Princess truly have to provide?

Even when I had my claim to the crown, I was still a nobody with nothing to offer.

He shrugs. "If anything, I hope this supply run is quick. No need to put my father in harm's way just because we are out of basic necessities."

I tilt my head. "You think Oresteia would be able to try something against us here? They'd have to get through the rest of the army still stationed at the Gate before that could happen!"

"I don't think we fully know what they are capable of," he says. "It's possible they've been living here all along, in disguise and biding their time."

Silence stretches between us as we pass through the front of the city. The Palace reaches up in the distance, its roof's peaks piercing the calm, blue sky. I squint against the noon sun, wondering briefly what the royals might be up to as we traverse across Paralia.

Our Captain barks orders, giving those higher within our company jobs that the rest of us wouldn't be able to handle. Like purchasing baskets of fruit to take back, or refilling water jugs at the wells around the city.

Things for experts only, truly.

I scoff to myself at my joke.

The rest of us are told to help where needed. We're each given a small stipend for lunch to spend at the many merchant carts. I follow Cal to his father's shop, weaving in and out of children who dart between carts, laughing and giggling as if they have no care at all.

I envy them. There was a time once that might have been me. Being the youngest in the Palace, many of my older siblings were much too serious and trained by the time I got to playing age. I spent most of my time with only myself for company. Then I met Callious, and my life as one quickly bled into a life as part of a duo.

Another memory tickles the back of my brain, one of another little boy I met once, an overwhelmingly sunny day at the Palace.

Couldn't be. My father didn't invite anyone within our walls. Must have been a dream.

The city thrums with life as we approach the Spathe's shop.

I begin to daydream. Of days after this war is over, of Callious and me returning here to retire. We might have our own merchant's cart, or perhaps he would take over his father's blade business so that Mr. Spathe can heal. Maybe I would learn a trade, one I was never given the chance to at the Palace. Baking, perhaps? Maybe...

I run into the door of the shop, not noticing that it's not standing wide open as it usually is.

Rubbing my forehead to ease the dull ache that begins to pound against my temples, I look back at Cal, who must have started trailing me at some point. I suppose I remembered the way to their shop after all.

He gives me a questioning look, just as surprised at the darkness in the windows as I am. Mr. Spathe doesn't close down for anything, working even on the holidays for those who might need a last-minute gift for a loved one.

He must really be in pain.

I try not to show my worry on my face, letting Cal take the lead on what we do next. I glance sideways at him, my hand not straying far from the dagger strapped to my side.

There's tension in his shoulders.

"I'm sure he's fine," he says, as if trying to convince himself. His eyes search the dark shadows of the shop. "We won't stay long. We'll head up to the family's quarters, check in, and head back out for food."

I gulp, apprehension and nerves flooding my system for some reason.

He's fine. He's fine, I chant internally.

Hinges creak as he pushes the door open. Cal walks in first, sword at the ready, heading straight for the door near the back that hides the stairs leading up to their quarters.

Just as he walks across the threshold, figures explode from the shadows, and the building is in utter chaos.

Knives flash in the dark, shouts rise and echo across the space.

No way this is happening.

Callious—no, in this moment, he is my Nightingale —whirls on them immediately. I try to match his quickness, drawing my dagger instinctively, but I barely parry the first blow that is dealt to me. The brunt of their sword was aimed at my still-ringing head.

My vision gets dizzy, and I clutch my temples in frustration.

Could this get any worse?

People outside notice the commotion going on, other soldiers rushing to our aid.

But they've already barred the door we came in.

How did they know we'd be here?

There are too many soldiers against us to count, their black uniforms blending in seamlessly with the dark shelves. Even if we were to disarm the ones in here once, there's an immense amount of weapons lying around the shop. We'll never be able to overcome them with these odds.

The clash of steel is all I hear as we fight. That, and a soft hum of something I recognize in the back of my mind.

Where is that sound coming from?

The figures dance around both of us like smoke, as if they are but wisps on the wind.

"Tidebreaker!" Cal's voice roars above the never-ending chaos. Somehow, he's across the room from me now. How did he get over there?

I turn from him, my eyes trying to focus, and I see a man stalking toward me, a sword raised.

But before he can meet me, sword to dagger, a heavy weight slams into my side, forcing all the air out of my lungs.

A distraction.

I stagger, doubling over. My vision swims, my blurry eyes catching sight of my opposition. They wield a dagger, one that looks like it's made of flames. There's a stone in the middle of the hilt gleaming against the dark metal, looking out of place.

I swing my blade at whoever might be close enough to hit. I slice fabric, and must hit skin too, as they cry out in quick anguish at the sharp bite of my weapon.

Blood scents the air.

Someone grabs me, arms strong and secure around my wrists. They haul me back toward the staircase, toward the back door of the shop. I kick, trying to force my weight away from this person.

"Let go!" I scream, hoping to alert someone, anyone, of my situation. The last thing I see as the back door closes is Callious on his knees, surrounded, hands behind his head in surrender.

It's as if time moves in slow motion as I am pulled away from the shop.

Cal's green gaze meets mine, worried.

He would do anything for me, I think. *He would follow me to the ends of this Kingdom, and into the next.*

I shake my head at him, ever briefly.

Stay. For me. I'll find you.

I try to relay this message with my eyes, urging him to stay put and not risk his life for mine.

There's a hand clamped around my mouth now, hardly allowing oxygen to ease my screaming lungs.

The door shuts.

Fear floods me. My dagger is still in my hand, but my wrist is trapped against my captor's body. I still fight against him, pulling my weight down, not wanting to be drug into the shadows of the building.

The street is eerily empty.

Quiet.

Where did everyone go?

He hesitates for a moment, and I think, maybe I've worn him out and proven to be too much of a hassle for what it's worth.

I kick more urgently, struggling against his grip. I

twist, trying to free my hands, but his hold does not relent. He shifts, grabbing something I cannot see.

I'm hit in the head *again*, the world tilting on its axis as I try to fight the dizzy spell that threatens to sweep me off my feet.

My legs buckle, the ground rushing toward me. Sand coats my tongue as my vision goes black.

I look at his face as my eyes close, trying to memorize his features.

Regret is the last thing I see as shadows swallow me whole.

* * *

I come to with a wave of sickness, my head lolling even though my body is bound.

My captor is carrying me—one arm around my back, one under my knees—and I feel weightless. His chest vibrates in a distinguished pattern, as if he's humming.

This must be easy for him if he's able to sing through it.

I'm sure I weigh him down, but he's quick at trudging through the sand. He must be hot under his clothes, the thick black fabric clearly not made for Paralia.

There's nothing around us but sand and sky. We are no longer in Komeus, but we *are* still in Paralia. I take into account where my dagger is, back in the belt at my waist, but still on my person.

What a silly mistake.

I could use it against him, if only I could reach it. I

decide to bide my time—wait to see where he's taking me. He might get tired and put me down to rest. Maybe I can pretend to still be out of it...

"You're awake," he says, surprising me.

There goes that part of the plan.

I strain against my restraints. "Where are we going?"

He doesn't answer.

We head for a small grove of kaluptos trees on the edge of one of our many cliffs. I do not recognize this one, but they all look the same after a while. He walks deeper into the trees. I shudder, the cliff's edge spiraling far below us.

The roar of the waters below attempts to calm my nerves, but all I can focus on are the jagged rocks cutting above the surface. Should he slip and fall, my fate would be sealed. I wouldn't be able to stop the inevitable.

The grove continues deeper, the small green leaves giving zero coverage to the sun's sinking rays.

How is it nearly evening already?

My stomach grumbles. I missed lunch due to the ambush. My heart sinks into my stomach.

I hope Callious got out of there, somehow.

This man pulls back a large amount of vine hanging from a kaluptos branch. We enter cool shade, a rare reprieve here in Paralia.

We are in a small, hidden cove—one I've never seen before. I'm enveloped in brisk darkness as the leaves exit his grasp behind us, the strands tightly woven to each other.

Far in front of us, there's an amber glow coming from the darkness.

Coming from… a tree?

Its trunk is thicker than anything I've ever seen before, planted amidst grass and sand. It sprouts tall and proud, towering over us with wide branches.

Curiosity gets the better of me.

"What is this?"

Something hums, as if coming from the tree itself. It prickles my skin, goosebumps rising along my arms.

My captor sets me down near its base roughly. I stumble, catching myself before I fall over, still bound.

I glance up at him, my eyes adjusting to the dark. His hair blends in with the shadows, so long that it touches his shoulders. His skin is pale, as if he's never seen the sun. It's a vast contrast to the color of his eyes, so overwhelmingly onyx that I cannot differentiate between his irises and his pupils. Those eyes stare at me, unblinking.

His appearance flickers, my dizzy spell still lingering. My stomach twists. I shake my head, trying to clear it.

He reaches toward the tree, causing me to flinch.

Foolish, I think. *You cannot show fear!*

He touches its rough bark, and as his skin makes contact, it changes and twists to create something new. There's now an opening in the middle of the trunk, a wooden door tucked inside.

I gape. I'm too stunned to try to do anything, to even realize that he's set me down. I should use this opportunity to make a break for my dagger. But all I can do is stare at what's happening before my eyes. He takes the smooth wooden handle in the center, opening the door.

A sweet smell comes from within, one of smoke after a fire. Darkness radiates with a welcoming warmth, an amber glow still radiating from seemingly nothing.

Before I can react and realize what this man is doing, he grabs the ropes attached to my body and pulls me through the door with him.

✵ ✵ ✵

We are wrapped in shadows. I know he still has a hold of me somehow, but I cannot see him. Everything vanishes from around me, the ground under me nonexistent.

Am I falling? Could I be dead?

I am both weightless and senseless, disoriented and confused.

In a blink, I'm dragged through the threshold of another door.

Gone are the sandy dunes of Paralia, the clear blue skies, and hot sun.

I sit in a mound of snow, body still bound. It's freezing.

My eyes adjust, the gleam of the white powder blinding me after my stint in pure darkness.

I shiver as I survey the mountains, their height demanding to be seen and appreciated.

A voice sounds from beside me, interrupting me from my stupor. I had forgotten he was here.

I had forgotten that my fate is no longer held in my hands.

"Welcome," he says, kindness somehow coating his tone. "To Oresteia."

I look up at him, puzzled. His voice sounds so familiar...

No—it can't be.

CHAPTER FIFTEEN
CALLIOUS

She slips from my grasp just as she always does in the terrors that plague my sleep.

And the moment those brown eyes no longer grace my own, the world spins around me.

I'm down on my knees, forced into submission by Oresteian scum, wholly surrounded. My body aches, breath coming in frantic bursts. My body is covered in bruises and cuts that won't fully heal.

More scars to add to my skin.

She knew I was going to fight to get to her. But she shook her head at me, spoke to me silently in a way that only close friends can.

Stay.

So I did. And that tight feeling in my chest? I know exactly what it is. I am all too familiar with its threatening grip.

Regret.

I shouldn't have listened to her. I shouldn't have let

her be whisked away from me. I *just* got her—she's finally *mine.*

To let her go so easily feels like admitting I'm weak and incapable of taking care of her.

Maybe I am.

Blood coats the ground I'm kneeling on as I look up at my captors. The crusty, metallic liquid might be theirs or it might be mine. I lost track of all the wounds I inflicted. They stare me down, and a scream builds in my chest. I want to yell at them, demand they bring her back.

But I bite my tongue, my teeth gritting in restraint.

I might be alive in this moment, but I feel as though I'm already dead.

The sound of Pen's scream rattles in my ears.

I have to go get her I have to go get her I have to—

The knife at my throat suddenly disappears, my train of thought interrupted by the absence of cold metal against my skin.

My vision returns to me. I hadn't realized I had tuned out my surroundings, my brain focusing solely on Nelly and getting to her.

Confusion floods me, adrenaline slipping from my fingers.

I push myself up from the floor of the shop, my scraped palms raw against the worn wood. A stench of smoke and metal lingers, just as it would in the middle of a workday. I survey my surroundings, slowly spinning in a circle to avoid disturbing the space.

It looks... untouched.

There's no blood coating the ground.

There are no Oresteian soldiers.

I shake my head. Maybe I've been knocked out and rendered unconscious.

Or I'm dead, and this is my afterlife.

But if this is eternity, then where is Penelope?

I glance around wildly, looking for something, *anything.* Any small piece that might tell me what just happened.

But there's nothing.

The soldiers… They were real. They *felt* real. They *fought* like they were real.

So, where are they?

The door at the front of the shop breaks open, men from my company flooding in, ready to assist and fight.

Confusion is written all over their features, too.

How could that many soldiers find their way into Komeus without us noticing?

Even more, how were they able to just… vanish?

I scoff, baffled at the irony. Theories begin to pluck at my brain, breezing in and out like a tide against the shore.

Before my comrades can ask any questions, floor-boards creak from behind.

"Callious?"

The sound of that scratchy voice makes me turn.

I forgot about my father.

I walk to where he stands, briskly, not wasting a minute.

"Where were you?" I demand. I don't mean to, but anger seeps into my words. If he had just been where he was supposed to be and in better shape, maybe all of this wouldn't have happened.

Used to my outbursts, he stands in front of me, tall

and steady. His hands are coated in calluses from years of hammering hot metal. Dirt clings to his fingernails, probably scraped off his heavy apron. His tool belt is slung around his waist, as if he was just working on another project.

I meet his weathered face, his green eyes that are all too similar to my own. City-dwellers always tell me I look just like him, that it won't be long until I'm running his business.

They're right. In his condition, it might be even sooner than that.

He slumps ever-so slightly, barely recognizable if you aren't looking for it. If you don't *know* him as I do.

"What happened?" he asks, eyes wide at those accompanying me.

A soldier steps up from behind me, clasping me on the shoulder. "We are wondering the same thing, Captain."

I wince at the title I have yet to get used to. I didn't tell Nel the whole truth when I told her they wanted me to begin training to be one. Instead, they offered me the position, impressed with my quick wit and battle-ready posture.

Because of my hesitancy, I might never get to tell her. To reassure her that this new position won't stand in the way of her and me—that nothing will change. But now, everything has changed.

"We were ambushed," I begin. "Recruit Tidebreaker and I slipped into my father's shop, concerned for his well-being."

I eye my father, not wanting to portray him as weak. But in the same breath, I must admit that I *am* worried about him. I know he doesn't want me to be. And now, my position has put him in more danger than I care to allow.

"Tidebreaker and I fought hard, but it wasn't enough. There were soldiers—Oresteian soldiers—everywhere. She was captured, taken out the back door. There were too many. I was prepared to go down fighting, ready to die for our city. But then... they vanished. Gone right before my eyes."

Their eyebrows furrow, all of them simultaneously.

My father speaks up. "I was upstairs. I heard the commotion. Something was keeping me from walking down and seeing what was happening. Felt like my limbs were bound. I'm not sure how I got upstairs in the first place—my memory feels blurry."

"How could this happen? How did they get here?" my soldier, Jaks, asks. "Where did they go?"

"Magic," I say, testing my most prominent theory with them. "I don't believe all of them were really here, except the one that carried Tidebreaker away. When that man left, that's when the spell broke and everything returned to normal."

They stand here stunned.

"This changes everything," I say, shattering the silence like glass. "Jaks, take the others and rally the Captains still in the city. We have work to do."

"Yes, Captain."

They leave, rushing to do my bidding.

So odd that my voice has sway.

My father and I stand in his shop, tension filling the space between us.

"I want to enlist. I want it more than anything. But I can't

leave you like this. I can't worry about your health while I'm away. I can't submit to the idea of me not coming back and you not having anyone else to take care of you." My voice barks at him, trying to make him see reason.

"I've done just fine on my own. I don't need you to stay behind, Callious. You're meant for this. If I could go with you, I would. But we both know I'd be a liability."

The pack on my shoulders weighs heavily on me. "I don't think of you as a liability."

He grabs me, pulling me in for a rough hug. It feels awkward, like we haven't had much practice at the act. Still, I relent, wrapping my arms around his broad back and letting my head fall into his chest as if I'm a little boy with a scraped knee again.

Tears threaten to fall, but I stop them, burying the emotion deep within me where it can't be touched.

Father separates the two of us, looking into my soul. "Do not come back here. When you get out—and you will, Cal—do not come back to me. Do not question my fate. Live a new life that is wholly your own."

I gulp, nodding, even though I won't do a thing he's asking me to do, and he knows it.

Walking away from him, I stop at the door to turn and give him one last piece of information. "I asked Pen to go with me. She said yes," I hesitate. "I'm afraid I won't be enough for her, that I won't be able to keep her alive."

"You do whatever you can to protect that girl. I couldn't be that for your mother—you know that. Do not let your story become mine."

And with that as my parting, I leave him, unsure if I'll ever see him again.

That memory haunts me now.

"I couldn't protect her," I admit. "And now I've lost her like you lost mom."

He frowns at me, the expression softer than anything I've received from him before. "We both lost Brenn that day—it wasn't just me. But you have to see that this is different. Penelope is savable. You *have* to find out how they did this Callious. We cannot lose this war."

I nod, taking in his demeanor. He looks like he hasn't slept since I left.

Perhaps he hasn't.

I begin to ask, to worry, but he stops me with a raise of his hand. "I told you not to come back."

My pulse hammers in my ears, my heart rapid in my chest.

I don't argue; I can't.

He would be better off without me here anyway, bringing trouble and pain wherever I go.

As I always have.

And with that, without a glance back or another word, I leave him behind once again.

※ ※ ※

The canvas flap opens before me, the air inside the commanding tent stifling. We sit at the edge of Komeus. Our recruits erected the tent while the rest of us gathered supplies.

The thick material traps the heat of our bodies, humidity hindering our breath. Three other Captains hunch over a worn map of our two Kingdoms, muttering as I arrive by their sides.

They fall silent, looking me up and down. I feel scrutinized by their eyes, still stepping into confidence within my newfound role.

"We heard," one of the men says. I don't know any of their names, just what they're known for. This one is Hammerhead, for the way he never stops moving.

And because his eyes are just a little too far apart.

He doesn't need to know that part, though.

I straighten. "They took the Princess. I believe that was their mission. I want to follow, find a way to get her back."

It feels weird not asking permission, and instead just admitting my wishes.

"She's not the Princess anymore," the only girl, Hawkwatch, says. "She's a recruit, and not a very good one at that. Who cares if she's been captured?"

Rashly, I slam my hand on the table in front of us. "I care!"

"We cannot risk the lives of many men for just one person. And you would bode well to bite your tongue on your emotions and think like a *Captain*, Nightingale."

I wince at the name Penelope gave me. The Captains had already asked what I'd like to be called. I gave them the one she picked.

Fuming, I look at Vengeance. He's been a Captain longer than I've been alive, and I know there's truth to his words. Still, my heart cries out for me to make this right.

"But," I begin slowly. "The reality of magic changes everything."

"The tales say that they can only carry magic within their land's borders."

I stare down Hammerhead. "And what if the tales are wrong?"

Veng eases the tension in the air, as he does. "They'll make fools of us all if we assume what we think is the truth."

Hawkwatch exhales. "That doesn't change that we cannot go after her."

"Then I'll go on my own. I'll slip through the Isthmus at night, see if I can catch whispers of where she might be held."

They look at each other, deciding without saying a word.

"If you do this," Veng says. "You will be on your own. We will not risk men to rescue you."

"I have to try," I respond.

"Then you'll need a plan."

I look at Hawkwatch, surprised.

The three of them nod at each other, then at me.

Oresteia doesn't know the weight of what they've started.

And so, we begin.

CHAPTER SIXTEEN

THE BOY WHO BROUGHT ME TO THIS TREE ISN'T THE same one standing before me now.

I rush to my feet, my head still spinning. My brain screams at me to avoid showing weakness, but I fear I may empty my stomach on his boots if I do not close my eyes right this minute.

I move backwards to try to create some space between us, but my shoe trips on a root. His arms catch me before I fall. His pale skin is bright compared to mine. He rights my stance, and I flinch against his contact, panic rising within my chest.

Breathing becomes difficult, the thin air causing my lungs to tighten.

His familiar gaze burns through me—as if he's able to see my soul.

"Penelope," he says carefully, as if testing how my name sounds.

"William." I grit my teeth, removing myself from his grasp. This cannot be happening. Surely this is just disorientation from getting hit in the head. There's no way that I am in Oresteia right now.

"Penelope," he says again.

"What?" I snap. "What did you do? Where is Callious? *Why* am I *here*?"

My vision finally stops swimming. The cold weather is a shock to my system, but it clears my head. Surveying my surroundings, we are in a small grove of peuko trees on this side of… whatever that was. Their sharp needles reach out to me, like they are hoping to trap me within their prickling embrace.

I look at William—truly look at him—and find that he appears different now. He surely was playing the part he wished us to see when we captured him.

He stands so confidently, like the royal he is. His dark cloak flows behind him in the brittle wind, embroidered with threads of silver that shimmer in the snow's reflection. His face is too sharp and too clean to be anything but a Prince.

I am so stupid.

He finally speaks again, as if sensing that I'm coming to terms with my current reality.

"You are here," he begins. "In Oresteia, so that I might continue what we started in Paralia. Callious is fine—I'm sure he's retelling the story of your ambush to all who will listen. I've done nothing but create a space for you and me to have a much-needed conversation."

I gape at him. "You kidnapped me to… talk? Haven't you heard of writing letters?"

He smiles at me, amused. "You never know who

else will read the words you write. I had to be thorough."

"I don't trust you," I say, just in case he's confused.

His ice-riddled gaze pierces me. "I don't expect you to. I just ask that you hear me out."

I'm freezing. Not just from the snow and the temperature change, but from the way he talks. Like I'm some pawn in a game he's playing. My throat feels tight.

I don't want to play this game. I only wish to go home.

He starts to walk away, motioning for me to follow him.

Perhaps it's time I put my dagger to good use.

I start to trail him, hand itching to grab my blade and stab him in the back. But my boots aren't made for the uneven snow-covered ground, and I'm having a hard time finding my footing. I begin to walk in the footprints he leaves behind, sinking into wet powder up to my calves.

A thought hits me. Could I not go back the way we came? He might not realize I'm not behind him until it's too late. I don't know how that tree works, and I don't know how we got there from Komeus, but surely I could figure it out, right?

I pause, trying to be quiet. He continues on by a few steps. I start to turn around and tiptoe my way back to the tree.

His voice sounds out from right behind me. "I wouldn't do that."

Turning around slowly, I find him standing merely a breath away. Sweetly, I say, "Do what?"

I try to bat my eyelashes at him, portraying a perfect picture of innocence.

"I'll just bring you back, Penelope," he begins, stepping closer to me. "And I don't think your head can handle that trip again."

As he gets closer, I whip my dagger out of its sheath, placing the tip of my blade under his chin. I'm careful not to draw blood, not wanting to provoke him or Oresteia into further anger, but I still want to make my point.

He sighs, lower lip pouting. "Penelope, I thought we were friends."

I hate the way he says my name as if he knows me.

"We're not." I push my dagger closer to his skin. He's tall—much taller than I am—and I have to reach to keep the upper hand. A swift wind brings a smell of vanilla and cinnamon to my nose, momentarily distracting me. "This is how it's going to go. You—"

I'm cut off by his quick grab at my dagger, his hand encircling my wrist. His fingers are cold, so cold, and I'm caught off guard. It's brief, but he takes advantage all the same. He sweeps his leg, catching both of mine, and I fall.

He relinquishes his grasp as I land in the snow, grateful for its cushion. A dagger is suddenly in his hand, the one I saw during the ambush. It feels out of place here, radiating something I can't name.

His knees find either side of my waist, pinning me into the white powder. A shiver runs up my spine as he leans forward, his dagger now stationed above my heart.

"It appears," he purrs. "As if you are no longer in the position to make demands. I have you."

I smirk. "Think again."

When he let go of my wrist, my dagger was free to find its way just above his waistline, its sharp point now shallowly sinking into his unprotected abdomen. "It seems I have you, too."

We stay there for a moment in an unspoken stand-off, each of our blades ready to do our bidding. Finally, in a surprising show of faith, he sheaths his and stands from where he's kneeled. He extends a hand to me.

I raise an eyebrow, not fully trusting this act. Still, what other choice do I have? I can't fight him. I'm hardly trained; barely able to do much but basic moves and blocks. He knows this terrain far better than I do. I'm outmatched in more ways than one.

Taking his hand, he lifts me with ease.

"State your terms," he says, his gaze amused.

"Tell me why," I respond.

He takes in the surrounding land, looking intently at the sky quickly darkening above us. "Paralia is holding you back from knowing the full truth. I had to find a way to talk to you."

"You're mistaken. Nothing is holding me back. For the first time in my life, I'm *free*," I pause. "And that is a poor excuse for needing to speak to someone. Especially when we hardly know each other."

He nods. "You're right."

I am?

"I am," I respond. I try to force confidence into my tone, but I have none left to spare.

"I'm taking you to a stable, where you can put on

Oresteian clothes so you don't freeze to death. From there, we'll take my horse to our city, Copolis. You'll be protected there. I won't keep you longer than I have to; I give you my word."

"You have horses here?"

He nods, smiling a bit. "Can we go? Before we get stuck in a snowstorm that neither of us wants to experience?"

"It seems I have no other option."

We begin the careful walk to the stables. He leads the way, often helping me down steep slopes. I slip multiple times on the frigid surface, ice beginning to pelt down from the sky. William lends me his cloak, covering my skin and the thin fabric of my uniform from the relentless drizzle. I'm grateful for its warmth.

When I'm not looking down at the ground to watch my step, I look around. The mountains of Oresteia rise into the sky, piercing it with beauty. The peuko trees are now few and far between. No picture in any of my school books could have done justice to the majesty that is this Kingdom.

Not that I'll be telling William that.

We come to a skinny gravel path, following it to a small wooden stable. Its gray wooden exterior blends into the snowy fog. Smoke rises from the chimney, and I nearly lurch at the prospect of sitting by a fire.

William opens the door for me, moving with a grace only a Prince would have. He offers his hand, but I don't take it, rushing inside to the awaiting warmth instead.

The smell of hay and earth greets me.

The door shuts behind us. "There's a washroom in

the corner. You'll find a knapsack of clothes in it; some things that will keep you warm the rest of the way."

I follow where he points, quickly changing behind the closed door and placing my Paralian uniform back in the bag.

I'm taking this with me, I think. *I'll need it when I'm returned to Paralia.*

I take a moment to look at my face in a small reflective glass hanging on the wall. Black looks foreign on my body, but it brings out the dark color of my eyes and curls. William's features are almost leached of color, apart from his eyes. I can't help but exude hues. They are my nature and birthright.

Exiting the washroom with the leather bag around my shoulders, I find William in the stall part of the stable. He looks at me from head to toe, and I feel suddenly self-conscious in my fleece trousers, heavy tunic, thick cloak and gloves.

The outfit was clearly well thought out—I'm so much warmer already. New socks and boots were among the articles, and I feel so much more secure in them.

"Thank you," I say, handing his own cloak back to him.

My hands feel less stiff and raw. I still have my dagger tied tightly to my waist, in sight and within reach, just in case.

I follow William to the end of the stalls, where a massive black beast leans its head out of the top part of the stall door. The horse huffs at me, its breath warm against my face.

William pats its nose. "This is Agrius, my closest and most trusted friend."

I blink, trying not to exude nervousness. "He's gorgeous. Does his name have meaning?"

"It means *wild*. I caught and broke him myself, but he'll never be fully tamed. Still, he'll take good care of us."

I gulp, mustering a smile. "Wow."

Reaching out my hand cautiously, I pet Agrius's nose. He nuzzles my hand, warm and steady against me.

Something rumbles in the distance, catching William's attention. "We should go. They'll be waiting for us."

I nod, remembering all too quickly that I've been taken prisoner, and this isn't just a fun trip to my rival Kingdom.

※ ※ ※

William helps me onto Agrius before swinging on easily behind me. I am thoroughly scared of being on top of this beast. But somehow, I know William would not let something happen to me.

At least not before he gets what he needs from me first.

We travel in silence for what feels like hours. I'm starving and tired. I can't imagine how long this journey would have taken without his horse. And for that, I'm thankful.

Arctic wind howls through the peaks, snow-dusted cliffs stretching on above us.

Agrius seems to know the way, leading us to the city William talks of.

Copolis.

We arrive as the storm begins to unleash its fury. William jumps off first while Agrius is still moving, grabbing his reins to halt him. He hands him off to a guard stationed near us, then reaches up to help me off gently. Immediately, my dagger is taken by another man, my wrists tied together fervently.

I wince, and William notes the movement. "I'm sorry," he whispers beside me. "I'll make this right as soon as you're with my General."

I nod, but I don't believe him. I should have expected this. They take me deeper into the city, guards stationed everywhere. Snow flutters past, blurring my vision from being able to take in anything about my surroundings. This late in the day, it appears no one else is out and about. I see doors shut tightly and windows covered.

We step into a two-story stone building. A girl about my age greets us, her black hair tied into a sleek ponytail. She twirls an arrow between her fingers, creating patterns in the cold air. "We'll take her from here. Thank you."

The guards hand me off, disappearing immediately. William and the girl stand in front of me, the rest of the ground floor empty except for a few wooden chairs and an empty fireplace.

They exchange a few quiet words. In the darkness, I watch as William hands the girl the dagger he's been carrying. She sheathes it quickly, whispered light from the window next to us glinting off the pale stone in the middle.

"Did it work?" the girl asks.

"Surprisingly well," William responds. "We can debrief later."

He eyes me then, noticing how intently I'm watching them. I avert my gaze, but not quickly enough. Leaning back on my heels, I try to become a perfect picture of nonchalance.

Hard to do when your hands are bound.

I must have grumbled that aloud by accident, because the next thing I know, a blade cuts through them like a hot knife through butter.

I look up, surprised that the girl was the one who cut them.

"Selene," William starts. "This is Penelope. Penelope, Selene."

I nod in greeting, trying to come across as polite and willing, though I am certainly anything but.

Is this his General?

Selene tilts her head at me, her long hair falling across her shoulder at the motion. She wears a maroon shade of clothing, and it's the starkest color I've seen in Oresteia so far. She holds herself with unnatural poise, as if she's been raised a certain way, too.

Could they be... siblings? No, they hardly look similar.

Besides the matching pale skin, they are vastly different in appearance. William is snow and ice, while Selene is dark shadows and burnt embers.

Perhaps, lovers?

The thought puts a bitter taste in my mouth,

though I can't explain why. It must be the cold getting to me. My stomach growls, a painful reminder that I haven't eaten since this morning.

"You look overwhelmed," she says, her voice playful and light. "Oresteia can do that to people. The two of us will take it easy on you. Everyone else," she motions outside with her hand. "Well, they won't. William and I have your best interests in mind, but you need to work with us."

"Why would I work with *you*? You've kidnapped me, tied me up, taken my dagger—". Before I can finish, Selene slings my dagger at me. The blade lands with a *thunk* on the worn, wooden floors. Still, I continue. "I don't know why I'm here. Oresteia is my enemy, and I do not wish to have a conversation with either of you."

She looks at William, as if asking for his permission. He briefly nods, and she takes a step toward me.

"You'll want to talk to us," she says, twirling that arrow again. Her red boots shine against the mud we tracked in. "In fact, I dare say you'll *want* to work with us. Once you know everything."

I huff, the forced breath causing a curl to fly up from my forehead. "And what is it that I don't know? Why are you both *so* cryptic?"

"Everything you believe about this war is a lie." Selene states this like a cold fact, as if there's no room for negotiation or rebut.

Those words hang in the air between us, and I shiver. My heart tells me that she's right, that there *is* something deeper that I'm missing. I can feel the tension sitting there, waiting to be addressed. But still, my head tells me no—that I *do* know everything. It's *them* who have the wrong story.

"What do you mean?" I ask, curiosity getting the better of me.

She just smiles at me, her eyes sparkling as if she's won.

Maybe she has.

"You and I are going to have fun together."

That's all she says before flicking her ponytail as she saunters out, leaving William behind.

The air threatens to suffocate me as I stand there, waiting for him to condemn me in some way.

"The house is yours. She'll be stationed in front of the only door. Shower, eat, sleep. We do not care what you do, as long as you respect the freedom we are offering you. We'll talk again in the morning."

With that, he leaves too. At his absence, I look out the only window. Sure enough, Selene stands there, her back to me.

Guards flit around the street, though it looks like most of them have tucked themselves away for the evening. Or maybe because of the incoming storm?

Either way, I'm as alone as I'll get.

I might as well go upstairs and get to know my surroundings.

Tomorrow could change everything.

CHAPTER SEVENTEEN

THERE ARE NO OTHER WINDOWS OR DOORS IN THIS building.

So thorough of them.

The stairs creak with my footsteps, the wood split in places that could only come after years of walking up and down the steps.

If this place has been so well-used, why is it so... musty?

I cough, dust in the air as I reach the second floor. There are only two rooms up here, barely separated by a thin wall and dirty wooden doors hanging off bent hinges. On my left, a bedroom. On my right, a washroom.

I might as well take my chances with the washroom first. Just in case they come back for me tonight.

Opening the door, I'm careful not to tug on it too hard. Candles are lying around, gifting a soft glow of light. A little table sits beside a large tub, both cleaner than anything else in this room.

A white towel is folded on the rim of the steel bath, and the water level is already full. Something fresh hits my senses as I watch steam rise from the bath—mint, perhaps?

It looks all too inviting, as if it's a trap laid especially for me.

I strip my cold, wet layers and step into the tub with ease. I realize now that, even after today's fight, my body isn't as sore as it was when I first started training. I've grown stronger. Things have become easier for me.

Maybe that's the true testament of time—that we grow better as days pass.

My muscles relax in the hot water's embrace.

It's cruel how peaceful this feels. What is Callious doing right now? He'll be searching for any sign of me, I imagine. Did they go back to the Gate? Or will they stay stationed at Komeus?

Not being able to tell him that I'm alright—to know if *he's* alright—is a sharp prick to my heart.

And while he's surely searching heavily for me, probably frantic and frightened, I'm *relaxing*.

I shake my head at my ridicule, knowing that I'm doing what I can. Should I be paraded around tomorrow, I will hold my head high, clean of every speck of dirt.

Scrubbing my body from head to toe, I rinse off, careful to avoid the tender spot on my head. There's still a dull throb there, but surely a little food and rest will take care of the remaining hurt.

Food.

Didn't William say something about dinner?

I dry off, wrapping the towel around my body as I head into the bedroom. Just like the washroom, there's not much, as if they made this into my jail-sanctuary last minute.

A bed takes up most of the small space, a scratchy gray blanket atop it, along with a white set of clothes.

I quickly dress, not willing to risk time or privacy here. The pants and shirt are just the right size, casually flowing off my body.

Definitely not made for fighting.

That thought reminds me—I left my dagger in the floorboards downstairs. Possibly the most foolish thing I could have done.

I wring out my hair, surprised at how easy it is now that my curls are much shorter, and fly down the stairs to retrieve my dagger.

It appears Selene must have entered while I was cleaning up, because the fireplace is now lit, and there's some sort of soup warming up in a pot above it.

My stomach growls.

I pluck my dagger from where it's still stuck and find a bowl underneath the pot. I grab the attached ladle and spoon myself a big helping. I don't care what's in here, only that I'm famished and won't be able to think properly with nothing in my system.

I moan. *It's so good.* I'm careful not to eat too much, lest I feel sick afterwards, but this and the bath is the perfect recipe for a restful night's sleep. I haven't slept in a real bed since...

Well, the Palace.

Never mind that. I don't *need* the Palace. Or my family.

Though I would love to see my father's face should he find out what happened to me.

But why would he hear of this?

I'm just Tidebreaker, an army recruit.

I shudder. I'm a nobody to them—someone easily disposed of.

And yet... William brought me here for a reason.

Perhaps it's all under pretenses. A way to get under the skin of our Kingdom and force me to lower my guard with the enemy.

I walk back upstairs, boards creaking with the weight of my unknown future.

Crawling into the bed, I place my dagger under my small pillow. The material is flat, and I can feel the shape of my blade through it. Still, it brings me comfort knowing it's there.

Lying on my back, I slip it out, surveying it in the pale light seeping in from the cracks in the roof. The gilded hilt shines brightly in the dim space, a depiction of waves winding around the grip that is the perfect fit for my fingers.

I brush my thumb against the middle of the cross-guard, where the sun sits in a deeper metallic color than the rest.

Paralia feels so far away and so vastly different than this place I don't know much about. Here, there are no waves, no sand. The heat isn't relentless; the cold is. My sun has finally forsaken me—replaced with the twinkle of small stars and an abundance of clouds and fog.

Sighing, I put my dagger back and turn on my side, the gray blanket clutched in my cold hands.

※ ※ ※

I don't know when I fell asleep, or how long I was finally pulled under from the waves of exhaustion.

But when I wake, I feel... rested.

I sit up slowly, my blanket askew at the end of the bed. I can't tell what time it is, but my internal clock tells me it must be morning.

The building is eerily quiet. Throwing my legs over the edge of the bed, my bare feet are met with the chill of the floor. I pad to the washroom, throwing some cold water on my face. Lacing up my boots, I piddle around.

I might as well take charge of the situation if I can.

I take the stairs down two at a time, my dagger secure around my waist. I look out the window to see Selene still standing guard in front of the door.

Did she sleep out there?

I peek out the panes and somehow, she hears me, turning toward the window with a grin on her face.

She waves, lighting up, pointing toward the door.

I tilt my head, confused.

Selene enters. Her long black hair is in a braid, resting over one shoulder. She's in black today, so she must have left at some point.

I'm clothed in the sleeping set they left me. Yesterday's outfit is still soaked.

"How did you sleep? The storm got a little crazy."

I didn't notice a storm at all. I must have slept *really* good.

I move away from the window, engaging in an odd stand-off with her. Ignoring her question and her kindness, I ask, "You're the General?"

She squeals, clapping her hands together. The sound makes my ears ring. "Yes! It's all I've ever wanted. William promoted me the minute we declared war on your people."

Tilting my head, I assess her. "Why you?"

Her eyes sparkle. "William trusts me. I've been training for years. *And* I beat everyone who tried to oppose his decision."

I open my mouth to speak again, but she cuts in. "You ask too many questions. William will be here soon." She leans against the wall across from me. "Before that, what do you know?"

"The truth."

She scoffs, kicking off the wall. "I'm sure you believe that."

The door behind us opens before she can say anything else, drawing our attention.

William walks in, as princely as ever. He's dressed head to toe in versions of white, silver threads binding everything together. His hair is a tad too long, as if a haircut is the last thing on his list of things to do.

He looks between the two of us, back and forth.

"What did I just walk into?"

Selene walks over to the burnt embers, kicking them with a boot. "She's surprised I'm General."

He looks to me. "Why?"

I cock an eyebrow, crossing my arms. "Why does it matter?"

"She's earned her position. I won't tolerate disrespect."

I nod. "I wasn't trying to be disrespectful. She's just... young."

He smiles at me. "So are we."

Good point.

"Can we cut to it? I'm tired of dancing around subjects and conversations."

"As you wish. Selene, go ahead."

She mumbles, rolling up her sleeves.

With a flick of her wrists, fire illuminates her fingers, dancing between each of her hands. In one breath, the flame catches. The next, it disappears. She lights the fireplace without looking at it, a snap of her fingers is all it takes. And as it's roaring to life, it's gone just as quick.

They stand there, looking at me.

I look at them, my hands shaking behind me.

Everything Mas said... the stories and hypothetical reasons why war inevitably came to our shore.

It all floods my system—a crown with a gem, a magical Tree connecting our Kingdoms sprouted from the blood of our ancestors.

What if it's all true?

What if we *did* steal some lost jewel?

Still... is that jewel not half ours? They took it first, claiming it as their own. What if we are just righting what went wrong long ago, making sure the jewel is in the right hands?

If that's the case... then where's *our* magic? And

what will become of our Kingdoms if it's not placed where it's meant to go?

My head spins as thoughts attack me. My next words are a mere whisper to myself. "Magic," I gulp. "You have… magic."

William steps closer, smiling gently at me. "Oresteia *is* magic."

CHAPTER EIGHTEEN

I CAN'T HELP BUT GAPE AT THEM.

William stares back, looking me up and down, watching my reaction.

"We need to show you something." Selene breaks the silence, looking between William and me.

Narrowing my eyes at both of them, I say, "Are we finally getting to the point of why you've brought me here?"

"I can't do it here," William lets slip, looking at Selene.

"Rhea's?" she asks.

He nods. "We can get breakfast there, too."

I hold up my hands as they begin to guide me out of this building. "Whoa, hang on. You can't do *what* here? I don't want to leave. It's…" I search for words. "Cozy?"

William runs his hand through his shaggy hair, as if debating how much to tell me. Which is ironic, considering that I feel like he's told me *nothing* this whole time.

When we make eye contact once again, there's an ice-filled determination in his gaze.

His voice is soft. "You've witnessed Selene's magic. I have... certain abilities... too. Under normal circumstances, I would be more careful with what you see, but the circumstances are dire. And we don't have much time."

Selene cuts in, a hand on his arm. "And because of that, we've decided to trust you."

I scoff, grumbling under my breath. "Great."

"I'm only asking that you hear us out."

I look up at him, trying my best to understand his intentions.

"Ask me," I say, mustering all the courage I can from the depths of once being a royal like he is.

"I'm sorry?" he questions.

"Ask me to go with you, rather than assuming I'll let you parade me around your city. If I'm not truly a prisoner—if there really is some deeper meaning behind all of this—then make this mutual."

Selene laughs. "And give you the chance to say no? Our Kingdoms hang in the balance."

"See, you keep saying that. But for some reason, I *still don't believe you.*"

She steps closer to me, as if itching for a fight, but William stops her with a lift of his hand. "Penelope, will you go with us? I wish to show you something regarding our worlds, but I cannot do it in the middle of Copolis."

My mind still wants to be stubborn, but my heart believes him.

Odd.

"On the condition that I may keep my dagger, I will go with you."

Callious would be proud of me for thinking that through.

William smiles at me. "Of course."

I nod then, taking my place between the two of them. Before we exit, William turns toward me, untying something from his waist.

He hands it to me. "It's a coat. You'll need it."

I wrap it around my upper body, the thick, fleecy layers warming me from the inside out.

I've never seen snow like this, flurries falling from the sky.

It flitters in slow, delicate patterns that vanish against my pale clothes before I can feel an ounce of their bitter touch. Flakes settle on the path as we walk, landing on roofs and branches like a dusting of sugar. My boots beat against the cobblestone, occasionally slipping on ice.

My first impression of Oresteia yesterday came in big chunks and jagged pieces of cold anger. Today, it feels thawed, as if it's letting me in just as much as I am it.

The air is thick with fog, so different than the humid mist I'm used to. This air smells of earth and pine and smoke. It clings to me, tugging at my senses like it wants me to be fully enveloped in its beauty.

I try not to look enchanted with their city when they look at me.

But I'm finding that to be difficult.

Copolis stretches along a slope, nestled into the sides of mountains. Warm, yellow lanterns glow on the sides of the street and on the walls of buildings, inviting me to come in and take a peek at what might be inside.

Roofs of booths and houses are steeply sloped to catch snowfall. Windows frost with the temperature difference.

I feel the hardness in my heart melting at the bustle of the crowd. People greet William and Selene, bowing their heads and grinning from ear to ear at them. Their breath fogs the air. I get some curious looks, but no one speaks. Even more so, no one turns away from me.

Still, I keep my hood up, letting it hide my sun-tanned skin that marks me as an outsider to all of them. At the end of the day, I'm unwelcome and their enemy.

Any kindness I'm given is simply because of who I am associated with. They wouldn't want to offend their Prince and his General.

I wonder if any of them question why he would be seen with a Paralian. Do they worry about their safety?

Or do they truly trust their authority that much?

Those questions feel too big for me to chew on right now. The implication of it all reaches down deep within me to ask myself the same of my own authority.

The market spills down the winding street, everything warm despite the chilly breeze. I pass by booths selling a variety of colored rocks. Another sells glazed pastries that smell of honey and yeast. One on my left calls out as we walk by, asking us to try their newest recipe.

"It's a version of bone broth, but lamb. Try, please." The older man spoons all three of us a small helping, smiling as he watches us drink.

I take careful sips of the warm liquid, not wanting to upset my stomach, but also not wanting to show disrespect. As I sip, I find that it's just as delectable as it is aromatic—filled with spices and herbs.

William and Selene gulp theirs, delighted. "It's *perfect*, Simeon. Allow me to stamp it, please."

Simeon bows his head, blushing. "Thank you, Prince."

William takes a piece of parchment from his pocket, and Simeon offers a small piece of half-melted purple wax to him. Selene holds the wax in her fire-coated hands, letting it melt just enough to be pliable on the paper.

Once it's dripping, William takes the ring on his first finger and presses it down onto it. He waits for it to cool, then pulls the ring from the parchment and hands it to Simeon.

At once, Simeon nails it into the wood of his booth, right next to his newest creation. He bows again, expressing gratitude.

William and Selene quickly pull me away from the booth, and I trip over my feet, not sure what the hurry could be now. We've been walking slowly around the booths for an hour.

Suddenly, an influx of people stampedes toward Simeon's booth, demanding helpings and portions of the broth to take home.

"It's an honor to have your items marked with the King's approval," William explains. "My father does not make it a habit to come to the markets. I try to make it a point to stamp something new every time I come, watching to see who hasn't gotten much business lately."

He shakes his head as he continues. "Simeon is always experimenting with weird recipes—things too outlandish for everyone else to want to spend their gold on. I am surprised this one was good, to be honest with you."

"That feels unfair to the rest of the vendors," I say. "But I suppose if everyone had a stamp, it wouldn't be special."

William nods. "I purchase from those who are desperate for the business. The rest do just fine with or without our approval."

I bite the inside of my cheek, wanting to ask more questions but stopping myself.

It appears things in Oresteia are much different than I thought.

A group of children runs past our small group, kicking up pieces of snow and flinging it at each other. They laugh, freely breezing past booths. I giggle as I watch them, remembering once again the days Callious and I would run through Komeus when my family was in the city.

William shoots me a look, clearly wondering what I'm laughing at.

I blush, feeling like I got caught in something I wasn't supposed to be doing.

Stupid Prince.

We arrive in front of a small building, large windows overtaking the outside walls. Cobblestone makes up the structure, clearly built to withstand storms. A white sign hangs from the roof, dark blue letters spelling out *Rhea's Place.*

Warm light spills out from the open front door, the smell of vanilla and melted butter wafting on the wind towards us.

I breathe in, allowing myself this one moment to enjoy the aroma of a place that shouldn't feel like home, but does somehow.

But I'm in enemy territory. Paralia is my home—a home I need to make it back to.

And soon.

Right now, I could lie to myself and say that the sandy shores of my Kingdom call to me; that I miss them dearly. But the truth is, I've always wanted something new to experience. And if this is my only chance, I want to reach out and grab hold of it while I have it.

I should hate this place. It's people. But I can't find it in me to wholly despise them, or to be angry with William for bringing me here.

I close my eyes for a moment, shutting out a vision dancing in my mind's eye—one of me walking this street like I know it, purchasing goods from these vendors just for fun, throwing snowballs and chasing someone through the booths.

I wipe it from my brain, knowing that if I stand here and keep dreaming, I'll begin to love what I see.

And I cannot afford to love the enemy. I cannot afford to stay. There's too much waiting for me back home. Callious, our army, a new life in Paralia when all of this is over.

I force my eyes to open, finding a woman—a decade older than we are— staring at me. Her pale hair is bound in a loose bun at the nape of her neck, the apron around her shoulders covered in flour and other spices.

"What do I owe this surprise?" the woman asks, Selene and William embracing her at once.

William smiles. "The emptiness in our stomachs, first. Second, might we use your upstairs room?"

"You know the answer is yes." She eyes me from where I hesitate, still in the street. "And who is this?"

Selene answers, surprising me by coming to my side and linking her arm with mine. "A guest of ours."

The woman nods. "I'm Rhea, it's nice to meet you. Please, make yourselves at home. I'll have food sent up for the three of you. Any requests?"

Selene ushers me into the bakery. I hear William's voice, being carried by the wind, as we leave. "Just that you'd lock the door behind you, taking a moment to stuff your ears after dropping off our food."

"Of course," Rhea responds with no hesitation.

I gulp, already being whisked away up the stairs.

What have I gotten myself into?

* * *

William joins us shortly after, all of us now sitting in a room with nothing in it but black curtains on the windows.

A knock interrupts our silence, Rhea ushering in plates of pastries—both savory and sweet—then pulling the door shut tight behind her. It locks with a click, and William waits for the sound of her footsteps to disappear from the stairs before speaking.

"We can eat," he whispers.

"I'm not hungry," I respond. And it's the truth. All thought of an appetite has disappeared at the mysteriousness of their actions and words. Anticipation builds in my stomach, nausea swimming around like fish in the sea.

William nods, brushing off his knees as he stands, walking to a door I didn't notice—one that blends in with the gray color of the walls. He slides it open just a crack, retrieving a tall, slender leather case from within.

He brings it back to us, holding it by the black strap attached. Lying it down, he opens it carefully, the hinges squeaking from the rust coating them.

Inside, there's a stringed instrument, one I haven't seen before. Its wooden material is sleek and a deep mahogany color.

Before I can ask, Selene cuts in, all business. "It's a violin. Leave your questions for the end." William cuts her a look of disapproval. "Please," she mumbles.

"Before I go any further, I need to tell you—what you are about to see, you cannot speak of. This is a closely guarded secret, one that only a few truly know about. I don't wish to use it against you, but for the betterment of my Kingdom, I *will* if I have to. So please, allow me to trust you, Penelope."

I hesitate. Should he trust me? *Can* he? We've known each other for only a handful of days. Our Kingdoms are supposedly in peril, and we are both of royal families, but that's where our similarities end. I could take this information and give it to my own General.

Maybe I'll tell Callious and see what he chooses to do with it.

But thoughts of betraying them like that make a shiver run down my spine for some reason.

I can't make any decisions until I see what it is he wants to show me. From there, I'll be honest with them about where I'm at. For how they've treated me so far, even though my circumstances are due to being kidnapped, it's the least I can offer.

Nodding, I release my breath, trying to settle my heartbeat.

"What you're about to see isn't our reality, but it will feel as though it is. If you get sucked into it too deeply, Selene will hold onto you. You're about to witness what will happen should we not right what has been wronged."

I brace myself, muscles tense.

And William begins to play.

CHAPTER NINETEEN
CALLIOUS

As I leave the other Captains, the hum of voices and the flicker of lantern light are a distant memory. Now deep into the night, I walk back to my tent, feet aching and jaw clenched.

The oppressive heat of the day clings to my dirt-ridden skin as humidity coats the air, suffocating me in a way that feels all too natural.

I can't shake the feeling that perhaps this is all just a nightmare—one I can wake myself up from. The day has passed in a daze of numbers and plans, theories and talk of possibility.

All of this—the mission that lies before me, decisions that need to be made, the idea that I might never see Nelly again—comes crashing down on me. I force myself to shove the uncertainty deep down and pretend that it's actually happening to someone else.

Someone far away from here, removed from this reality.

My thoughts spiral as I wander our makeshift camp

on the outskirts of Komeus, calling me back to the moment when she slipped out that door. Her eyes were so trusting, so certain that she would be okay.

Why didn't I fight back?

How could I just kneel there, helpless and beaten, and let Oresteia take her?

In truth, there's no way I could have known that the fight was a ruse, an illusion meant only for us.

Still, being hard on myself is the only punishment I've ever truly known.

I should have tried harder. I should have been more ready for what may come when we saw my father's shop dark and closed. My heart was in my throat, my pulse pounding in my chest. Visions of my father knocked unconscious, dead even, took over my usual discernment, and I acted as such.

"Get it together, Cal," I mutter under my breath, clenching my hands at my sides, aching for a fight.

I exhale sharply, realizing that sleep won't find me tonight. I make my way to my tent. As a Captain, I've been promoted to a singular person tent back at camp, one a tad bigger than the others. But we weren't planning on spending the night in Komeus.

Most of us are shoved in small tents for the night, eight or nine of us lying on the ground atop each other. Mess supplies are scattered carelessly everywhere you look.

I grab my flask from my backpack, taking a long swig of the lukewarm water. Every plan we came up with tonight—every strategy to breach Oresteia's borders and try to hear talk about Pen's fate—feels like it's missing something.

I feel like I'm missing something. The reality of magic changes everything.

I don't know how I'm going to get her back.

I slip into my tent, bodies already sprawled out on the floor, most of the men snoring to some extent.

Lying in my small spot, my backpack under my head, I focus on my breathing—on steadying my heartbeat. Tomorrow, I'll need to release some pent-up energy and take out my restlessness on someone who surely doesn't deserve it.

But for tonight, I'll try to rest. And trust that P is okay. Maybe even taken care of.

Wherever she is.

⁂

Up with the sun—but awake much longer than that—I wander, adrenaline churning in my stomach. I go through the motions for most of the morning, attending meetings and barking out directions and orders to those who don't know why we are still here.

Maybe we should send the rest of them back. She's not here—we've looked. There's no point in staying here much longer.

I walk to a post stationed nearby, dull practice swords hanging from the beam. Grabbing one, I swing it around, feeling the thickness of the leather hilt in my hand before striking the weighted, crusted metal against the air.

"You need a partner?" Vengeance yells from somewhere behind me.

I spin, careful to watch where I wave the blade. "You've got things to attend to, I'm sure."

He grabs another of the practice swords, shifting it from hand to hand. "I've always got time to beat you."

I huff, recognizing his verbal spar for what it is.

A distraction.

But one I will welcome wholly.

I strike at him, trying to catch him off guard. He blocks it easily without looking, pushing back against me with built-up strength.

He might have years of practice on his side, but I have frustration coiling beneath the surface of my skin, and anger always comes to play.

Voices begin to yell around us as recruits and guards alike circle our sparring, words taunting us and betting like this is just a form of entertainment. For me? This is personal. This is the war I came to fight, the life I came to fight *for.*

With the girl I want to hold forever.

That thought spurs me into reckless action again, my sword driving toward Veng of its own volition. I stab at his gut, a coward's blow, hoping he'll block so I can use that momentum to swing my elbow into his chest.

He blocks me again, but holds me there, not bouncing my sword off his like I was hoping. It catches me off guard, confusion at what to do next blocking all thoughts from my brain. In that moment, he kicks out a leg, sweeping mine from under me all too easily.

I hit the ground with a *thud*, my sword clattering out of my hand. Sweat soaks my back and drips off my forehead into my eyes.

Venge takes his blade's tip and points it under my chin, holding me there for a moment.

His storm-filled gray eyes penetrate my soul, bearing my weaknesses to him in front of everyone.

Lowering his voice and his blade, he says, "You're going to find her."

Sand coats my sweaty palms. My chest heaves. "What if I don't?"

He throws his sword to the side, offering me an outstretched hand. "You'll figure it out. With us."

I take his grip, hauling myself to my feet. The weight of his words sinks into my brain. I don't want to imagine a world in which she does not come back; one where we do not leave it together.

No, I can only think of success right now. That is the only way forward for me.

No matter the cost, I will try to make this right.

My heart cries out for it, and it's a cry I cannot ignore.

The rest of the afternoon, as the sun is high in the sky, I spar with everyone who offers. My emotions are more regulated now, anger not fueling my movements as much as it did with Vengeance. And that is the service he gifted to me—a place to unleash my fury at myself. He could see that I needed it.

That's the kind of Captain he is, and why he is widely respected by our army. We see something special in him, just as he sees something special in us.

Recruits come to me, looking to make a mark on my skin and impress their friends. And maybe, some of them, to try to prove the Captains wrong. That *they* should be the ones in my position, not me. Chatter falls silent when I spar this time, focus and resolve rippling from all those who watch.

I don't speak to those who try to overtake me, matches lasting between seconds and hours. I know the weight of my practice blade well now, honing it to become an extension of my arm.

I move like the tide, an overwhelming wave of strikes, lunges and blocks. Fluid, I stay on the balls of my feet, ready to maneuver. I see Pen's face every time I blink, so I try to keep my eyes open. Still, I hear her scream in the back of my mind, echoing off the ridges and dips that are the torture of my memory.

Having won against my most recent partner, I toss the sword down in the sand and meander around camp once more, my boots kicking up particles as I stomp and huff. I roll my neck, releasing pent-up tension in my shoulders that I can't help but hold onto.

Evening is upon us, and I haven't eaten a thing all day. Even then, my energy levels are high. The stress of the day is keeping me upright.

By sundown, the Captain's tent is a map-strewn mess of half-sketched plans and possibilities. I cross-reference every other Captain, getting their opinion and thoughts on how far they think I could travel into Oresteian territory without getting caught, and how long it might take.

We don't know much about their land or where things are—only that it's a cold, frosty territory.

Hawkwatch enters, probably sensing my stress. I run my fingers through my ragged hair as I look at her, my eyes feeling tired and desperate.

"They wear black," she says.

I tilt my head at her, unsure of what she means. "Who?"

"The Oresteian soldiers. They don't have uniform color ranking systems like we do. Their whole army is outfitted in matching onyx uniforms. You'll need one in order to blend in and get as far as possible into their territory."

I chew on the inside of my cheek, mulling this over. It could take days, even weeks, to have a uniform crafted for me. Thankfully, being in Komeus, it will be easier to find a seamstress who can craft a design and take my measurements. Maybe I could pay them to expedite the process...

Hawkwatch throws a bundle of something in my direction, interrupting my thoughts. Without thinking twice, I catch it, finding myself holding a thick pair of pants and a shirt.

A black uniform.

I look up at her, startled. Her mouth is upturned, amused at my reaction. "They're from a prisoner we kept long ago. You'll need to get them tailored to fit, and there's a hole in the pants' knee. You know Komeus—I'm sure you can find someone to take care of those things for you."

My heart starts beating quickly again, adrenaline my only friend.

"Good luck, Nightingale."

And with that, she walks out, head on a swivel as she leaves the tent and surveys what's happening through the rest of camp.

My fingers toy with the rough, thick fabric. It smells as if it's never been washed, and sand coats the various nooks and crannies of the seams. Still, it's my first step in getting Nel back.

I stare back down at the maps in front of me, one hand tracing hypothetical locations of where she could be.

Wherever they took her, I'll find it.

Whoever is behind this, I'll take them down.

Even if I have to leave Oresteia in ruins to do it.

CHAPTER TWENTY

A MELODIC TUNE BREEZES THROUGH THE SALTY AIR, catching my attention.

Hot wind flows through my curls, whipping them around my face in a dance I know too well. It rushes in off the Neronian, both sharp and alive all at once. The scent of sea tangles with that of fresh fruit and flowers wilting in the brutal sun. Paralia's sands hum beneath my bare feet, the warm, coarse grains soft.

A stone path lies before me, bathed in sunlight, leading to our family's Palace. Laughter spills from within, a sound I'm not used to hearing. Birds of all shapes cry out overhead, their wings spread wide mid-flight. Somewhere far away in Komeus, bells ring.

Breathing in deeply, I tune into my every sense. The sounds, the colors… this is *home*. How could I ever forget that?

I begin to walk the worn cobblestones, wondering where my siblings are, when an inaudible sound begins to vibrate throughout Paralia.

The earth beneath me is groaning, knocking me off my feet.

I tear my palm against rock as I catch myself from falling flat. My knees are scraped now, blood welling up from my wounds. I look up, wild and desperate, my face a portrait of confusion. As I help myself back up carefully, something feels different. Something is *missing*.

I turn around slowly, my gaze back toward the Neronian, trying to make sense of what just happened. Are we about to be swept away to sea?

Gasping, my hand finds my mouth. Every muscle in my body freezes, and my skin prickles with apprehension. My beautiful ocean, the waves that pull ceaselessly against me as I swim, my favorite place in Paralia...

Gone.

The sound of the tide hitting the shore has been silenced, the roar of the waves quieted. Where emerald waters once sparkled as if alive, there's only boiling ash. Steaming smoke peels off the surface in thick coils.

My foundation shifts again, this time the stone cracking in half as it gives way. I run toward the Palace, unsure of what's happening, only knowing that I *need* to be with my family. We need to get somewhere safe— somewhere we will all be okay.

We need to alert Komeus's residents. I need to find Callious and make sure he's alive. My feet pound against the cracked rock, my balance unsteady as it moves beneath me. I trip on rocky outcroppings, scraping my feet raw.

My arms pump as I run as fast as I can, gulping air

down my lungs as if I'm drowning. The oxygen is no longer clean, but now smoke that burns going down.

I run up the stairs to our Palace, looking for a familiar face. Walls crumble in the distance, falling into the black sea. Remnants of white dust float through the air, obstructing my vision. The Palace feels eerily still.

I pause, assessing. Where do I go from here? Should I look for my family first? Where are they?

Then people begin to panic. Running, screaming, crying. Flames chase servants down hallways. I can't breathe, the ruins of all I've ever known suffocating my lungs.

My chest rises and falls in quick succession, desperate to make sense of what's happening. I can feel my heart in my throat, the pounding of blood accompanying the roar in my ears.

The sky begins to darken above me, the ceiling now nonexistent. I can't find the sun… where is my sun? My bright, relentless star that warms my back? The one that lights my way, and asks me to bask in its never-ending heat. I once begged it to hide, to *leave*.

And now I realize maybe I didn't mean that. Maybe I didn't know what I was wishing for. Where are its rays?

My nose burns with salt and something metallic— blood? I plug my nostrils, gulping air with my mouth instead, hoping to avoid whatever might be burning. I don't want to think about it. I don't want to face the reality that might be my own.

Tears slip down my cheeks, streaking wet spots against the soot now covering my skin.

I begin to run again, picking up my pace, unsure of where I'm heading.

"Mother!" I scream, heart racing. "Father? Carter?"

There's no answer from them. Not one I can hear, anyway. Their potential responses and my screams are drowned out by the tragedy unfolding before me.

I'm in the front grounds now, unsure of how I got here. My body was acting on its own, memory carrying me far. Surveying the Palace, all I see is ruin. Cracks run like vines through the walls as flames lick up the columns of our Palace.

We've never had an issue with fires. The sea protects us from its wrath. But now, the ocean is gone, and we are vulnerable in ways we've never known. I squint, seeing someone standing on the balcony near the top of our Palace, waving frantically at me. I yell, trying to see who it is through the smoke.

It's my brothers, my sisters—all of them. I shout, gesturing at them to stay there, that I'm coming.

But before I can move a step, an ear-splitting *crack* weaves its way toward me as the balcony gives out.

And they fall.

I cover my mouth, holding in the sob that threatens to overtake me. I want to throw up, I want to cry. I want to scream and rage and die with them…

"Penelope!"

I turn in a hysterical daze. Callious stands before me. How did he get here? Where has he been?

My heart gives out as I throw my arms around his neck and collapse in his comforting embrace.

He shoves me away, gripping my arms and shaking me.

"This is *your fault*," he snarls.

I stare, unblinking. "What…"

"*You did this.*" He throws me away from him in disgust, his upper lip curled. I trip, falling backward, landing on my back with a *thud*.

And I'm… cold.

I open my eyes, having not realized I closed them in the first place. All the breath has been stolen from my lungs as I witness the impossible.

Snow. I landed on… snow.

It's frozen against my hands, sharp and wet against my bare legs and feet. My tears freeze onto my face as I peel myself off the icy powder.

How did I end up in Oresteia?

Mountains rise into the dark sky like broken glass— jagged and empty. Trees are down, cracked and burnt to stumps. Ash flows through the air like the snowflakes I once enjoyed.

Copolis stands in ruins in the distance, the buildings and market demolished. Somehow, I can see blood running along the streets, flowing like rivers.

Everything around me keeps getting darker, my vision struggling to keep up. I take a step and hear a whimper over the sound of destruction. My neck whips to the right, searching.

William. Selene.

Crimson pools around both of them, their skin paler than normal as frost lines their lashes and lips.

I run to them, falling onto my wounded knees. Shaking, I touch their necks, looking for a pulse.

There's one there, but barely. They are cold—too cold. Unmoving. William's eyes are open, but glassy—unblinking.

Crying out, my voice breaks. "What's happening?"

I'm desperate, so desperate. How could all of this ruin come to us so quickly? Where did this come from?

He looks at me, shifting his head slightly so that our eyes lock. Grief overcomes his features as his frozen lips move.

"Help us," he murmurs.

My chest splinters in two as they both stop breathing. I scream, sob, plead, but there's no one to answer me. There's only silence and snow.

"I don't know how!" I yell into the oblivion and to whatever being might be listening.

The ground rumbles again, vibrating my teeth and skull. Then, everything around me crumbles into dust, falling into a never-ending black hole.

I go with it, my fate no longer in my own hands. I've resigned myself to this ending. I clutch the seashell necklace around my neck, closing my eyes and awaiting death to greet me.

Eternity is so dark.

I gasp, choking on stolen air, throat raw as I scream into the oblivion. Hands grab at me, holding me down. My limbs thrash as I claw at my captor. I'm soaked in sweat—both freezing and burning at the same time. I can't see. I can't breathe.

The sound of the violin is gone.

"It's not real," William murmurs, over and over, trying to get my attention.

I look back and forth from him to Selene, reality coming back to me in pieces and shards.

Selene's hold lessens as she sees me calm down. "You're not there. Everyone is okay."

I gulp. My eyes sting from all the tears I've cried involuntarily.

I'm lying on the floor, Selene kneeling next to me.

My chest heaves, the sobs still coming. I can't make them stop.

"Paralia was… and Callious… my family… they—"

"It's not real," William repeats, hand running through his hair. Did he have those shadows under his eyes earlier, or are those new?

I scoot from Selene's grasp, pulling my knees up toward my chin to tuck my body into a ball. "It felt real."

"It's not."

I look at him quizzically. "There's a 'but' in your sentence. I can hear it in your tone."

He hesitates.

I throw my arms into the air. "You can't put me through whatever *that* was and not give me all the information I need."

"Yet. That's the 'but' you're hearing. It's not real *yet.*"

"What do you mean?" My fingers start to shake, so I tuck them into my lap, hiding them from my captors.

Selene gets up from the floor, dusting off her pants. "I'll tell Rhea she's okay to go about business as normal and leave you two to talk."

Before she leaves, she comes over to where I am on

the floor and wraps her arms around me. The tight hug is almost too much, crushing me in a way that is too personal, too intimate. But somehow, it feels... natural. She whispers into my ear, "Hear him out. Please."

She releases her hold and walks out the door, shutting it behind her.

"Are you hungry?" William asks, breaking up the silence.

I shake my head. "Please don't ask me to eat anything. Not after that. Not before you tell me what's going on."

He nods, just slightly. "We are at war because our most prized possession, The Queen's Heart, has been taken and replaced with a fake. My father, King Kori, believes the Frey to be the ones to have taken it. You were meant to come with us to aid in our search, but also to serve as a bit of... collateral... for Oresteia. That didn't go the way we planned, obviously."

I blush. "I wanted to make my own decisions."

William smiles gently. "It's admirable that you decided to take your life into your own hands." He pauses. "The Queen's Heart was created from the combined magic of our two bloodlines—Paralian and Oresteian—and grew out of the Janus Tree, where my ancestor found it. I'm sure you've heard the story?"

Nodding, I motion for him to continue.

"From the research I've found, The Queen's Heart was never meant to be separated from the Tree. This is no longer merely a war between our two Kingdoms based on hearsay—it's a matter of life or death for our world. The Queen's Heart *must* be returned to the Tree, but both of us must be present to do so."

"I don't have it. And I'm sure no one in my family does. We can't return something that is still lost."

"What you saw, Penelope… it was a vision gifted to me from the Janus Tree. That is our future reality; should we not mend what has been broken. And it must be us—both of us, together. We can turn the tide of this war."

"How did you show that to me?" I whisper. "And why did it feel so… real?"

"My magic gives me the ability to portray realistic illusions while playing an instrument or singing. I was merely passing on an image that was given to me, so you might truly see what is at stake. For all of us."

He says this so matter-of-factly, as if the idea of having magical abilities isn't unheard of.

Everything is so different here.

"I will help you as much as I'm able. But I still wish to go back home. If you are truly searching for the Heart, I will too, and I will write to you of any information I find. And when we do find it, because I know we will, you can come get me again." I eye him pointedly. "But there will be *no need* to stage a kidnapping this time."

He laughs, head tilting back, and the sound soothes my aching heart. It feels out of place after what I just witnessed, but it's nice all the same. "Fair deal."

Silence penetrates the distance between us. I unravel myself from my protective cocoon to sit on my knees.

"What we saw, Penelope... we will not let it happen."

I look up at him, and for once, I don't see an enemy. I see a boy with the weight of our Kingdoms on his shoulders—one that hasn't been sleeping. One that might need a friend to help him carry that burden. I swallow. "How do you know it's real?"

I'm not sure I truly want the answer to that question.

He meets my gaze, steady. "I don't. But I can't take a chance on it coming true because I decided to stand by and not do what I could to stop it."

CHAPTER TWENTY-ONE

.

I DON'T KNOW HOW LONG WE'VE BEEN IN RHEA'S Place, but somehow, the pastries are still warm.

The flaky, buttery layers fall apart between my fingers as I sit curled up on a cushioned chair downstairs. My legs are crossed beneath me as I watch customers flit in and out the front door, a bell announcing their presence every time it swings open. Copolis is busy—busier than it was when we first arrived.

The filling of the pastry I'm eating tastes like some sort of tart fruit—perfectly sweet and sour, but sticky going down.

For a while, I sit next to the fire in silence with William and Selene and pretend I'm just… here. That there's no impending doom in the near future. That I wasn't dragged across a border I never wanted to cross. I pretend I'm not a Princess, not a recruit. I'm just… Penelope.

And who is Penelope, really? Will I have time to find the answer to that question, or am I out of chances?

Selene hands me a mug filled to the brim with something hot and thick.

"Rhea calls it hot chocolate," she says. "Careful, you might burn your tongue."

I take a careful sip, letting the warm liquid coat my throat. I roll my eyes back in delight, a gasp slipping out of my lips involuntarily. "This is *delicious.*"

William joins in, taking a mug from Selene as well. "It's especially good on a stormy winter night."

The room quiets between the three of us, but I feel compelled to break it. "It's easy to forget where I am right now. What's at stake. What I've left behind."

"Dangerous thoughts," Selene murmurs. She watches me carefully, though it seems she's pretending not to as she stretches out her legs.

"You feel comfortable here?" William asks.

"Where is 'here'?" I ask. "Rhea's Place? Oresteia? In the presence of both of you? I feel my answer is different for each of those options."

He mulls that over, speaking slowly and carefully. "With us."

"Right now I do."

Though he doesn't meet my eyes, I see a small smile creep onto his face as he takes a big bite of something with salt and cheese atop it.

"An unknown fate doesn't have to be used as a weapon," Selene says, tone light. But as she looks at me, I see something deep within her gaze. A weight— as if she knows what it's like to be dragged somewhere you didn't want to be.

"What's your story?" I ask, motioning to both of them.

They look at each other, quiet smiles on their faces as they reminisce. William nods at Selene, waving for her to go ahead. Her smile grows tenfold, creases in the corners of her eyes deepening.

"We're cousins!" she proclaims. "Our mothers were sisters." Her tone turns somber. "My parents were killed when I was ten, the culprit thinking they might gain some sort of leverage over the royal family with the act. Instead, they earned themselves a worse fate. And I found myself part of the royal family overnight, Uncle Kori declaring me as one of his own."

William cuts in. "Selene has been many things in the time I've known her. My cousin, a royal, a soldier. But my favorite thing is that she is my friend. That's why she's my General—not only is she skilled, but I trust her wholeheartedly. She's been training her whole life to be part of Oresteia's army."

"King Kori expressed that I wouldn't be allowed to enlist unless William got sent to the lines first. He would do anything for me, even if that meant risking his life so I can fulfill my lifelong dream." They share a look, one of deeper secrets that only the two of them know.

I begin to put pieces together, thinking that maybe Selene felt she was denied what she thought was her whole purpose. It truly is kind of William to make sure that reality got to happen for her. Perhaps I've misjudged these two and their land. Maybe all I've learned *is* a lie.

But if Paralia's version isn't the truth, where does

that leave me and *my* Kingdom? Does that make us the true enemy?

I shove those questions down, burying them beneath piles of denial. I don't want to look at those too closely yet, lest I find an answer I don't want to.

"And hear me say this, Penelope," Selene retakes my attention, her look full of resolve. "I won't let him down."

I nod, understanding. "I won't let you down either."

※ ※ ※

Later that afternoon, I find myself wandering the streets with William. The walls had started to close in on me, the weight of all that is at stake making it hard to breathe.

I needed a space to think, but unfortunately, I'm not allowed to walk around without an escort.

And they don't trust anyone else to walk with me. So William it is.

The bite in the air doesn't bother me quite as much today, but that might be because of the thick layers Selene gave me to put on before we left. The white of the material is blinding, and William's own blends in well with our surroundings.

His footsteps are soft beside me, his hands in the pockets of his coat, face tilted toward the people milling about.

I see him looking at me from the corner of his eye.

"You—"

"Do—"

We speak at the same time, our voices overlapping. I huff a small laugh as he motions for me to go first, shutting his lips tight.

"Do you get used to the cold? The snow?" I ask.

"I suppose we are used to it in the same way that you would be used to your heat and sun," he responds.

I tilt my head, thinking. "I don't think I *am* used to Paralia's weather patterns."

He laughs. "The same is true here. It still affects you just the same, but you begin to expect it. That's what makes it less noticeable."

I motion for him to talk now, giving him his turn.

"You look radiant in Oresteia white," he says, voice low.

"Why white? I couldn't help but notice that I don't see anyone else in this color." Other questions are on the tip of my tongue, but I hope that he hears the unspoken words.

Why was Selene wearing red that first day? Why are your guards and soldiers all in black? Where are the bold colors that I've grown so accustomed to in Paralia?

"White is for the royal family only. It helps us blend into our surroundings. But at the same time, if we are hit in battle, it shows others where our wound is and just how bad it is. There's no sun here, as I'm sure you've noticed. Black is for soldiers and guards, helping them blend into the shadows and fog."

"Why red for Selene?"

He smirks. "She likes to do things her own way."

I giggle a bit, weaving in and out of people going the opposite way. "I can tell."

Snow crunches beneath our boots. "Can I ask you something?"

"Didn't you just?" he teases.

"Funny." I pause, and he waves for me to continue. "How did you get out that night? After we captured you?"

He chews on the inside of his cheek, hands behind his back in a picture of poise. I watch as he considers this question, exhaling through his nose as if he's debating how much to say. "I was never really there."

He glances at me, gauging my reaction. I stop where we walk, crossing my arms, waiting for him to continue. "Like the illusion I showed you this morning —the vision of what could happen to our Kingdoms. I'm also able to project myself and others; to make you see what I want you to see in other ways."

I frown. "You felt real."

He laughs, almost embarrassed. "Yes, that's the point."

"So were you... nearby? How does that work?"

"I was in the area, yes."

"But we didn't see you." My voice pitches up at the end of that sentence, as if I'm asking a question. I suppose I am—the implications are making my head spin.

"No, Penelope, you did not."

I shuffle my feet along the ice, kicking at the dirty clumps with my boots.

"It's not my intention to deceive you. I needed to know if you were there. I was... looking for you," he admits quietly.

"Why? To tell me about all of this?" I wave my

hands around, gesturing. I want to be angry at him, at Selene, at *Oresteia*. But I can't. Wouldn't I do the same if I were in his position? There's a strain in the way he talks and honesty in his eyes. Somehow, I feel like I can trust him.

"Yes, that."

"And?" I prompt, hearing unspoken words in that sentence.

"And," he pauses, visibly stressed. "And, you remind me of someone. Someone I once knew, long ago."

"Tell me about them." We resume walking, nodding and saying hi to all of those we pass. Steam billows off the houses, their warm insides so vastly different from the temperatures we're experiencing out here.

"She was… vibrant," he begins, wonder in his voice. "I could have written poems regarding how pretty she was, even as a young girl. Her laughter was a song on the wind, her eyes golden like fresh honey. She was wild, free. Everything I wasn't allowed to be."

He points at the scar just under his left eye, barely visible in the bright light. "She gave me this. My father was in a meeting of sorts, one of high importance. Because I was young, he didn't want me in the way. She and I were about the same age, so we started playing together. We were throwing a rock back and forth after a day of running around and having fun. My father stormed out of the meeting, furious, yelling at me that we were leaving that instant."

William's hands wave wildly, voice loud and animated, fully pulling me into the story. "I wasn't looking when she threw the rock that last time. It hit me under the eye, cutting it deeply. I was pulled away from her without a goodbye, blood streaming down my face." He pauses. "She was my first friend."

My stomach churns, my palms sweating for some reason. "She sounds lovely."

He smiles at me, warm and bright. "She is."

Before I can question his wording choice, Selene prances out of the building to our left, one swarmed with guards. "Hey! There you guys are. Come in, it's time to play!"

I shoot a questioning look at William, but he goes right in after Selene, not sparing a look back at me.

Play what?

※ ※ ※

Evening descends on us, the wind howling fiercely outside.

The leather chair I sit in envelops me. Selene places a box on the wooden table in front of us. She opens it to reveal a deck of worn cards, the corners curling from too much use.

"Do you play?"

"What are your rules?" I ask, sitting up to pay better attention.

"Our version is simple," she says, shuffling the gray cards. "If you lose, you share an honest answer. Winner gets to ask the question."

I arch a brow. "Seems easy."

Her dark eyes sparkle. "Perhaps."

We play their version of this game. It appears to be the same as ours, but the cards have different icons. There are two sets of fifty different pictures, all of various Oresteian things. Mountains, snow, vendor booths, food, people.

The goal is to grab as many matches as possible, asking for specific cards when it's your turn in hopes that your opponent has what you need. If they do, you keep it. If they don't, it's their turn.

I win the first hand. I ask her if King Kori knows I'm on Oresteian soil. She says no, that they've tried their best to keep my interactions with them a secret.

Appreciation floods me.

She wins the second hand, sweeping me, as if she was going easy on me the first time. "What do you love most about Paralia?"

I think that question over as she deals our next hand. "Truthfully, I don't love Paralia that much."

"There must be something you love about the only home you've ever known," she prompts.

I nod. "Yes. Callious. He's what I love most about it."

We continue to play, and as we do, we trade stories, laughter, and memories. I get to ask what her favorite thing about Oresteia is. She says William's leadership.

She asks me about my relationship with my family, and how my days are usually spent. I give her little pieces of truth, careful to not say too much.

Candles burn low as soldiers head to their posts for the night. There's something else between Selene and me at the end of the game, too. Not friendship just yet. But something mutual. Something… free and *fun*.

William walks over from where he's been talking with commanding officers. "Having fun?"

Selene and I link arms as we stand, both of us giggling. "I beat Penelope five to two."

He tsks. "Seems unfair."

He eyes me while I laugh, enjoying this feeling of normalcy. Noting his seriousness, I quiet, waiting for him to continue.

"I came to tell you that we are staying the night here. We'll be traveling in the morning."

"Am I going back home?" I ask, hopeful.

He shakes his head, regret brimming in his eyes. "Not yet. First, we'll be going to the Oresteian Gate. And you'll be coming with us."

CHAPTER TWENTY-TWO
CALLIOUS

I LEAVE THE PARALIAN GATE IN THE DUST, SAND shooting up from beneath my boots as I trudge forward in the night.

I shouldn't be here.

But what other choice do I have?

Thoughts spin circles in my head as I run the length of the Isthmus, not wanting to give up a single bit of shadow cover that was gifted to me tonight. It's as if the sun knew I would need its presence completely removed, as if the stars heard my cries for Pen.

It's risky to cross the Isthmus alone. The water on either side is relentless and chaotic. The length of the land is narrow, and I feel I am just one big wave away from being pulled under.

I shake that thought off, watching my steps carefully. Wet sand turns into dirty snow; humid heat into bitter cold. It's a thing of wonder and beauty—how our Kingdoms connect and intertwine at this spot. I can't think about that too long, though. There's no time.

I need to get to Oresteia.

My eyes are fixed on their own Gate and watch-tower—on the way it pierces the night with glowing lantern light. I creep low as I get closer, slowing myself to an almost crawl. My borrowed Oresteian uniform has been shoddily patched. I didn't want to waste any time.

I tug on the collar. It's rubbing against my scar, making my neck itch.

I need to know what is happening to Nelly. Where she is, if she's okay. I crave that information like I crave the air pumping in and out of my lungs.

Sticking to the shadows, I survey their Gate. There's no one stationed on the Isthmus side, so I'm able to get as close to the iron bars as possible. The bars have just enough of a gap between them that I might slip through sideways if I release all my breath, so long as no one is watching.

A pair of guards talk idly by torchlight near the watchtower, their words drifting this way but falling on ears that don't care what they're saying. If it's not Penelope's name, I'm not listening.

I hold my breath, counting the seconds and minutes and hours. Waiting. Watching. Wondering if I'll even get farther than this, or if my trip will be cut short here and I'll be forced to turn back with my tail between my legs.

A Captain who couldn't complete his most important mission.

No, I can't think like that. *Strength, stealth, security,*

sight. I repeat those words to myself, over and over, reminding my body what I've been trained to do. Reminding my brain what I know is true.

The guards' heads turn toward the watchtower, maybe hearing someone call out for them? Regardless of the reason, they open the door at the bottom of the tower and slip inside. I move, quickly and silently, not willing to give up this chance.

I'm light on my feet, my boots hardly crunching on snow as I slip through the metal bars. I grunt accidentally as I fall out the other side, catching myself, looking around to make sure no one heard me.

Nothing.

Feels too good to be true.

Their gate is wider and bigger than ours. Usually guarded to the teeth with soldiers milling about. Thankfully, it seems as though the only ones out are those on watch at a specific post, the rest in bed or unaccounted for.

I drop low behind a stack of old crates. Do I dare walk as if I belong here, hoping they only see my uniform and don't look too closely? Or should I stay hidden, creeping through their camp, trying to slip past undetected?

I choose the latter, not willing to risk someone asking why I'm out and about. I don't know their rules and regulations. Better to be unseen and unheard.

My lungs burn from the run down the Stenos Isthmus, but I try to keep from breathing heavily, only allowing oxygen to slip through my nose. Their air is so thin, but I won't risk my breath fogging up and alerting them to my presence.

Dozens of soldiers stand posted in various places, cloaked and armed, the steel of their weapons glinting in the lowlight.

I packed only my dagger, thinking it would be lighter and easier to carry. I have it tucked in my waistband, in a pocket I asked the seamstress to add last minute. The metal is cold against my leg, but its existence beside me is reassuring still.

A patrol shifts formation, swapping with another group of guards. A few of them step away for a moment.

Now is the time.

I press my hand to the leather cord tucked around my chest, letting its familiar weight ground me.

Leaping from behind my cover, I run, slipping through the gate on the other side of their iron fence. Ice threatens to take my feet out from under me, but I don't pause to catch my footing. The slick surface carries me further and faster than I could have without it.

Trees align the distant hill, and I make a break for them. I sprint, leaving footsteps in the snow behind me, hoping they don't notice. Or, if they do, that they don't care to follow.

There are no shouts behind me as I slip into the shadowed forest cover. No alarms ring, no one cries for help.

I'm in.

✵ ✵ ✵

I head south, following where the trees are taking me, allowing the cruel winter to fully envelope me in its dark cocoon. The peuko branches lean heavily with snow, and starlight gleams off the powder like blades waiting to cut me.

Every sound I make carries too far, the crunch of debris like a death wish.

I don't know where I'm going, not exactly. I follow the maps we've pieced together, unsure of exactly where their city lies. We thought Copolis would be my best bet in hearing whispers of a Paralian prisoner, commoner gossip hopefully spreading like wildfire. I just... don't exactly know where Copolis is.

Still, I *do* know she's here, somewhere. And that's what keeps me going.

I press deeper into the woods, trying to keep a straight path, steering away from where I believe their own Palace resides. I don't think it would be smart for me to try and invade their well-protected castle. Not unless I have to.

By the time my hands start to go numb and my knees begin to pain, I see something up ahead: a flicker of warm light half-hidden by a slope in the hills.

A cottage.

It's small and worn down, as if it's not used regularly. There's no path in the snow leading up to it and no footsteps left behind from another weary traveler. Smoke does not climb up the chimney, gracing the air with its heat. No, the only sign of use is the single light turned on beside the wooden door.

Night is dissipating quickly, a new day beginning just as fast. I don't know who lives here, if anyone, and

I don't care. I need shelter for the day so I can rest and recuperate before heading back out tomorrow evening.

I told the other Captains to give me three night cycles. And that if I wasn't back by then, to not count on my return.

I knock softly, chancing the sound, listening intently for footsteps. Should I hear any, I'll forsake this plan, finding shelter within the forest instead.

No answer.

I try the door, rattling the rusted metal knob.

It's unlocked.

It's a simple structure—just four walls surrounding everything you might want in a home. The cold wooden floors penetrate the soles of my boots.

Tall, grand windows overtake the walls, letting in what little light Oresteia has to offer.

A dark gray leather couch looks inviting, a wood-burning heater in the corner just waiting for me to light a small fire—enough to get warm again.

A piano sits in another corner, an odd piece to see. Perhaps an older person lives here, spending their days by the fire and in the accompaniment of music. Truthfully, that doesn't sound like an awful life to live.

I can imagine Nel and me living in a house like this, spending our days in each other's presence, swapping stories and laughter like it's our second nature.

I shake those thoughts from my brain, not allowing myself to dream.

I have to find her first.

This place is clearly lived in, but somehow, I've lucked out in finding it while no one is home.

I go back and shut the front door behind me. I

collapse before the fire after lighting it; just a spark. I don't dare use the tub in the washroom, or sleep in the bed in the other room. My back stays to the fire, my front toward the door, alert and ready should someone enter without notice.

Even on edge, I allow myself to breathe and refocus. Warmth seeps in slowly, my eyes drifting shut with every second that passes.

☼ ☼ ☼

I wake up with a start, realizing night is upon me again.

I snuff the embers of the fire. It's still hot, but I don't have time to wait.

The maps must be outdated. If the information I have is mostly correct, I'm near the edge of Oresteia. The Khionean Sea shouldn't be that far off if I keep going south. I need to start my trek toward the north, then, and try to avoid their castle at the same time.

Nothing I can't do.

I keep to the snow-coated coast. Mountains loom beyond the forest I've been trapped in, spilling into the dark sky. I don't know how far I walk or how long I'm out in the cold. Only that by the time I see a glimpse of city lights, I could weep with joy.

Finally.

I walk right in, assuming the position of just another person who lives in Copolis. I keep to the shadowed alleys behind their market street, listening.

I hear her name.

Not her name exactly. But whispers about a Paralian visitor. About their Prince and General.

"That Paralian girl must be nothing but trouble. She used to be a Princess, you know. Left them behind."

"Should have left her there, then. What a coward."

"I bet she's just here to spy on us."

Their grumbled words grab hold of my chest. I ball my fists, rage rising from within, but I force myself to shut it down.

Not the time, nor the place, nor the people.

"Prince William wouldn't let someone he didn't trust within our borders. I think there's more to her than we know."

That makes my head tilt, considering. What *does* their Prince want with *my* girl? It sounds like the people don't know.

"Either way, I'm glad they're going back to the Gate. Might get the King off our back."

The Gate.

They're going back.

I bolt out of the city, sticking to the dark corners and ridges. I'm out of breath by the time I'm back on the mountain overlooking Copolis. Pausing to clear my head, I breathe in the crisp winter air.

Snow has begun to fall, flakes covering my uniform and hair in light drops. My breath fogs up the air in front of me in thick bursts, showing just how cold it is here.

And somehow, I no longer feel its bite. Adrenaline burns in my veins. I reach up to touch my necklace, to ground myself, but my hand does not find the worn leather cord or the old metal ring.

I grasp at my neck, my chest, searching for it in my shirt.

It's gone.

I dig through my pockets, look around me on the ground.

Nothing.

It must have fallen somewhere in the snow during my trek. Perhaps in the city, or maybe in the cottage.

My heart pains. The family heirloom my father gifted is me already gone. I had plans for that ring— plans to grace it upon Penelope's finger, to pass it down to my own son, after all of this is over.

Regret threatens to drown me. But I cannot let it hold me back from doing what needs to be done. I don't know what they're planning, or what they have for her when they get to the Gate. But if she's going to be there, it's the best chance I've got to get her back.

And to strike at them before they can strike at us. At her.

I'm going to go back to Paralia and will return with a blade between my fingers and revival in my blood. I will make them pay for whatever they've done to her, and everything they haven't.

I begin the journey west, toward where the Isthmus beckons me. My army will be behind me—that I know for sure.

And if what Oresteia wants is a battle, I'll give them *war*.

CHAPTER TWENTY-THREE

THE SMELL OF CINNAMON GREETS ME AT THE GATE. The chill in the air hits my bones, reminding me I'm still deep into enemy territory, even though if I squinted my eyes, I'd be able to see the Neronian.

Home.

It's peaceful as we walk through camp, William and Selene ahead of me as we pass by tents of all sizes. Campfires are lit all around, constantly blazing, soldiers sharpening blades and playing cards.

Where are the people training? Are they that sure of their abilities that they do not believe they need the daily practice?

Selene whistles at me from ahead, waiting for me. I hadn't realized I had stopped in a stupor, taking in everything I could. Not that I'm sure I would relay this information to my own Captains, but… they will ask questions. And I should be prepared to answer them.

It would be suspicious if, when I return to Paralia, I had nothing to offer regarding our enemy. I probably cannot tell them the real reason William brought me here.

Right?

I shake my head, clearing the concern creeping up internally. That's not something I need to worry about right now. I jog to Selene, catching up with her. "Like what you see?" she asks.

"It seems like everyone is taking today off," I reply.

She shrugs. "When William and I are away, people relax. It's just the nature of our positions and our relationship to them. I'm sure they haven't heard we're back yet, or they'd all be trying their hardest to kiss the ground we walk on."

I suppose my surprise shows on my face, because she tilts her head at me and asks, "Do you not receive the same treatment at your camp? Surely being a Princess has its weight with those around you."

Ashamed, I turn my face away. "No," I whisper, not wanting to give away to her what it's like for me in my father's Palace. More than that, why I decided it was best to leave everything altogether.

That's a story for another day. Another time.

She just nods, eyes now looking toward the horizon where the largest tent is erected. She smiles, the act brightening her face. "I have an idea. Follow me."

I don't argue, trailing after her while she walks proudly through those she's in charge of. Here in the depths of camp, a few people are sparring, soldiers clashing wooden staffs with precision I could only dream of.

It's as if they are dancing to a song only they know —the moves and hits and feints spotless. One of them pauses mid-strike to salute Selene, and she just gives them a quick nod of her head, hardly even glancing at them.

There seems not to be much of a ranking system here; everyone is milling about with whoever they'd like to. Paralia's camp is much more divided. People laugh loudly, joking with each other, slapping them on the arms.

There are no masks present—no pretending to be something you aren't. Just soldiers having a good time.

I scoff under my breath. How could they be having a good time while in the midst of *war?*

Selene peels back the tent flap for me, letting me enter first. The smell of cinnamon hits me tenfold, so pungent I can hardly breathe. Warmth pours out of the space, so I immediately shed my fur-lined cloak.

I wrap it around my waist, tentatively stepping toward the brick-laid oven, Selene on my heels. My boots crunch on the gravel rocks intermixed with melted, dirty snow.

A woman stands in front of us, her back facing me, kneading something soft and doughy on the steel table next to the oven. Her dark, flour-coated sleeves are rolled past her elbows, her silver hair pinned up in a messy bun.

Her hand finds my shoulder. "Tarsha," she calls.

The woman turns, her smile so big her eyes seem to disappear. She wipes her hands on the apron I didn't notice she was wearing, then holds them up to grasp Selene's upper arms. She squeezes, coming in to kiss Selene on the cheek.

Selene kisses back, pulling away to push me toward Tarsha.

"This is Penelope. Keep her occupied for a bit?"

Tarsha nods, looking me up and down.

"I'll be back later. Tarsha will keep you good company."

I look at Tarsha as Selene leaves, mustering a nervous smile. She points at another gray apron crumpled in a ball next to the table, mimicking that I should put it on.

Raising an eyebrow at her silence, I grab the apron, replacing my cloak with the linen strap. I wrap it around my neck and waist, tying it tightly.

She points again, at a wash bucket in the corner. I follow her orders, washing my hands with the small piece of soap beside it, dunking everything up to my wrists in the warm water. I scrub, removing all the dirt and grime underneath my fingernails from our trip here.

Agrius carried William and me most of the way, Selene behind us on her horse. The soap smells like lavender, so deeply contrasting the smell of baked goods elsewhere. I'm hoping it covers up the scent of horse and hay still lingering in my hair and on my clothes.

I dry my hands on my apron, the fabric coarse against my skin. As I return to where Tarsha is, she's back to kneading the dough, having split it into two bundles now. She motions towards one, and I mimic what she's doing.

I've never kneaded anything before, let alone baked or cooked. I hope she doesn't think I'm incompetent or incapable because of it. It seems as though Selene values this woman, and she values her just as much.

For some reason, I want to be a part of that and make her proud of the work I do in this kitchen.

My forearms begin to burn as we finish kneading, and I shake out my hands, my palms going numb. I've wiped more flour on my forehead than I have my apron, sweat beginning to perspire on my arms and face.

The oven is *hot*, and I hadn't realized just how inherently cold I've been in Oresteia until I wasn't cold anymore.

Tarsha hands me a wooden rolling pin, showing me how to flatten my dough as she is. I follow her motions, flattening it as best as I can. It feels like I'm suffocating in here. I roll up my sleeves, realizing why she did so long ago.

I'm used to humid conditions, but this is ridiculous. Can't we open that tent flap a bit or something?

I keep my grumbling internal, not wanting to hinder our progress or make Tarsha send me on my way. Selene wanted me here, out of the way, so it's out of the way that I'll be. If I'm compliant, following along with what they want, maybe I can go home soon.

To Callious.

Suns, I miss him. It's been so hard learning this life, but it *has* been fun doing it with him by my side. I wonder what he's doing right now, what the army is preparing for next, what whispers I may be missing while away…

Tarsha waves her hand in front of my face, grabbing my attention. I smile at her sheepishly, putting my rolling pin down. She grabbed a tub of butter from somewhere else in the kitchen while I was stuck in my daydream, now handing me a knife and motioning for me to watch what she does.

She takes a slab of butter from the steel container, the bottom of it icy from where it must have been on snow or ice. The butter on top is melted a bit, just enough that it drips as she plops it onto her flattened dough. She disperses it evenly, covering almost every inch of it.

I follow, doing the same with mine. The knife catches on the dough in places, cutting up my mostly flat handiwork. I huff, curls escaping the tight ponytail at my neck to get in my eyes. I begin to feel faint, my legs swaying from under me.

It must be the heat.

I finish, taking much longer than Tarsha does. She waits patiently, watching me work, not saying anything about what I might be doing wrong. Perhaps this is a test—seeing if I'll break with something as simple as pastry making. I might, to be honest. It's so hot in here, I'm going to melt just like the butter.

I look at hers, then look at mine. Back and forth, comparing the two.

You can tell it's my first time.

Tarsha takes the butter, popping a lid on the top and placing it in a wooden chest nearby, cool air rising from it when she opens it. I breathe a sigh of relief.

She notices, tilting her head. She must be so used to the heat that to watch me struggle with it isn't something she expected, especially because I'm from such a sunny, coastal Kingdom.

Unless… she doesn't know where I'm from? Surely she does. My skin tone and hair color practically paint a picture that says, 'outsider—does not belong here.'

She beckons me toward the front of the tent, holding the flap open and tying it to a pole so it stays.

I step outside for a moment, letting the frigid mountain air replenish me. Goosebumps pop up all over my exposed skin, but it's a feeling I revel in. The air bites going down, drowning me in its chill. My sweat begins to freeze on my forehead, which cools me down faster.

Relaxing a bit, I roll my shoulders, shaking out my legs and arms. I move my neck back and forth. Feeling better, I turn back to Tarsha, who gives me an apologetic glance. I just smile at her, softly. There's no way she could have known how I was feeling. Of course, I could have told her…

But I didn't want to be seen as weak.

We go back in, the open flap letting in the right amount of air to curb the overwhelming heat. She hands me a metal shaker, and I take a whiff of what's inside, realizing it's what I've been smelling since I first arrived.

Cinnamon.

I moan, the smell so delicious I can almost taste it. I see her giggle a bit in the corner of my eye, her shoulders moving up and down in laughter as she layers her butter with the spice. Following what she's doing once again, I layer mine heftily, covering the dough's surface—and the table's surface—with the rich particles.

Next, she takes a sharper knife, cutting her dough into four strips a couple of inches wide. Once she's done, she hands the knife to me. I cut mine carefully, trying not to catch the corners of my dough, lest I ruin my hard work.

I look up at her when I'm done, and she smiles at me, nodding at my pastry. I feel a sense of accomplishment begin to take hold of my heart, pride at what I'm doing a seed rarely planted within me.

She rolls her dough up into tight spirals, placing them on a stone baking circle upright. I add my four spirals, mine not nearly as cohesive and wound as hers are. I hope they still bake okay.

Tarsha takes out another baking stone from the oven in order to put ours in. On the hot stone, there are eight perfectly baked rolls that look just like the ones we just made. Their dough is now golden and crusted over, the butter and cinnamon in the middle melted just enough to create a concoction that would rival any pastry I've ever had.

Once they've cooled a bit, Tarsha offers me one, and I take it greedily. Biting into it, I groan, the sweetness of it exactly what I needed.

"Having a good time?" a voice asks from behind us.

I spin around, Selene leaning against one of the eating tables, watching us. Her eyes catch the roll in my hand, gooey butter dripping down my fingers. "I would love to be a baker," I reply between bites, mouth full.

She laughs, coming over to grab another pastry from where Tarsha offers it to her. Taking a bite, her eyes roll into the back of her head. "William is going to be *so* jealous he missed this."

Tarsha waves her hand in front of her, shooing off

the compliment. She grabs the rest of the rolls, placing them in a lidded glass container, and leaves the tent.

I finish my treat, noticing that my whole body is covered in flour and other elements. I take the apron off, putting it back where I found it, and place my cloak around my waist once more.

A slow warmth has settled into my heart, one of quiet peace. Maybe I shouldn't feel comfortable here, but somehow, I do.

And that unsettles me.

"She's not very chatty," I remark.

"She's been our head kitchen server as long as I can remember. King Kori does not allow the staff to speak in our presence. He says it would cause too many unnecessary opinions flying about."

My heart sinks. "That must get lonely."

Selene shrugs. "She's well taken care of. She normally resides in the Stronghold, but I think she wanted an excuse to keep an eye on us."

"Does she not have family?"

"Rhea, whom you met." I nod. "She's her only daughter. Tarsha has always treated both William and me like two of her own. She's really special."

I wonder what it would be like to have someone who isn't your parent love you *that* much. To choose to pour into you and take care of you because they *want* to, not because they have to.

And with Selene's parents succumbing when she was such a young age, I'm sure Tarsha filled much of the gap their loss left.

"Thank you for letting me spend the day with her."

Selene grins. "Anytime."

CHAPTER TWENTY-FOUR

As day transitions into night, fog drapes itself over the Gate like a second skin. I find myself peering up into the dark sky, searching for stars alone, the snow glowing faintly under their light.

I think of Callious.

Of home.

William and Selene have been in briefings most of the day, and they allowed me to wander camp. People here recognize that I am not one of them—the soldiers most of all. I've been met with a few sneers, a few verbal jabs as I walk.

Which is what led me here, to the edge of camp. Searching for any sort of solitude I might find. I'm close to the iron fence where we entered from Komeus, but there's no one stationed here right now. I could just slip out into the wilderness, no one the wiser.

William could surely track me down on the back of Agrius, covering much more ground than I'd be able to. But if I could find the Janus Tree, I could send myself home. Maybe they'd be too busy to notice…

The ground rumbles under my feet. I look back toward camp, eyes wild, unsure of where the shaking is coming from.

A vibrating sound crashes through the air, long and *full*. A second sound answers it—a horn? I start to run before thinking twice, heading back to the middle of camp to see what's going on.

My cloak tugs on the air behind me, the tie around my neck choking me as I sprint. I weave through people running toward their tents, putting on armor and grabbing weapons.

What is happening?

I crash into someone wearing a black uniform, yelping as I do.

"Penelope! Where have you been?" Selene asks, hands holding tightly to my shoulders to keep us upright. There's a dagger in her right hand, pinned against my arm—the one I saw William with when he kidnapped me.

I open my mouth to respond, but close it quickly because how could I explain to her that I was thinking of leaving them?

She shakes her head at me, eyes darting back and forth between me and the chaos of our surroundings. "Never mind that. Find the kitchen's tent. Hang back with the staff while we get this sorted out."

I shout over the loudness of the clash of steel. "What's happening?"

"We're under attack." Her voice is low—the voice of a General.

I stop breathing.

Callious. He's come for me.

My heart quickens, anticipation flooding my veins. She steps closer, holding onto me tighter. The dagger's blade begins to pinch against my sleeve. Her eyes narrow as if reading my mind. "I mean it. Go there and do not leave. No matter what."

And with that, she pushes me in the kitchen's direction, vanishing into the disarray.

Everyone is awake now and on high alert. Boots thud around me, armor clinking as it's met with metal. Voices bark orders. I spin in a circle, overwhelmed, watching all that's happening.

I should go back; do what I'm told.

But if Callious came here to get me...

I have the information I need. Shouldn't I just go back with them now, then? Instead of waiting for William to drop me off at his leisure? I've agreed to work with him and help save our Kingdoms, but that doesn't mean he's the final say in what I do.

And I know Callious. If I don't return now, he's just going to keep coming back. I can't risk all these people's lives over something as trivial as which Kingdom my feet are placed in.

I run toward the front of the Gate, whipping my dagger out of its sheath. Most of the fighting is happening near the Isthmus.

The Gate is chaos.

Soldiers spill into it on either side, a combination of black and brown intermixing above snowy ground. The gates have been ripped off their hinges, now lying in piles on the ice.

Snow falls all around me, the blur of flakes keeping me from seeing clearly. I squint, peering at faces and bodies, trying to find my person.

I'm looking at beige uniforms first, thinking he'll be with the recruits. When I don't find him there, I keep searching the other shades of brown. It's there that I find him.

Callious.

Dressed in a Captain's uniform, dark brown gracing his figure.

Did they promote him while I was away?

My heart speeds up as I watch him battle two Oresteian soldiers, wielding his sword as if it's another arm. He slices at their legs, one of them falling as the blade cuts across his shin.

The other looks down for a moment, eyes wide. And in the few seconds he takes his attention away, Callious disarms him, upper lip curled in a snarl, holding him at sword point.

The Oresteian holds his hands up in surrender, falling onto his knees. Cal grabs the soldier's sword, tossing it to someone behind him. I look around, watching the Kingdoms fight. Paralia is vastly outnumbered.

Shades of red begin to coat the white powder.

"Callious!" I scream, taking a step forward toward him. There's still so much distance between us, but it's space I would travel if it meant I could be next to him.

His head snaps up, somehow hearing me over the sound of the battle waging on. His eyes soften as they land on me.

"Pen!" he shouts. "Come to me!"

I begin to walk, to jog, to run. I weave in and out of arrows flying, swords swinging, bodies falling. I duck beneath someone's arm trying to punch at me —unsure of whether that was a Paralian or Oresteian.

The clothes I wear say that I'm the enemy, but my heart is a traitor to William's people. It's as if both sides are against me.

I'm almost to Callious's outstretched hand when a figure lunges in front of him—a tall Oresteian soldier with a curved sword. Cal doesn't notice in time—he's too focused on me. The blade's pointed tip catches him across the thigh, slashing his pant leg nearly in two. I wince, as if feeling his pain.

His last wound was because of me—because his attention was divided.

Now this one is too.

Blood gushes from the wound as he stumbles, teeth bared, slashing violently in the man's direction. Another Paralian Captain—an older one I've seen around before—comes in from behind, stabbing the Oresteian in his lower back. He falls.

"We need to go," the Captain yells, his voice full of authority and power. I'm caught behind two Oresteians holding them off, tears streaming down my cheeks as I witness Cal's wound begin to bleed. "We need to go, Callious!"

"I can't leave her!" he screams back, trying to hold himself up. His knee gives out, and the Captain catches him, bearing his weight.

"We will die if we don't."

Cal looks at me. I wonder what he sees. I'm stuck

behind the enemy, wearing their colors, my face filled with grief and shock.

"I *will* get you back, Tidebreaker. I *will*." Conviction coats his tone, spanning the space between us. He spits on the ground, angry, as Paralia turns away from us.

I nod, clutching my shirt, my heart split in two.

Paralia retreats, limping their way back across the Isthmus. We don't follow, Oresteia making sure to bar off the gate again. As beige and brown uniforms reach halfway across the narrow strip of land between our Kingdoms, our side begins to cheer, clasping hands and clanking metal in celebration of a battle won.

I stumble, stepping back as I focus on Callious in the far distance, watching Paralian soldiers go. My chest tightens as realization hits me.

How could we ever win this war?

Colors begin overtaking my vision as I turn back to Oresteia, vibrant yellows and blues and blacks fading in and out. I'm overwhelmed with emotions of all kinds: fear, joy, sadness. I choke on it all, suffocating. My hand finds my temple, and I squeeze my eyes shut, trying to block it all out.

Dizzy, I stumble, nearly falling to the ground.

Gloved hands catch me, white fabric holding tightly onto my forearms. My vision swims as I look up into bright blue eyes, concern etched into his every feature.

What is happening to me?

CHAPTER TWENTY-FIVE

THE SNOWY NIGHT AIR BURNS AS I STUMBLE BACK INTO camp, William holding me up, my breath ragged and shallow. Cheers of victory fade in comparison to the sound of my heart pounding in my ears.

I feel as though helplessness is clawing at me, ripping me apart from the inside out.

I collapse on a wooden crate just outside the kitchen tent, clutching my head so tightly I get a headache. The world around me blurs into smoke and fog.

Blinking at my surroundings, I try to refocus, but all I see are colors swirling and shifting like pulses around people. Panic rises as my throat tightens. I put my head between my knees, trying to shut everything out, but colors deepen beneath my dark eyelids, invoking emotions I can't bear.

"Penelope." William's clear voice cuts through the storm as he kneels in front of me, hands on my legs. Still, I can't focus on it—on him.

"What's happening?" Selene says, popping up behind William as if she's been there the whole time.

Maybe she has.

I shake my head, wishing desperately the motion would clear it. My breath hitches as I try to speak. "I don't know. I feel... all these things. That aren't my feelings. And I'm being attacked by colors." My voice is hoarse, hardly a whisper as they lean in to hear me. "It's like I can see people's hearts."

William's grip on my legs softens, his thumb gently brushing the top of my knee in a soothing circle. I can feel his gaze go to Selene, his neck whipping back to her in a violent and quick action. I try to peek at them, to see what they might be conveying silently to each other, but my head continues to pound.

I groan, nausea swirling around in my stomach.

William's eyes are back on me, handing me something. "Drink this," he murmurs.

I oblige, taking the small cup from his fingers. I take a small sip at first, testing it. Finding that it's just cold water, I down it, hoping the freezing of my brain may distract me from the rest of the pain.

"Penelope, I need you to focus on me."

I look up at him, the colors dimming around me as everyone else departs. Soon, it's just the three of us, sitting in the dark.

William's glow is a slight orange, barely visible around him. "Better?" he asks.

I nod, my body rising to sit up straight, my hands clutched around my middle.

He breathes a sigh of relief. "Good. Now, it seems we may be in a little bit of a predicament."

My eyebrows furrow.

Selene gets straight to the point. "You have magic manifesting."

I look back and forth between them in disbelief. "But… I'm not Oresteian."

"No," William begins, relinquishing his hold on my knees to stand. "But you are of royal blood. And truthfully, no one in your family has been on our land long enough for us to discover if this would have happened to them, too."

"I don't *want* magic. I just want to go home. To Callious… he's hurt—he's…" My voice breaks, tears welling in my eyes.

Selene steps forward. "Don't worry about him. You need to focus on yourself first—on figuring out what this magic is and how you can keep it from overwhelming you. We can't have you becoming a liability." She looks at me pointedly. "You were *supposed* to be in the tent."

I frown at her, my own anger exuding red out of the corner of my eyes. "And *you* don't tell me what to do."

William holds up a hand to both of us. Ever the Prince.

"We can figure this out. Quickly. Together."

I stare at him. "Why are you helping me?"

Something flickers in his expression, but it's too quick to catch. "Because no one helped me when my magic revealed itself."

He extends a hand to me, offering a bit of peace. "Come with me, I want to show you something."

I take it, shakily rising to my feet. William waves Selene off, sending her on her way.

He takes me to his horse's post on the north outskirts, untying Agrius and hoisting me up onto his back. William jumps up behind me with ease, swinging his leg over easily.

I lean back into his chest, my eyes drooping from the weight of it all. I let the rhythm of Agrius moving lull me to sleep, darkness overtaking me.

❅ ❅ ❅

I awaken what feels like minutes later, peuko trees surrounding us. Agrius has slowed to a walk, so I sit up a bit, trying to find a steady seat on his back.

Pulling back a vine from one of the branches, William reveals the amber hue I've seen once before.

The Janus Tree.

It towers over us, glowing faintly. This color isn't overwhelming, though. It's one that beckons me forward, as if begging me to touch it so it might take me back to Paralia.

Agrius stops, and William slides off, grabbing hold of my waist to help me down.

"I told you that you aren't a prisoner, Penelope, and I meant it. You can walk back through this Tree right now, if you want."

That catches me off guard. I look at the Janus Tree, as if able to see home on the other side.

A cold breeze stirs the leaves surrounding us as I hesitate.

"You'd let me leave?"

"Yes."

"And you wouldn't follow me, or try to kidnap me again. You'd find me when you're ready for my help—like you said?"

"Yes." He answers without hesitation, as if everything he says is the absolute truth.

Maybe it is.

I walk to the trunk, and it hums at me, as if sending my presence. The pull of its magic feels fainter than it did the first time I was here—or was I just not paying enough attention?

Reaching out a hand to touch it, I notice black lines creeping up from where the roots hold onto the earth. The leaves of the Tree have begun to wither, the tips of them tinged with shades of brown.

I look over my shoulder. William watches me carefully, pieces of blue bouncing off of him, as if he's trying to hide his emotions from me.

I stare at the Tree again, considering.

It calls to me.

But so does something else.

The magic I didn't know I could have, and the truths regarding our Kingdoms I've only begun to unravel.

Callous is fine. He can take care of himself. I'll be home soon enough.

I turn away from the Tree.

"I'll stay," I whisper. "Not forever, but long enough for your help. I don't want to leave with unanswered questions."

William's breath catches at my words, just enough

that I notice. He nods at me, grabbing Agrius's reins once again.

"We'll take it slow, but I'll make sure you get home soon."

"Thank you," I respond, letting him hoist me back up onto his horse.

As we trot out of the grove, I look back at the dying Tree, grief holding onto my heart.

I have to do what I can to save our Kingdoms. Not just for me, but for William too.

CHAPTER TWENTY-SIX

Silence follows us the whole way back to the Gate. I squint my eyes in the dark, mapping out the way between the Tree and camp as best as I can, just in case I find myself needing to come back here alone.

I shudder.

I feel different. Not necessarily more magical, or healed from the hurt that held me captive. But… awake. *Alive.*

Free.

When we reach the edge of camp, my back and legs are so sore I can hardly walk. I wince as I limp up to where Selene is waiting for us, William grabbing Agrius by the reins and tying him to the post next to the other horses.

Her expression is unreadable, but her eyes are dark with something akin to wariness. A faint, muddied yellow exudes from her shoulders.

I wish I understood what all of this means. But I suppose that's what my staying is for—to learn.

"You took her to the Tree," she states, all business.

"I did."

"Has anything changed?" she asks William. He gives a quick shake of his head. Selene looks at me, an eyebrow arched.

"I'm still here, aren't I?"

"That you are." She smiles at me, stress obviously melting off her body in radiant greens. I wonder if she thought I would have chosen to leave.

"I like having you on our team, Penelope." She loops her arm in mine, whisking me toward the tent we've been sharing.

We fall asleep nearly immediately, heads propped up by bags, lying next to each other on the tarp-covered ground.

"I think I'm getting used to the cold," I whisper, an admission that feels like betrayal to my Sun.

She yawns, eyes already closed. "I knew you would."

❈ ❈ ❈

In the pale light of the early morning, my training begins.

William and I sit in the middle of camp as soldiers arise, a harsh wind nipping at my nose. My head is clearer today, less pain flooding through my senses. Still, I barely slept, too much anticipation for what today might bring keeping me up.

Every time I closed my eyes, I saw Callious falling, again and again, the pain in his cries a brutal lullaby.

I don't feel ready for any of this. But will I ever be?

William's eyes flick over to where I'm picking at my nails. He lays a hand over mine, stopping the motion. "You don't need to be nervous."

I give a half-hearted laugh, removing my hands from his. "That's easy for you to say. You've had magic your whole life!"

He shakes his head. "Not my whole life." He sees the look of apprehension on my face. "Okay, most of it, yes."

I scoff, turning my head from him.

"My magic manifested just after my mother died," he begins. Knowing he has my attention, he continues. "I have always loved music—have always leaned toward the melodies and harmonies that make up Oresteia. I was always creating a song, humming or singing around the Stronghold. But one day, something changed with the tunes coming from my mouth. Suddenly, my father's innermost desires would begin playing out in front of our eyes—so real we could touch them. The longer I sang or played, the more detailed everything became."

He sighs. "My father was... unimpressed. He felt embarrassed that so many of our servants and soldiers had seen my magic manifest in that way. That so many of them had seen the true *him*. My father's magic is... more impressive, you might say. He created a space for me within the Stronghold, and I taught myself piano. I have taken the time to discipline myself so that I only create illusions when I want to, rather than anytime I play or sing."

William looks at me, finally. "I tell you all of this to

tell you that you do not need to be scared of what may come for you and your magic. You cannot cultivate this beautiful ability by being angry at it, or by fearing it. Your gifts can't grow if you aren't willing to care for them."

I smile at him, whispering, "Thank you."

He smiles back, the scar beneath his left eye turning up at the motion. "I'm here to help you."

We look back out at the people walking around, all taking part in various duties. I try to focus on their emotions, but the colors begin making my head swim again.

William notices, putting a hand over my eyes to cut off all stimulation. "You're going too fast. That's why we're up early—to help you figure out how to take it slow. If the colors you're seeing are others' emotions, you don't want to suppress those."

"It feels like drowning—like I can't get enough air."

He hums. "With training, you'll be able to focus on one at a time. My magic works similarly—if I start singing under my breath, my magic reaches to everyone around me to give them each their own illu-sion. It's exhausting. With practice, I can focus on one person at a time. It helps me if I keep my eyes closed."

His hand is cold against my skin. *Why isn't he wearing gloves?*

I sit up straighter, trying to focus on the footsteps I hear nearby, and not on the chilled fingers attached to my brow.

"Reach for the feeling, deep within you. For me, it feels like a tug in my lungs. I might guess for you, it feels like—"

"My heart," I interrupt. "It feels like it's coming from my heart."

I focus on my chest, on the tight feeling within—one that often comes just before crying. I imagine it spreading throughout my body, rather than straight to my head, letting the rest of my limbs share the burden.

Breathing in deeply, I exhale just the same, picturing the emotions of those around me flowing in and out of me like a steady breeze on a warm day.

It feels... gentle. Kind.

With my eyes still closed off to the world, I focus on the boy sitting next to me. I picture his hand glowing, a vibrant orange radiating from his own heart. There's a tinge of pink there, too. Just barely enough for me to make out, but it's there.

"I'm going to remove my hand," he whispers.

I nod, swallowing. Keeping my eyes shut, I wait for him to fully pull away. I keep my hold firm on his aura, trying to depict what his colors mean. Is he happy? Boastful?

That feels right.

My head no longer pounds against me, and my body doesn't feel like it's going to retaliate.

I block out the noise from everyone else and slowly open my eyes.

The first thing I see is William's soft gaze and smile meeting my own. His head is tilted, just a bit, as he searches my eyes. I see something swimming underneath, and I realize I was wrong before.

Pride. That's what he's feeling. He's... proud of me.

My smile widens, encouraging him to do the same.

"How's it feel?" he asks, just loud enough for only the two of us to hear.

"Easy," I respond. "Like breathing."

"And what is it I'm feeling, Penelope?" he jests, a small blush creeping up on his cheeks.

He just wants me to say it out loud.

"You're feeling extremely full of yourself. Thinking you're a brilliant teacher, and all." I knock my elbow against his, laughing.

He roars, delight coating the sound. "Funny."

I smile. "Thank you."

"Anytime. Let's take a break."

We walk toward the kitchen tent to get breakfast, and I allow myself to focus on individuals we pass, tugging on that feeling in my chest with every glance. The colors aren't quite as overwhelming, and the emotions aren't nearly as suffocating.

I take a deep breath, confidence my companion.

Maybe I'll get to go home sooner than I thought.

※ ※ ※

I sit next to Selene at the fire she just lit.

"Would you like a pastry?" I ask.

"Yes!" She grabs it quickly, eating the whole thing in one bite. She moans, licking red jam off her fingers. "Tarsha's recipe?"

I nod. "I think it's a cherry-filled scone."

After breakfast, William and I played around with my magic a bit more. When my head started to hurt again, he left for some war council meetings, leaving me with Tarsha for the afternoon and evening.

I learned how to bake three different treats, finding my way easily around the kitchen now. She gave me some peppermint tea to drink when my headaches began to overwhelm me, and it helped a lot with my concentration.

Still, magic is exhausting. But after today, it does feel more manageable.

Shadows and light flicker across Selene's face. She's sharpening a blade, one I've seen before. Up close, the dark blade looks like it was cut from liquid flame. The jewel in the middle matches the color of the snow beginning to fall around us, glowing as if alive.

"Is that yours?" I ask. She nods. "I saw William with it. When he," I pause, refraining from saying kidnapped. "When he borrowed me from Paralia."

She huffs a laugh at that, caught off guard. "At least being borrowed means you'll go back."

I snort.

"Yes, I let him use it for that mission. It came in handy for him," she says, sheathing it and crossing her legs out in front of her. "I prefer to use a bow. I don't love short-distance combat."

"You must be good at both, though, if you're General?"

"Yes. But that doesn't mean I want to get blood on my outfit."

I chuckle, silence stretching tautly between us. The fire's crackle is vibrant, embers bouncing around the cold air, smoke dissipating into the stars.

"You're doing a good job adjusting to all of this," she waves around, gesturing toward camp.

"I'm trying to make it easy on you guys," I admit sheepishly.

She raises an eyebrow at me. "Why?"

"I want to help," I start. Slowly, I let my other truth slip out. "And, unfortunately, I've realized I like you guys. And I might like to be friends—when all of this is over."

She leans forward, her two elbows resting on her knees, gaze toward the fire. Flames flicker in her pupils. She clasps her hands, wringing them.

Selene just nods, not looking at me. "When all of this is over," she pauses. Her eyes flick toward my own. "Sounds nice."

As the fire begins to die, we sit in silence together until I can't stay up any longer. She doesn't say anything else to me as we stand, returning to our shared tent.

That night, I slip into an easy sleep—dreaming of home. Of Callious. Of... whatever might be after all of this. In the dream, there's a distant song playing some-where—one I recognize. I turn, searching for the sound, but I find no source.

❅ ❅ ❅

A horn wakes me from my slumber—sharp and high-pitched, three blasts in a row. I shoot up, curls amuck. I blink the sleep from my eyes, realizing I slept straight through the night for the first time since being in Oresteia.

I look beside me, but Selene is already gone.

"Suns above," I grumble, lacing my boots back up and wrapping my cloak around my shoulders.

I pull back the tent flap and nearly run right into Selene. Her eyes are wide, and her usually slick ponytail has pieces flying out of it at all ends.

"Thank the stars you're awake," she says, pulling at my arm. I struggle to keep up with her pace, ice from the freezing temperatures causing me to slip.

"Where are we *going*?" I ask, exasperated.

When she doesn't answer, I pull my arm from her, stopping in my tracks. "Selene!"

She looks back at me, apologetic. "He's here."

I tense. "Who?"

Her shoulders droop, the General within her evaporating with every second that passes. "King Kori. He's come to see you."

The mountain air stills, and it's as if the temperature drops tenfold.

A chill skates up my spine, and I clutch my cloak around me tighter.

She reaches a hand back out, silently asking me to take it.

My stomach drops, recognizing I have no other choice but to go.

Because he will find me regardless.

And choosing to stay might have been far more dangerous than I realized.

CHAPTER TWENTY-SEVEN

I CAN FEEL THE STARES OF HUNDREDS OF EYES permeating the back of my head.

Every step I take toward the commander's tent echoes off the mountains, as if warning me to turn back before it's too late.

But it's already too late.

Selene walks beside me, biting the inside of her cheek. Her jaw is tight, and her footsteps fall quickly against the uneven ground.

She's never looked like this before—like she wants to run but can't.

I gulp. *What does that mean for me, then?*

Reaching the tent at last, two guards I haven't seen before flank the entrance. Adorned in black uniforms, they both have shorn dark hair and cracked knuckles.

The one on the left stares straight ahead, not bothering to look at us. But the one on the right nods his head in our direction, hands clasped around a longsword's hilt.

"Haldor," Selene says by way of greeting.

He smirks just a bit. "General."

I look at Haldor, noticing a branding on his collarbone, black ink barely peeking up from the top of his cloak on his pale skin.

It looks like... mountains?

Selene squeezes my arm once, letting go just as quickly as Haldor and the other guard open the tent flap before me.

"Don't let him walk all over you," she whispers to me as I enter, staying behind with the guards.

Inside, the tent is warm. A low fire burns in the middle, smoke escaping out of a hole in the top. Shadows flicker across the canvas walls.

King Kori stands with his back to me, hands clasped behind him.

"Close the flap," he calls out.

The guards do, encompassing me in a glowing darkness.

He's dressed in white, blending in with the layers of snow beneath our feet. The air smells like burning wood, a haze coating the space between us.

His silver crown fits perfectly atop his cropped blonde hair; hair that is more white than anything.

William looks just like him.

He turns, slow and steadily, as if he has time to waste. I try to calm my beating heart as his ice-blue eyes freeze me to the spot—as if they can see all my failures with just one look.

There's a difference between the Prince and his father. William's eyes hold a softness that the glare in Kori's never could.

"Penelope Frey."

I nod, attempting respect. *I have not been looking forward to this reunion.* "King."

"You've been on my land for how long now?" he asks. His voice is low and smooth, and I recognize the question for what it is.

A trap.

I feign confusion. "I've lost track. Time works differently here—you do not have the sun to guide your days."

He waves a hand, beginning to pace. "You don't realize, lamb, that I know when you're lying."

I tilt my head at that, questioning his words. Still, he continues. "It appears you've integrated quite well in the time you've been here. Surely you're ready to go back to Paralia?"

Sweat beads at my hairline. "I do not believe that's my decision to make. Might I remind you that it was your son who kidnapped me to bring me here?"

He looks at me, sharply. "I have good word that you were given the chance to return. And you chose not to."

I blink. "I didn't ask to be brought here."

Kori spits in my direction, losing resolve. "And yet, you've stayed." Pausing, he stands up straight once again. "Why?"

I don't want to let him know about my magic, or about what I'm helping William do. Is it possible that Kori knows about the true risk of the missing Queen's Heart? Could all of this just be a test to see what I'll give up under pressure?

When I don't answer, he resumes his slow pacing,

walking to a table filled with maps and miniature figures and flags. "Perhaps you've forgotten, lamb, that you caused your father to breach the terms of our agreement. *You* caused this war by running away, rather than coming to Oresteia with me. Seems quite suspicious, then, that you happen to end up on my cold soil anyway."

"I did what I had to." I attempt to straighten my back, infusing confidence into my voice. I was a royal once, after all. Maybe for him, I need to act like one.

He hums, tracing lines over the worn parchment. "It seems I have to jump to the point. Who sent you?"

I take a step back. "What?"

Kori turns to lean against the table, crossing his arms across his chest. "*Someone* stole The Queen's Heart."

I hesitate. "So I've been told."

He watches me, assessing, like a predator that's snared its prey and is ready to pounce.

"Have you come to spy on us, Frey?"

"No," I breathe.

He laughs, cold and quick. "You expect me to believe that?"

"I didn't want to be here."

"And now, for some reason, you do." He pushes himself off the table, coming to stand in my face. He towers over me, dominant and leering. "*Why?*"

My fingers begin to shake, so I shove them in the pockets of my pants, trying to keep a nonchalant composure. "I'm not here to spy on you."

"Prove it, then."

I want to scream in his face, to stomp on his feet

and rush out of this tent. But I plant myself in the snow, nose turned up. "How?"

The King studies me for a long, long moment. "Who took The Queen's Heart?"

"I don't know," my voice croaks. *For sure.*

He scoffs. "You're not a good liar."

"I'm not lying!" I screech, my emotions getting the better of me. I can feel his distrust leeching off of him in waves, wariness radiating in muddy grays.

Taking a deep breath, I try again. "You believe your jewel was stolen by someone in Paralia."

Silence. I'll keep going, then.

"Whoever took it *wanted* war between our Kingdoms. It has to be someone who knew what would be at stake—someone who all of this would benefit."

He looks down his nose at me. "You think I stole it."

I shrug, flames crackling in the background.

His voice drops. "Accusations like that have consequences."

I meet his stare. "So does war."

Minutes pass.

He turns away from me, back to the maps and papers. "Get out."

I don't move, too stunned to do anything. The tent opens behind me, cold air rushing in. It spurs me into motion, and I walk out of the King's frosty presence as fast as I'm able.

The guards shut the flap behind me, and I take a deep breath of cool, mountain air.

Not once did he ask me about what's truly at stake,

or mention any sort of hope that we could spare our people and end this war.

Maybe Kori didn't steal his own jewel.

But it doesn't seem as if he minds the lives being lost, or the retribution that he's finally taking on my Kingdom after twelve years of strife.

And maybe both of those things are just as bad.

* * *

Selene grabs me, whisking me away from the commander's tent without a word. She takes me to the tent we've been sharing, where William sits inside, waiting.

He stands just as we enter, looking me over from head to toe, the ridges in his face softening.

"You're alright," he says. It's not a question—not exactly, but I answer it all the same.

"I'm fine."

He nods, looking between Selene and me.

"Your King thinks I'm here to spy on Oresteia."

Selene scoffs, letting go of my arm. "I'm not surprised."

"He doesn't trust anyone from Paralia—especially a Frey," William admits, as if apologizing.

"It feels like he doesn't want to *try* to trust me—like he's looking for any reason not to. And I might know why."

They look at me, questioning.

"I believe Kori wants this war to continue more

than anyone else," I say, quietly. "More than he wants his precious jewel to be found."

William doesn't speak, but he glances once at Selene, so quick I barely catch it.

"What if Kori took the Heart and had it hidden, so he could finally have reason to go to war on Paralia? What if this is just a personal vendetta and that's all it's ever been?"

Selene looks grim, her mouth turned down in a frown.

"That's quite the accusation," William says. "I hope——"

I cut him off. "I told him as much, too."

They both gape at me.

Selene shakes her head while she speaks, her voice calm and collected. "We can continue this later. William and I have a meeting we can't be late for. Will you be okay on your own here, or should we see if Tarsha is free?"

My words come out harsher than I intend them to. "I don't need someone to watch me. I'm fine here."

She's taken aback at my bite. I almost apologize, my mouth open with words ready, but they slip out of the tent before I can utter them.

I sit, defeated. I didn't mean to make an enemy of everyone around me.

I'm only trying to survive.

"She's trying to figure things out," Selene's voice rings out as they close the tent flap.

I lean in, trying to hear what they're saying.

William's voice is like gravel. "She suspects my father."

"For now," Selene responds. They're walking away, heading to wherever their meeting is.

I grapple for their words as I pull the flap back, hoping the breeze might send the rest of their conversation my way.

I watch William exhale. "I hate lying to her."

Selene grabs his arm, stopping them both just a few paces from the tent. I close it, just barely, keeping it open enough that I can press my ear to the gap. "She wouldn't understand."

William pauses. "She might."

Selene's voice hardens. "We can't take that chance."

Silence follows, and I take a moment to risk looking out.

They're nowhere to be seen now. My heart pounds, drowning out my many thoughts.

I return to the floor, sinking to my knees in a blur.

What am I missing?

What do they know that they aren't telling me?

CHAPTER TWENTY-EIGHT

"I HAVE TO TAKE YOU BACK."

William stands before me, out of breath, having run here from his meeting with Selene and the Captains.

I've been sitting here contemplating, running ideas through my mind. I eventually fell asleep, too tired to keep thinking.

I squint at him, groggily nodding. "Okay," I whisper. I saw this coming after my meeting with Kori. I just didn't think it would be right away.

Standing, I start to gather my few things. I strap my dagger around my waist, tie my cloak around my shoulders, and lace up my boots.

William doesn't move as I get ready. He stands there, watching me. Clearing his throat, he says, "I know you didn't want to stay here as long as you did. But thank you—for listening. For your help."

I look at him. His shoulders slump unnaturally,

dark circles under his eyes. Tentatively, I say, "Of course."

I still don't know what to make of the conversation I heard between him and Selene earlier. Do I bring it up and risk him lying to me? Or do I take this information to Paralia and see if our Captains can make anything of it?

I decide on the latter, realizing that if what William says about the Heart and the Tree is true, he will have to come for me again.

And when he does, I will get the answers I'm looking for.

Silence stretches between us, but it's a comfortable feeling. I allow it to wash over me as he catches his breath and finds his composure. A tinge of deep blue bleeds from his chest, coating me in grief. I try to take hold of his own feelings so that I might not have to face my own.

There are so many things within me that I don't want to unbury yet—the ache of trying to trust him, the weight of our Kingdom's fate, the pieces of me that I will undoubtedly leave behind once I'm back on Paralian sand.

He averts his eyes from my own. "Let's go."

Without another word, he stalks from the tent, leaving me in his wake.

I take in a deep breath, looking once more at what I'm leaving behind. I should be feeling nothing but gratitude and excitement, but I cannot help the sadness that takes root in my heart. Why it won't let me go, I'm not sure.

It's probably William's emotions getting the better of me. I need more practice in differentiating between the two.

Fresh snow wets my shins as I trudge out of the tent, tucking my gloved hands into my pockets.

And I follow.

※ ※ ※

Selene stands in the training circle, guiding two recruits through a shooting routine. They're using bows, and it looks like it's the first time they've ever held one. She spots us as we walk past, stopping her instruction to run up to us, bow still in hand.

She crushes me in an embrace, wrapping her arms around me. I stiffen, caught off guard, before relaxing in her hold. I put my own arms around her, grateful for this act of friendship. I'm not sure if I'll see her again as allies, or if the next time we meet will be on the battlefield.

I've enjoyed getting to know her, and sharing a tent with her. Regardless of the hesitations I have about her true intentions, she's a good General, and I can tell people love her.

"We'll see each other again soon," she says as she loosens her grasp.

I smirk at her. "As friends or enemies?"

Her eyes sparkle with mischief. "You should hope it's as friends. You wouldn't want to be on the other side of my arrow, Penelope."

With that, she swings around to face a target thirty meters away, nocking an arrow as she does. In one smooth motion, so fast I can hardly blink, she shoots, the arrow landing with a *thunk* in the wooden board.

Suns above. I didn't know she could do that.

"Is that bullseye supposed to frighten me?" I tease, trying to make it sound unbothered.

She just winks at me, sauntering off to begin teaching the soldiers once more.

William taps my elbow, regaining my attention. He points at the kitchen tent, where Tarsha stands in front of the opening.

She waves at me, smiling broadly, a white cloth in her hands.

I jog over to her, giving her a quick hug. "Thank you for teaching me how to bake," I say. "I enjoyed the afternoons I spent with you."

I mean those words, truly.

She holds up a finger, as if asking me to give her a minute and wait here. I do, shifting on my feet. William didn't follow me over here—he's now talking to Selene. Their faces and hands are very animated, their two shades of red fighting just as they seem to be.

I cock my head, wondering what it is they could be arguing about, when Tarsha returns.

She holds a small loaf of something warm, the crust toasted on top. It smells like yeast and spices.

"Thank you," I whisper as I take it from her.

Then, she slips something from her apron pocket, a vial of a purple liquid. A waft of lavender rises from it as she holds it to me, and I take it.

My eyebrows furrow. "What is this for?"

She mimics falling asleep, holding both her hands next to her tilted head and closing her eyes.

I don't know what to say. I didn't speak to her about my restless nights, but maybe she can just tell? Do I really look that tired?

Footsteps sound from behind me. She takes both of my gifts, wrapping them in a cloth to tie them securely.

She pushes it into my hands and gives me a quick kiss on the cheek before William gets to us.

Tarsha slips back into the tent. I turn to face William and nearly collide with him. He rights my posture, holding me up, his grip on my elbows firm.

He looks down at the bundle in my hands. "A parting gift?"

I nod, still confused. "Yes," I croak.

William gives me a small smile. "Ready, then?"

"Are you taking me back through the Gate?"

He shakes his head. "The seas have been restless the last two days, their waves cresting the top of the Isthmus. I can't risk you walking it alone, and I can't go with you."

"Oh," I say.

Attempting a broader smile, he lets go of me, taking a step back. "To the Janus Tree we go, then."

※ ※ ※

Agrius deposits us at the Tree; the trip this time was much faster than before.

With William holding the reins, we walk toward the grove, slipping through the prickly green branches.

The Tree stands still, but on closer inspection, the

decay is more visible than last time. I touch a brittle leaf, and it turns into ash in my hand.

William watches the encounter, gasping.

"I hadn't realized…" he trails off, lost in thought.

There's no hiding the tension written across my face. "We're running out of time, aren't we?"

"It's a good thing you're going back, then, so we can move on to the next phase of the plan."

I nod. "What do I need to do? I can talk to my Captains and see if they know anything. Maybe our Kingdoms can come to a temporary truce as we work all of this out—"

He cuts me off. "You can't tell them."

My forehead creases. "They could help."

"They won't understand."

I scoff. "That's funny that you'd say that, considering that's the same thing Selene said about me yesterday."

He pauses, speaking slowly. "I hadn't realized you had overheard that conversation."

"You understand, then, my position." I regain my composure. "I can't lie to them."

He nods grimly. "I suppose you can't."

I turn, laying my empty palm against the Tree's trunk. A door appears, the blood within me a key.

In a moment of bravery, I whip around to face William, my words careful as they slip from my mouth. "We might be allies now, William, but if I find out you know more than what you're letting on, war and our Kingdom's fate won't be the only things you'll be answering for."

Facing the Tree once more, I take a step toward it when I hear him say my name.

I look over my shoulder at him—at the person I might have considered a friend if things were different.

I have a Kingdom to save. There's no time to think of anything else.

He holds out Tarsha's gift, offering for me to take it.

I grab it from him, our hands briefly brushing. He takes the opportunity to hold on to my wrists, gently keeping me in front of him.

"Please, Penelope." His pale eyes look into mine earnestly, searching for... something. "If I can ask this of you, I ask that you keep our fate a secret. I *will* come to you soon. We will right this wrong. Don't drag more of our people into this than need be—enough damage has been done."

My stomach turns. "That's not fair of you to ask. You have Selene to talk about this with—someone who is on your side. I have *no one.*" I choke on the words, realizing how isolating Paralia is about to feel. If I can't even tell Cal, who do I *really* have?

"None of this is fair."

I step back from his grasp and look at him. At his tight jaw, his sad eyes—at the way his hands hang limp at his side. There's so much buried under the surface— so much that he's choosing not to say.

And I think, just for a moment, that if he asked me to stay, I might. If only so that I could unravel those threads and see what truth lies beneath them.

But he won't. And I can't.

With a small smile as my parting, I step toward the dim amber glow of the Tree. The pulse of magic is less than before, and my heart pains. "We'll fix this," I whisper to the Tree, and to whatever else might be listening.

Without another glance back, I step through as darkness overtakes my vision.

※ ※ ※

Suns above, must it be so hot here?

I lay facedown in the sand, dizziness from the trip disorienting me enough that I could not catch myself.

Maybe someday I'll get used to that.

I rip my gloves and cloak from my body, leaving them at the Tree. I'll need them the next time I walk through, and I'm sure no one else will be coming here anytime soon.

The ocean roars nearby, and the sun beats against my face from where it shines.

For a moment, I stand there, trying to get my bearings. It feels like my body is here, but my brain hasn't caught up yet. I pick up my loaf bundle from where it lies in the sand—a tangible reminder that everything that happened was not merely a dream, but real life.

I sigh.

I guess it's time to head back to the Gate, then.

Having no idea if that's where the army—and Callious—will be stationed, it feels like my best bet. At the very least, most of the recruits and some commanding officers will be there, and I can have one of them send a message to alert the Captains that I have some *very important* information for them.

I start walking, eventually taking my long sleeve off and wrapping the black fabric around my waist once I'm out of the shade of the grove. My under-tank allows for a small amount of saltwater in the breeze to coat my skin.

I've lost some color since being in Oresteia, but I know that I will gain it back quickly. I take my boots and thick socks off too, rolling up my pants to let the warm sand slip beneath my feet.

As I walk on the cliffs near the coast, I watch the waves, marveling at the magnitude of their power. William was right—the waters are restless, as if they know what's happening to our lands, too.

I can see where the Khionean meets the Neronian, dark blue intermixing with ice and glaciers. It's a wonder to behold—the way they swirl together, pushing and pulling like old friends.

The day is almost over by the time I reach the far end of the Gate, the sun dipping below the horizon.

I'm exhausted and coated in sweat. As I've travelled, I keep reminding myself of all the things I need to tell our officers. I mumble out loud, replaying the illusion William gave me in my mind, not letting myself forget a single thing about their city and how their camp is laid out.

I slump near a lone tree that grows tall despite all odds. I need a moment to gain my strength back, so that I don't walk in weak and tired. Maybe I'll spend the night here and take a quick swim in the sea so I can wash the grime off my body.

I need water. Drinking water. What if I die before I get to taste fresh water again?

My brain feels delirious as I nod off. Just a quick nap, I tell myself. Then I'll clean up, get going again…

"Pen?"

His voice cuts through my haze, shocking my system like a bucket of cold water on my skin.

A figure moves through the glow of the sunset, walking toward me.

No, not walking. *Running.*

I scramble to my feet, brushing sand off my pants as I run to meet Callious, tears springing to my eyes. We collide, and his arms wrap around me, lifting me into the air to spin me around until I'm dizzy.

I bury my head into his shoulder, laughing, feeling weightless as I grip him tightly.

A hand finds the back of my neck as he sets me down, the other around my waist, as if he can't bear to let go of me.

"You're here," he murmurs, voice breaking. "You're actually *here*."

His eyes are so much greener than I remember, the freckles dusting his nose more pronounced after all these days spent in the sun.

"I'm back," I breathe, already crying. We lean our foreheads against each other, and a tear from his eye makes its way onto my face.

I start. "There's so much I need to tell everyone. How quickly can we get the Captains together for—"

He shushes me. "Don't worry about that yet. There's plenty of time. *We* have plenty of time."

Cal pulls back just enough to see my face, his thumb brushing away the tears lining my cheek.

"I wasn't sure I'd ever get you back. And I realized —I don't know how to breathe when you're not here. There's nothing more important to me than you. I would burn Paralia and Oresteia to the ground if it meant you'd be on the other side of the ashes."

I choke on a sob, smiling.

And then he kisses me.

It's soft, and kind, and everything I ever thought it would be. He's tentative at first, as if wondering if this is okay—if we are okay. I nod as he kisses me again, more sure this time. I curl my fingers into the front of his shirt, pulling him closer.

This feeling is sweet, the culmination of years spent chasing each other, fighting, giving up everything for the other. It's also promises unsaid, ones of a future and a life after all of this—whatever that might look like.

I melt into his embrace like ice in the sun, allowing his love to thaw my aching heart. There's a desperation in his hold as he presses his hands to my face, as if reminding himself that this is *real*.

When we finally pull apart, his eyes are still closed, like he's scared to open them and find that I'm gone.

I nudge at his face with my nose, lifting myself up on the tips of my toes. "I love you," I whisper.

He looks at me with that sea-green gaze, and it's right then that I decide it's the only color that matters in this world. I crave it—that jaded hue. I want it on my walls, adorning my clothes, in my garden. I want to bottle it up and drink it, so that I might feel wholly *alive* inside.

"I love you, Penelope," he says quietly. My full name slips naturally from his tongue, as if it's not one of the only moments he's ever done so.

I bury that moment deep down within my heart, where I might replay it both in my dreams and in my wake, so it can fuel me for the rest of my days.

He slings an arm around my shoulders, and we walk back toward the Gate.

Together.

CHAPTER TWENTY-NINE

CALLIOUS WALKS BESIDE ME, SLOWER THAN NORMAL. Torchlight illuminates his face as we enter the main part of camp. He hesitates as we arrive at the commanding tent, slowly removing himself from my side to open the flap for me.

It's subtle—just a shift in his weight and a wince—but I can't help but notice it. I've always *seen* him—every little thing about him.

"You're limping," I breathe.

He looks down at his leg, where a wound from the last battle must hide beneath his dark brown pant leg. "I'm fine. Don't worry about me."

I reach for him. "You shouldn't have run to me. I would have found you—"

"I would rip a limb from my body if that is what had to be done to get to you," he states simply. *As if it really is that simple.*

I wrap my hands around his middle. "I can handle

this meeting on my own. Go rest, Callious. I'll tell you about it in the morning."

He shakes his head, looking down at me. "Now isn't the time to rest. Besides, I know these three far better than you do. I can help."

I exhale, resigning, as I remove myself from our embrace. Steeling my nerves, I straighten my spine, hoping to portray a portrait of confidence.

Inside, the air is heavy and humid. A single lantern glows in the center of a massive wooden table, maps and papers and pieces thrown halfheartedly all over it.

Long shadows paint themselves across the tired, hardened faces of Paralia's Captains. They look like they haven't slept; uniforms pressed clean, but eyes heavy and wrinkled.

Swords are strapped to each of their backs in various lengths, as if they expect to be ambushed at any time.

One paces in the back of the tent, mumbling to himself, hands waving in the air. Another stands stationary, her dark glare peering at me—*through* me— as if she already knows everything I'm about to say. And the last smiles at me kindly, his white-peppered hair contrasting sharply against his dark skin.

I take a deep breath, careful not to show too much.

"You're back," the older man states.

Callious steps forward, leg dragging a bit. "Vengeance, Tidebreaker has come to tell us of Oresteia," he pauses. "To tell us about the enemy."

I bristle at his words, trying to hide the motion, but the girl narrows her eyes at me all the same.

Callious gestures for me to begin, leaning on the table now.

"The Oresteian Prince kidnapped me. He took me to their Gate and their city. I met his General, his soldiers—listened to their conversations. And in the end, he brought me back as he promised."

The Captains murmur to each other. The overly active one pauses to look at me through a raised eyebrow. "How did he get here?"

He resumes his pacing before I'm able to answer. I gulp, feeling guilty to be giving up family secrets—even if they weren't secrets my own family taught me.

Still, I'm sure the rest of my siblings know. But I can trust these Captains. And if I want to do my part in saving our Kingdoms, I need to give them the truth.

"There's a tree... the Janus Tree. It connects our two Kingdoms by magic, giving the royal family a way to travel back and forth quickly and safely."

The oldest one—Vengeance, Callious called him—whistles under his breath. "So it's real."

I nod. "I've entered it both in Paralia and in Oresteia."

The girl jumps to sit on the table, the wood creaking under the motion. She makes me more nervous than the others in the room—there's something about her that makes me feel like she can see everything. "Why did they take *you* in the first place?"

Callious elbows her from where he leans nearby. "Play nice, Hawkwatch."

I ignore both her tone and Cal's attempt at placating the situation. I try to keep my voice steady as

I speak again, but I can't help the slight tremble that forces its way in. "Oresteia searches for what they believe we stole—The Queen's Heart. It's a jewel that was created through the blood of our ancestors. I assured Prince William that we had no part in taking the gem. He believes that the gem was never supposed to be separated from the Tree where it was crafted. Should we not return the jewel to its rightful place, it could mean ruin for our Kingdoms. William..."

I hesitate, not wanting to paint him as a saint, nor as a villain. "William wanted my help. To tell me of the true stakes, to see if I would be willing to aid their search."

Hawkwatch scoffs. "He snuck into Paralia through a magical Tree, captured you *and* surrounded Nightingale with soldiers that did not actually exist, just to take you to Oresteia to... chat?"

I shuffle my feet in the sand, confidence slipping.

Vengeance speaks up, voice kind. "What Hawkwatch means is that it's a lot of risk for an only heir to take on for a simple conversation. Had he come to our Gate and requested a meeting with you, or if his father and yours could have reached some sort of agreement, we could have made it happen. So the question is, Tidebreaker, why did he choose the more secretive route?"

Chewing on the inside of my cheek, I consider my answer. Why *did* he choose the secretive route? I still hold some belief that Kori could be behind all of this, so maybe he didn't want his King to find out he was asking for my help?

The one in the corner shakes his head violently, scoffing at me under his breath.

"He needs me. It has to be a Paralian and an Oresteian that return the Heart to the Tree." My attempt at certainty is met with silence. They all look at each other, as if deciding how much of what I've said they believe.

Hawkwatch looks at me again, stripping me bare with her gaze. "And are you?"

I hesitate. "Am I what?"

Hopping off the table, she creeps closer to me. "Are you willing to aid their search, Tidebreaker?" She pauses, tilting her head. "And while we're asking *real* questions—what secrets did you give them while you were over there?"

My mouth opens, words trying to form, but nothing comes out.

Cal steps in. "That's enough. Nelly wouldn't give them anything." He looks at me, those green eyes full of trust and love. "I know she wouldn't."

The one pacing quickly joins in. "You may be blinded, Nightingale, by things that we are not. Besides that, you are not supposed to be here in the first place. You were placed on bed order, were you not?"

Callious grumbles. "I'm fine, Hammerhead. I told you—it's just a scratch. And if I stay down, it's just going to be worse the next time I get up."

Hammerhead flicks a short knife into a post, one holding up the tent. "Still, you disobey orders now. Who is to say you won't disobey mid-battle? You're too distracted, overwhelmingly prideful—"

Hawkwatch interrupts. "Don't forget, incredibly reckless."

Before arguing can erupt, Vengeance holds up a hand. The tent quiets, all attention returning to him. "That's enough."

He walks over to me, placing a worn hand lightly on my shoulder. "We do not have what they seek. We've heard whispers here of a jewel stolen. We know nothing of the ruin you speak of regarding the fate of our Kingdoms, and therefore, we must treat it as hearsay by the enemy. They're hoping to distract us in an attempt to win this long-coming war."

I slump a bit. Oresteia isn't lying. I *know* they aren't —I saw the vision myself. But I'm reluctant to share the specifics of their magic and of the things they can do. Does that mean I'm sympathizing with the enemy? Maybe, but I can't help but think that maybe they aren't our true enemy. Our enemy is whoever took The Queen's Heart.

And with William and Selene's help, we can right this wrong and find even ground between our two Kingdoms.

Besides, William has no reason to need to distract me. It's not as if I'm someone of importance.

Vengeance removes his hand from my shoulder, motioning for all of us to follow him to the maps.

"Now, are you able to fill in some gaps for us regarding Oresteia? You said you traveled a few places."

I nod, stepping forward into the glow of the lantern light.

We don't have much on Oresteia—just bare bones.

I look at the jagged edges of their land surrounded by the Khionean. My finger traces our connected Isthmus, noting the locations of our Gate and theirs.

I walk my hand up, toward the north, circling a forest depicted on the map. "I think this is where the Janus Tree connects in Oresteia. The ride wasn't too far from their Gate to it. Maybe a few hours."

"Ride?" Cal asks.

"They have horses. I rode primarily on the back of William's horse, but they have more—both wild and tamed."

"We used to have horses," Vengeance states wistfully. "It was a trade made long ago. Where else did they take you?"

I hesitate, not wanting to give up the location of Copolis.

"You said you went to their city. *Where is it?*" Hawkwatch nearly shouts.

I think of those little kids running through the streets, their laughter bouncing off the merchant booths. We would never do anything to harm children —I *know* that. So why am I hesitating?

"Their city," I begin. "It's called Copolis. It's here."

I point to the northern tip of Oresteia, circling the general area.

They all nod, making marks on the various maps in front of us.

"What else do you know?" Vengeance asks softly.

"Just about the jewel—the warning they gave me about what could happen if it's not returned."

"What *else?*" Hammerhead spits.

"I don't know anything else!" I shout, throwing my

hands up in the air. "And everything I've told you is the truth."

"Is it?" Hawkwatch's voice sharpens. "Because the way you talk about them doesn't sound like they're the enemy to you. And that's a very dangerous place to be."

Callious speaks, low and steady. "Leave her *alone*. I know when she's lying, and she's not."

Hawkwatch focuses her venom on him. "You just know her so well, then, Captain? Will you be responsible for the lies she's spewing when they come about?"

Vengeance stops them again, ever the mediator. I can't focus on all that's happening; their discourse is flooding my senses. "Nightingale is too injured to fight, but he isn't decapitated enough to not understand the weight of what he's saying. Should Tidebreaker prove to be unreliable, we will deal with *her*—not her Captain. Understood?"

Both Hawkwatch and Hammerhead nod. Cal just grips the table, looking down at his shoes.

"Good. Callious—go get your wound checked. Make sure you did not tear the stitches open in your haste. Penelope, you may leave. Clean up, change, rest. War is still on the horizon, and we must be ready."

I look down, remembering the state of my person. My bare feet grace the sand, my black Oresteian clothing barely a uniform at all. My cheeks turn red. I shouldn't have come in like this.

"Dismissed," Vengeance states.

As I walk out with Cal, I look back at the three Captains. "You don't have to believe me," I say. "You don't even have to trust me. But the Tree is real—this *war* is real. And the jewel must be found."

We leave the tent, letting the flap close behind us. Callious shifts, and I reach for his arm, steadying him as his balance wavers. He gives me a small smile in a quiet thanks, leaning into me.

As we part, going our separate ways for the evening, I know all of this isn't over.

If anything, it's only just begun.

CHAPTER THIRTY

THE NEXT MORNING, WHEN I STEP OUT OF MY TENT, the air smells like salt and lingering fire.

Voices call out drills in the distance as I squint my eyes against the rising sun. I didn't mean to sleep for so long, but after a night of dreamless slumber, I couldn't help but stay in it.

The space between me and the rest of the recruits milling about feels stretched thin and delicate.

They don't know what I've seen—how dire this whole situation is.

They don't know that it might be too late.

Walking through camp, I slip by training drills and sparring matches quietly. No one stops me, but heads turn as whispers follow me.

I didn't know what they thought of me before all of this, but I do now. The girl who was kidnapped by a Prince—a girl who came back alone and unharmed.

I shake my head, clearing those thoughts. I'll need

to get back into practice today to make sure I didn't get too rusty while I was away.

I reach our mess tent, the air filled with burnt spices and warmth. Scanning the area, I realize the tables are almost filled, the volume of various chatter noisy to my ears.

Joining the food line, I grab my tray and let the servers heap piles of whatever onto it. My memories pull me back to Oresteia—to the food and baked goods I was given there.

So much better tasting than this stuff.

It feels treasonous to think that Oresteia's meals are preferable and more fulfilling than what we have here. I shouldn't complain, truly. Mas and his staff do the best they can with what they have.

As if my thoughts conjured him out of nothing, the cook spots me from where I leave the food line and walks right up. He smells like grease and fire. His voice is gruff as he talks.

"Heard that Prince caught *you* this time, darlin'."

I wince. "He did."

He strokes his beard. "Mighta been better for all of us if you had stayed there."

Frowning, I stare at the stains on his apron. "Nice to see you too, Mas."

He holds his hands up in surrender. "I'm just sayin' what everybody else is. Sounds like there's a lot we still don't know, and I think you could have figured it out. That's all."

Mas turns and meanders away. I tilt my head at what I *think* was a compliment? Hard to be sure with him.

Still, I grumble under my breath. "I'm doing everything I can."

I walk to a full table, placing my tray down with a *thud*. Everyone looks at me from the corners of their eyes. I don't pay them any attention, shoveling my food down as fast as I can so I can get on with my day.

Alex happens to walk by, and I choose to smile at him, feeling guilty for all that he got roped into. He looks at me, hesitating, then looks around as if to see who's nearby. Deeming it safe, he slides into the bench next to me, barely on the seat.

"You came back just in time," he talks slowly and quietly.

I hunch over toward him, leaning in. "Just in time for what?"

"Captains have been restless. We've been prepping to ambush, so I hear. But not a small one—all of us. I think Cal—I mean, Nightingale—originally wanted to do it to get you back. But I think the other Captains just want some blood."

He looks me up and down, an eyebrow quirked. "You don't look like somebody who was kidnapped and held behind enemy lines."

I choose my words very carefully. "It's different than what I thought it would be, over there."

He nods as he stands. "Well, good thing we won't have to waste any manpower on your rescue. Now we can all just focus on winning this war."

My eyebrows furrow. "Weren't we doing that anyway?"

He shakes his head, walking backwards. "Not Callious."

I look down at my half-eaten food, pushing the tray away as I stand and leave the table.

I need to find Callious.

※ ※ ※

He's leaning on a post, watching other soldiers spar, barking out orders and moves.

I walk up behind him, wrapping my arms around his middle, reaching up on my toes so my head rests on his shoulder. "Hi."

Turning, he smiles at me brightly. "Good morning."

I release him from my grasp, coming to stand beside him. He leans in to kiss me on the cheek, a giggle escaping my lips. "How's your leg?"

Callious huffs a breath. "I'm mobile. I tore a few stitches running, but it's nothing I wouldn't do again—if I had to."

My hand finds his arm, giving it a quick squeeze. "That's what I came to talk to you about—I hear your priorities might need shifting."

He looks at me quizzically. Yelling at the soldiers to take a quick break, he refocuses his attention on me. "And what *are* my priorities, Pen?" His tone is amused.

I shuffle my feet. "From what it sounds like—me."

He nods enthusiastically, but his eyes are serious. "Yep."

Just those three letters, as if that's the only possible answer. He turns his head away. No way does he think this conversation is over that easily.

"You can't just focus on me, Callious. This is serious. You could get hurt if you aren't all in when you're fighting or if your attention is diverted elsewhere."

Turning back toward me, he takes my hand, his thumb brushing across my knuckles. They're riddled with scars now, fighting and training roughening up my hands like they've never been before.

"Do you remember what I said? When I asked you to come with me?"

I smile, the memory pulling at my heartstrings. "That you want us to be together. To trust each other, watch over each other."

He interrupts my thoughts. "You gave up your crown to be here, Nel. Your *life*, your plans—you threw them aside to follow me. I do not take that lightly. You are mine to protect, to cherish, to be there for."

"And I would do it again. But that does not mean I cannot take care of myself. I can't be worried about you while we fight, Cal. Which means you can't be worried about me—or we are both doomed."

He kisses the top of my head. "Then let our hearts beat in tandem until we die together."

I roll my eyes at this, at the words he's stealing from himself. "You aren't going to listen to me, are you?"

He laughs, warm and easy. "No."

I'm not surprised. This is the Callious that I know —the one I fell in love with. Wrapping my arm around his side, I lean in. "Then whatever may happen, know my heart is with you."

His lips find my forehead this time. "Mine is yours."

※ ※ ※

Later that day, as the sun reaches its peak, Cal and I spar. He takes me through a few dynamic stretches, warming up my body to new movement after a long time off from my normal routine.

"We wouldn't want to risk any injuries," he smirks.

I shove his shoulder a little as he tries to straighten his hurt leg, causing him to lose balance. He glares at me as he uses my arm to catch himself, and I laugh.

Limping as he separates from me, he hands me a wooden practice sword and assumes the position of the defender.

The sand is packed under our feet, hard from the constant movement this piece of land sees. A small breeze drifts in from the sea, catching a stray curl and pulling it in front of my face. I tuck it back with ease, not taking my eyes off of Callious.

"Ready?"

I take in a deep breath, letting the scent of ocean and salt coat my lungs. Rolling out my neck, I shake out my arms as I nod. "Ready."

Cal spins the sword in his hand, testing its weight. "Show off!" I call, circling him as he does me.

"Only for you," he laughs.

We begin only when I get impatient, advancing on him, hoping to catch him off guard. But nothing I do ever does—he's always one step ahead of me, even injured. Still, our sparring is fluid, and he moves as if he has no injuries.

His sword cuts through the air toward my shoulder,

and I lean toward the left, barely avoiding it. I swing my sword wide and low, aiming for his shins. He hops it, not thinking twice about the motion, and his knee nearly buckles on the way down.

"Are you okay?" I cry out, lowering my sword.

He reaches out, as if wanting my help. I step forward, extending a hand. In one quick motion, Cal grabs my wrist, pinning me against his body with his sword blade under my chin. My sword arm is tucked too tightly for any attempt at defense.

"Show off," I huff, mumbling.

He throws his head back, roaring with laughter as he lets me go. Dropping his sword, he pries mine from my fingers and takes my head in his hands.

He takes a second to search my features, his eyes bouncing back and forth between my own. I think he might kiss me, but suddenly, a worried furrow begins to grow along his eyebrows. "Do not show them weakness, P. I know you saw things over there. I know you care for the people you spent time with."

I open my mouth to interrupt, but he shakes his head at me. "I *know* you, Nel. You have a big heart, and you long to be involved; to help. It's why you were going to follow your father's wishes to travel to Oresteia in the first place—a part of you *wanted* to be of use. But you can't show them weakness. Not when we can end this war."

"What if I didn't make the right choice? We could have avoided all of this. Every wrong could have been made right before we resorted to war."

He frowns. "This is what you chose. The tide moves forward, and so should you."

I let my body lean into his, as if melting under the hot sun. Lowering my voice, I whisper, "I don't want to fight."

I don't say out loud what I'm afraid of most—that the Queen's Heart won't be found. Or worse, that it will be, but not in time to be returned.

That our Kingdoms will fall to ash as they did in the vision, but this time it will be *real*. And it will be *my fault* that I lose everything I hold dear.

He leans his forehead against mine. "No one really *wants* to risk their life, Pen. We just do what we must."

I let that sink in, the roar of the waves a symphony behind us. "I'm worried that nothing I do will ever be enough," I admit.

That I won't be enough for you.

He lets me go gently, sadness creeping onto his features.

"It sounds like you need to hit me harder."

That forces a smile to emerge from the depths of my emotions. I pick my sword back up, waiting for him to as well.

And I give him all I have left.

CHAPTER THIRTY-ONE

Sunset begins with a flurry of activity. Boots hit the sand after dinner, running around preparing for tonight.

The night we'll catch Oresteia off guard.

That's what I've been hearing, anyway.

I follow orders, rushing around to sharpen weapons and pack medical supplies in bags.

Callious finds me as the sun dips below the horizon, both of us dripping in sweat and covered in salt.

"It's time," he yells at me over the roar of the waves. I'm sitting on my knees in front of the Neronian, using the ocean's water to clean pieces of armor.

I wipe sweat from my brow. "Time for what?"

He smiles at me, clearly knowing something I don't. "Time for our secret weapon."

I grab the armor, hoisting it in my arms as I follow him back toward the Gate. I drop it off at a table on our way, running to catch up with him as night hits

Paralia. Despite his small limp, he's still much faster than I am. "Callious! Where are we going?"

He doesn't answer, and he doesn't look back. He just expects me to follow him. It feels good to shake out my legs after kneeling for the last few hours.

We climb down the cliffs on the south side of Paralia, on the shore closest to Komeus. There's already a slew of people waiting there, whooping and hollering with all their might. I look around, confused.

What am I missing?

"Are we going for a late-night swim?" I joke, trying to get Cal to answer me. But he's too focused on what-ever we're doing next.

I grumble under my breath as people come from behind us, running to meet up with those waiting. It seems as though the entire army is in on something that I don't know anything about.

Maybe because I was gone for so long?

For a moment, it feels like I'm back in the Palace. No one cares to fill me in on anything. It's always been like that. Usually, I can do a bit more sleuthing on my own to read what people aren't saying and fill in the gaps I'm missing.

Today, though, I'm much too tired to try.

I walk up beside Cal, who's talking with a few guards. He's grinning like he's mad, hands waving excitedly in the air.

He turns to me, grabbing hold of my upper arms, passion alight in his eyes. The water's reflection seems to catch his stare, giving him an ethereal glow.

I smile up at him. "Why is everyone cheering?"

Horns go off from the south, loud and low—somewhere from the middle of the ocean. At first, I think I'm imagining it. Dark shapes rise from the sea like the cliffs on our shores.

I squint, looking, trying to see what could be out there in the midnight waters.

"They're here!" someone yells to our left. Everyone starts pushing each other to the shoreline, some wading up to their waists in the waves.

Gasping, my hand finds my mouth as I see what all the commotion is about.

Boats.

We have… boats.

Four massive ships, each one taller than I could have imagined. *And they're coming straight for our coast.* Our Paralian flag waves from their masts, sails rippling like the sea. The creak and groan of the wooden hulls carries to us over the slight breeze.

I clap my hands together in delight as I realize just how important this is for us. With these, we can sneak into Oresteia without needing the Isthmus. With boats as our vessel, we can turn the tide of this war.

The closer they get, the more my heart pounds. This is *it.* This could be the end of everything.

Cal looks at me, seeing realization bloom on my face. He chuckles. "You're on my boat, Pen."

Shocked, I fluster my words. "Are you… commanding one?"

He nods. "Each Captain has one."

"Who's steering yours now?"

"It's tied to Vengeance's. Someone had to stay back and keep order while they sailed to us. They picked me because of my 'injury'." He quotes the last word, rolling his eyes.

I look, noticing the tethers between his boat and the one in front of it, where Captain Vengeance stands at the wheel. Pushing forward like everyone else, I let my feet find where the sand meets water.

Excitement hums through the crowd as the ships loom over us, sergeants and guards grabbing ropes to tie them off along our shore.

The first anchor, Hammerhead's, drops with a heavy splash. A ramp slams down against the water, bridging the sea and land like the Stenos Isthmus. Hawkwatch follows on her boat. Vengeance pauses at the bow, staring down at all of us below him.

I feel as though I've already left Paralia behind, as if the Neronian has already whisked me away. My hands shake, thinking about the thrill of riding the seas.

I can't wait.

Vengeance's voice rings out strong and true. "To the soldiers of Paralia. We have come today with a secret weapon—one that Oresteia will not see coming."

He pauses, letting the excited whispers and murmurs die down. "The last twelve years, we have been in strife with our connecting Kingdom. It was inevitable that war would come to our shore. And when it did, we swore to be ready."

People start to hoop and holler, cursing Oresteia in one breath and praising Paralia in another.

Vengeance holds up a hand, commanding our attention. "We have painstakingly built these ships south of Komeus over the years, in the cliffs and caves that line the sea. With these ships, the Neronian will carry us to Oresteia. With these ships, your Captains will carry us to VICTORY!"

The crowd shouts, screaming at the top of their lungs as Vengeance lifts his sword in the air. Cal claps people on the back, pounding chests and crying out for all of Paralia to hear. I chime in, watching the excitement on people's faces.

Still, a small voice inside of me worries for my friends in Oresteia. I know they're ready—I've *seen* their army and their camp. And, they're lying to me about something. I can feel it, deep in my bones.

But my heart still pinches thinking about the harm we may do to them.

And the harm they may still do to us.

I'm pushed to the side as the crowd shuffles, each of us awaiting direction in where to go. Our supplies and weapons are already here.

We are ready.

I follow Callious as he takes command of his ship. Surveying the boats, I find words burnt into the hulls. Now that I'm in the back of the ship's line, Vengeance's boat is the only one I can read.

The Juliet.

My chest wrenches. I don't know much about our Captains; just that they've been around a long while. Everyone has their scars and their reasoning for fighting in this war. Juliet must be his.

Callious shoves my shoulder playfully, noticing what I'm looking at. "Juliet was his daughter. They were traveling merchants before all of this—before our

Kingdoms hated each other and the Gates were erected. He let her go alone. Just once. She was killed there during an exchange. I don't know much else other than that. He doesn't like to talk about it."

He gulps, sadness creeping in as he looks toward Vengeance. "When the Gates were being built and the Isthmus closed, he was the first to sign up to start training. He's been waiting for this ever since."

I squeeze Callious's hand, mourning for the man whom I know he considers a friend. Squinting toward Cal's boat, I look at the letters the burnt lines make up. I can feel him looking at me, smiling like a love-sick fool, just happy to be here.

Tidebreaker, it reads.

My eyes find his, and we stand there, as if it's just the two of us. I open my mouth to say something—anything—but no words could properly display how I feel about him. Especially right now, in this moment.

We have come so far from when we were kids, learning so many things about each other. He has been a constant for me when my family was not, someone I could lean on when I had no one. He is playful, kind, and encouraging. We fight and get angry, but only because we care so deeply about each other.

It's always been that way, and I wouldn't give that up for anything.

"You're the reason I fight. For the life we might have after this. Everything I do—it's for you, Penelope."

I reach up, standing on my toes to place a light kiss on his lips. Tears begin to well in my eyes, and I have to look away to keep them from falling.

Looking out at the slow crash of the waves, I watch the push and pull of the tide. It reminds me of us—the way I had to push him away for so many years, thinking my family would never let something like *us* happen.

I never would have thought I'd have the chance to create the life *I* desire—letting him pull me toward him as effortlessly as he always has. "I like it when you call me by my full name."

He laughs a little, but I can hear slight confusion in the sound. "You don't like your nicknames? Everyone calls you those."

It's the first time I've ever said as much. "I know. But maybe you could be different."

Before he can say anything, Vengeance begins making the rounds, barking at us to start loading the ships. "Ten minutes! Grab what you can and get on board."

Cal gives me a swift kiss on the cheek, whispering in my ear. "Whatever you want, *Pen*."

He leaves my grasp, heading to command his ship's soldiers. I quickly stick a leg out as he walks away, tripping him. "Brat!" I call.

He falters, turning toward me as he catches himself. He smirks and mouths something at me, winking. I roll my eyes, but still I mouth the three words back to him. *"I love you."*

Smiling as I turn away, I begin loading the boat with weapons and rations, just in case this were to go sideways. It seems as though they've thought of everything, but then again, they've had twelve years to prepare.

It's that thought that makes me sick to my stomach. We've been planning this for over a decade, and Oresteia has had the same amount of time. What surprises might they have up their sleeve? And with the reality of magic... I really don't know what to expect.

No one does.

CHAPTER THIRTY-TWO

OUR BOATS CUT THROUGH THE DARK WATERS OF THE Neronian, passing under the dim light of the stars into the icy waters of the Khionean. We all stand aboard the deck, wrapped in our various shades of brown, weapons ready.

I'm familiar with the waters we're leaving—I know them like I know my hand. The sea has always had this sense of… unpredictability about it. It might be why I love it so much—never knowing what to expect.

Through the years, the shore has changed exponentially. But day by day, it seems as though little changes.

Like me.

The waves have a strange way of going silent. The roar of the ocean is no longer a numbing sound to behold in the background. It's as if the sea knows we require stealth to complete this mission.

As if it's on our side.

The pull of the tide brings us closer to Oresteia's

shore, snow-capped mountains and frost-covered ground lying before us. Waves crash against our hulls, frigid waters splashing on our bodies.

The Captains truly did think this night through, commissioning many Komeus seamstresses over the years to craft gloves and cloaks for us. The only thing exposed is the skin on our faces, our noses donning a red tint as we glide closer to Oresteia's frozen exterior.

I stand near the bow with Callious, covered fingers curled around a salt-crusted railing. Wind snaps at my cloak, my pant legs, tangling my curls against my mouth. I don't bother retying the short ponytail it's in.

No matter what I do, it will not stay. I might grow it back out after all of this, just because I can. Maybe I want to know who post-war Penelope is... who she could be.

Squinting in the dark, I watch the dark smudge of land grow clearer on the horizon.

Oresteia.

We're coming from the south, their Gate further north with the Isthmus. The waves grow in intensity as we sail closer, jagged black rocks rising from the sea. We maneuver them with ease, our boat the fourth in line behind the other Captains.

Cal's crew moves around the deck with nervous energy. Blades are checked, re-checked and checked again. Boot laces are tied tighter, and cloaks are wrapped around mouths and noses to make breathing the cold air easier.

Footsteps sound from behind me, and I know it's Callious. They're heavy, but familiar.

"And who's steering your ship while you're away, Captain?" I joke.

"Alex begged."

His tone is serious. He stands beside me without saying a word, and we watch the coast draw closer together.

"We'll be at the back." He breaks the silence, his words but a whisper.

I sneak a glance at him, his unruly hair coated in salt. "The back of what?"

His breath comes deep and slow, his eyes not leaving our destination. "Our crew will make up the rear of the formation when we land. The other Captains… they think I'm a liability."

My chest hitches. "Because of your leg?"

I watch him look down at his injury, shifting his weight on it a bit. Then, his eyes make their way up to mine, captivating me. "Yes, my leg. And our crew got quite a few new soldiers, ones that are much younger and inexperienced than others."

I nod. "I'll follow your lead, Captain."

Our first boat, Hammerhead's, touches shore. Bumps rise on my skin as the rest of us follow suit, a chill seeping into my bones that isn't really there.

Callious and I grip the railing as our boat slams into the slip of land before us, nearly knocking all of us off our feet. Cal reaches for me, laying a hand on my lower back to steady me.

I slip him a quick smile, heading toward the ramp with everyone else to begin disembarking.

My heart pounds like a relentless drum. Every decision I've made has led me to this moment. Every word spoken, every thought. Every promise broken and kept —it has all brought me here.

Steadying my breath, I hop down from the ramp, boots crunching on the snow and ice. We gather in the middle of this small piece of sanctuary, awaiting orders.

Other soldiers hold gloves out to catch falling snowflakes, running the powder through their fingers. For most of them, this is their first time here.

And possibly their last.

A shiver runs down my spine at the thought.

The piece of Oresteia we've docked on is just big enough for the tips of our boats to anchor themselves, some ramps lying in cold, shallow waters. Crews are split back up as we configure our formation, Cal and I at the back.

We'll have to climb a bit to get to where *they* are, scaling the short cliff with nothing but our hands and feet. We are warned to watch for patches of ice and to take it slow.

There's no rush, they claim. They do not know we are coming.

They don't know we are already here.

Callious is behind me as I climb to catch me if I were to slip. I begin to drift in thought. I once imagined our big battle would come with horns and battle cries, shouting and furious emotions. Instead, it's quiet. Slow. Cautious. And I feel... numb.

Numb to the cold air circulating me, trying to penetrate my uniform. Numb to the emotions wrapped up in my heart and mind. I feel like we are all missing something. Something that could change *everything*.

I just don't know what it is.

My dagger is strapped to my waist, the leather belt tapping against my leg as I heave myself up this small mountain. People in front of us reach down to help us scale the last bit, pulling soldier after soldier up by their arms and hands.

I make it to the top, my knees hitting the ground with a *thud*. Shaking off the snow, I reach back to help Callious make it up. He scales it with ease, even with a hurt leg, practically jumping up the rest of the way.

He has twin blades strapped across his back, and his shoulders are tense as he surveys our surroundings.

Wind cuts across our faces, stealing the breath from our lungs.

We wait for the rest of our crew, everyone making it up with hardly a scratch.

Moving as one, our unit sticks to the shadows of the peuko trees, weapons ready in case we are ambushed. The units above us seem to be moving with no problem; Vengeance's unit is barely within our eyesight.

That's how they planned it—wave after wave after wave of Paralian soldiers seemingly coming out of nowhere.

We didn't plan a retreat. We are going to leave everything we have at Oresteia's Gate.

They probably thought their waters and cliffs were impassable.

They thought wrong.

"Soon," Callious says, slowing to a creep as we watch Vengeance's crew do the same. Hammerhead gives a brief whistle from somewhere far in the distance, and Hawkwatch returns it.

Cal waits for the third whistle before giving his own, showing the rest of them that we are *ready*.

My stomach churns. *As ready as we can be.*

We come into full view of the Gate, the other three units already breaching their fences.

There's seemingly... nothing. No soldiers keeping watch, no arrows being fired. There are no sharp shouts alerting the others and no cries for help.

Where is everyone?

I bend to a sit, waiting for Cal to motion for us to keep going.

He smiles at me, one full of mischief and secrets.

Digging in his pants pocket, he pulls out a small cylinder with a fuse atop it.

"Time to wake Oresteia," he shouts before flicking a match across the bottom and lighting the top.

It sparks wildly, the flame catching immediately. A ball of red flies into the sky, illuminating all of us hiding in the shadows. It gives a piercing scream as it ascends into the night, eventually fizzling out and falling back down to the cold earth.

Shouts cry from in front of us in all areas of camp. Cal draws both of his blades, and I grasp tightly to my dagger, rushing to my feet like everyone else. We slip through the iron fence, finding the rest of our unit.

Thousands of us roar, our boots pounding against the earth and making the mountains shudder.

We rush in like we are the tide itself—endless, wild, free.

The Gate appears, looming before us, its lanterns

snuffed out. I cock an eyebrow, slowing as we search for an enemy to fight.

All the lanterns are snuffed out. Every. Single. One.

Not even a fire is lit.

I open my mouth to say something to whoever might be standing nearby, to alert them of the wary feeling that has bloomed in my stomach.

It's as if it happens in slow motion. I turn my head to speak to the boy to my left—a recruit, like me. One moment, he's standing next to me, searching wildly as everyone else is. The next, an arrow protrudes from his stomach, his mouth open in surprise and agony.

He falls face-first into the snow. I fall to my knees next to him, searching for a pulse that's not there. My eyes shoot to their tall stone building, searching.

A quick glimpse of red catches my attention as it runs around their watchtower.

Selene.

A quick shout—her voice, no doubt—and then arrows rain down on us.

"Find cover!" Callious calls, weaving in and out of enemy soldiers that were sitting in wait.

Selene's arrows find their mark one after another. They've engulfed us in darkness, knowing we are not used to the dim night sky.

But *they* are.

Have we been outmatched? Have we lost this battle before it started?

I can't think like that.

Another arrow takes down someone next to me as I crouch behind a tent. It's not a fatal wound, but there's no time to help. Hopefully, they can wrap it themselves… somehow. Callious peels off right, carving a path toward the sleeping tents where Hammerhead and Hawkwatch's crews fight.

My heart cries out to me to follow him, my eyes catching his slight limp as he runs. I stick behind tents and barrels. Eventually, the archers will run out of arrows and be forced to come down and meet us.

In the meantime, other parts of camp need to be taken. Other soldiers who need help. We wanted to overwhelm them, scatter them—burn it all down if we have to.

And we will. The Captains will, I know.

Screams echo around me, soldiers on both sides shouting as steel meets steel.

The first Oresteian I encounter is a boy around my age, maybe younger. He lunges at me wildly, and I parry his sword, my dagger hardly a match for the wide blade.

I twist to the right as we lock eyes for half a second, swinging my dagger around to cut across his neck as he stabs the air where I just stood.

My blow lands. His does not. Shock fills his face, and I'm certain it mirrors my own.

My first kill.

I side-step around his fallen body, hands shaking as crimson stains the perfect white we fought on. I choke back a sob, holding back my instinct to reach for him and see if there's anything I can do.

There isn't. I know that. You did what you had to do.

I whisper apologies as I leave him behind, running more fervently toward the rest of my crew.

Tears blind me. I do not look back.

✵ ✵ ✵

Now fully inside the Gate, chaos leaks from every corner of camp.

Smoke curls from the north, where Hammerhead was told to set fire to as many tents as possible. Flames lick at the dark sky, burning images into my brain.

Someone screams my name, running at me quickly. Too quickly.

I ready my dagger until I see it's one of our own—Alex.

Blood blooms from beneath his beige uniform. "They're circling back!"

I shout back over the sound of agony and triumph. "Callious too?"

He nods, grabbing my arm to steer me back toward the Gate. "They set fire to every tent. Hawkwatch is already back at the Gate, trying to find a vantage point to throw knives at the archers."

My eyes search for Cal in the smoke and snow, flakes of embers and frozen water falling from the sky.

Alex and I push back toward the Gate, fighting our way to where our most seasoned fighters hold our front line. Our formations have been thrown to the wind, soldiers fighting however they know best.

My dagger feels heavy in my hand. I swear the fence walls are closing in on us.

Despite the exhaustion, I keep fighting, trying my best to focus on debilitating blows—not killing ones.

I never want to do that ever again.

Then I think of Cal—wherever he may be—and

his injury. If killing is what is necessary to save him, I would do it. I would take a life without hesitation if it meant he could live the rest of his days with me.

A horn blows in the distance, high and sharp.

I whirl, looking for the sound. It's not ours— our horns are low-pitched.

White clothing cuts through the shadows like a ghost. I blink, looking again, but I can't find it anymore.

Focusing back on where I am, I see Hawkwatch's crew taking down archers one by one as they throw delicate, sharp knives in their direction. They're on a small hill near the watchtower, just outside of the Gate's fencing.

My heart pounds as emotions begin to bleed in the air, blues and golds mixing as joy and grief threaten to overtake me. I center myself, taking a moment to take charge of my own feelings, pushing those to the forefront.

Confusion wrecks my chest as something bright and hot flies in Hawkwatch's direction.

Flame. Selene is throwing fire.

I suppose the magic is now out to play.

Thankfully, I warned our Captains of the reality of magic. I did not tell them all the specifics of William's exactly—only what they already knew from the vision. I did tell them of Selene's abilities... but I did not know she could throw it *that* far and with such intensity.

Tears blink at the corner of my eyes as snow begins to melt in the presence of her light.

A small hum sounds from somewhere close to me, low and musical.

William.

I see Paralian guards and soldiers begin to run toward the Isthmus, shoving each other and screaming. One of them latches onto me, nearly pulling me off my feet. "It's coming! It's going to rip us to shreds!"

I wrench my arm from him, nearly pulling it out of its socket.

The further they get away from the song, the slower they run, as if realizing what they are running from isn't real at all—but an illusion.

"That Prince," I huff.

Arrows clothed in fire begin shooting toward us, catching the rest of the tents and wooden posts on fire.

It seems too... intentional.

Smoke begins to choke my lungs. Alex is next to me again, worry lining his eyes. "Should we fall back?"

I gasp, lungs searching for clean mountain air. "Why are you asking me?"

"I'm not!" he shouts, looking behind me.

Callious emerges from the fire, blood splattered on his uniform. My heart drops, utterly relieved. He's lost both of his swords, the one he now swings something he must have picked up somewhere. "Stand your ground! This isn't over yet."

Alex exhales, exasperated. Oresteia's soldiers have swarmed the Gate and watchtower, letting Selene's archers cover them.

This isn't all the soldiers they have. It can't be.

I know there were ten times this many when I was here. The question rings in my head, over and over.

Where are the rest, then?

Cal finds a sure footing, standing back to back with me. "Until the end, Pen."

I swipe my dagger at a man much larger than me, slicing his wrist so that he drops his own dagger. "You and me, Callious."

We've backed them into a corner, hazy light beginning to bloom from the east as night departs.

Archers lay across their tower's stone, blood running down from the stone walls. I search for red, for white—but I do not see them.

I wish I didn't hope they're okay.

Cal limps next to me, leaving to find a moment to speak to Vengeance about something in hushed tones.

He returns, dark smoke following him to the rear of our new formation. Grabbing my hand, he motions to the right—toward the hill Hawkwatch stood on before she fell.

She did not die until her task was completed—the archers were rendered unable to shoot. There's victory in this—remember that. Do not let her death be in vain.

Cal ducks his head toward me, and I lean in to focus on his words alone—not the shouts of dying men or the ringing of blades. "We're climbing that hill, Nelly. We're ending this—once and for all."

I clutch his fingers, fire lighting in my veins. I'd follow him anywhere. We run together, in the dim light of early morning, with smoke at our backs and the battle on our heels.

It's time we turn the tide of this war.

For good.

CHAPTER THIRTY-THREE

WE CLIMB THE SMALL HILL, TAKING CARE TO WATCH where we step.

And not trod over the bodies of the fallen.

We're going to surround the last of the Oresteian soldiers, Callious and I, pushing toward the watchtower so the remaining forces are forced to fall back to the earth.

Where Vengeance and Hammerhead's crews await.

The top of the mound is wrapped in smoke and shaking beneath our feet—the cries of battle echoing off the mountains and stone walls. Blood runs everywhere my eyes can see, and if I look at it too closely, it makes my stomach churn.

I was not built for this... for violence. I never thought this would be my life.

But I can't take it back now.

The tower's platform rises just beneath us, and we stay crouched for a moment behind peuko trees. I look to my left, seeing Hawkwatch's body where it fell—four arrows protruding from her chest. She fought until the very end.

There aren't many women in our company—not many girls have the desire for war. But she was someone I thought I might look up to—someone I might want to become after all of this.

Closing my eyes tightly, colors once again dance in the dark. I don't understand the coming and going of this magic—or where it came from. It seems to grow stronger when Selene and William are nearby, and I wonder: could that be a coincidence? Surely not. I open my eyes to search, skimming the dawn until...

There.

Selene is at the top of the watchtower. She doesn't see us. Or at least, she's pretending she doesn't. I can't imagine anything gets past her here. Her silhouette cuts through the haze, her bow raised and arrow ready, peering at our soldiers below.

Callious told me we would jump from the hill to the tower's platform, landing ready to swing. We don't know exactly how many guards are left—just that it might be few enough that we'd be able to take them.

We stand slowly, and I follow his lead, knowing what he's thinking just by watching his body language. It's familiar—this thing between him and me. Something I always wanted but denied myself. I thought I'd never receive it. I've never been anything to anyone—just my parents' daughter.

The last Princess.

My father is King, and my mother is lovely. The rest of my siblings have their defining characteristics:

Everett the heir, Ana and Eva the twins, Finneus the kind, and Leila the creative. Even Carter, just a year my senior, is the mischievous one whom all the maids and cooks adore.

Where does that leave me? Who am I?

I am Callious's. I remind myself. *Perhaps that's all I need.*

As I creep behind him, a *snap* rings through the air.

Wide-eyed, I look down at my boots and the branch that just broke.

Time slows as I look up to Cal, my face wincing and apologetic. Surely over the loud sounds of battle, a branch is merely a whisper in comparison. Still, he whips his head toward the tower, checking to see if anyone heard.

A shout comes from the platform, an Oresteian soldier alerting others to our presence, pointing at us in the dim dark.

He's coated in blood and wild-eyed, a massive wound on his right shoulder where a knife must have been.

Where he must have torn it out.

His uniform is nearly in tatters as he rushes toward us, using the full length of the platform to leap onto the short stone wall and *jump*.

He smiles, utterly crazed, his sword at the ready. One of his front teeth is chipped, and blood is dripping from the side of his mouth. He spits at us.

Callious charges, meeting this soldier blade for blade. I hesitate on the sidelines, feeling like I should jump in, but I don't know how or when.

I curse myself for not continuing my training in

Oresteia—for letting myself get kidnapped in the first place. For all the days I spent stuck in my room while most of my other siblings learned how to do these sorts of things...

A cry of pain grabs my attention, but my heart slows back down once I see it's not Cal, but the soldier. Callious sliced him across the arm, and he nearly dropped his sword. Anger bleeds from this man's entire body so violently, I can't help but lean into it.

I shout a curse to Oresteia, to their army, to my family—wishing so desperately all of this could just *end*. I begin to run into their duel, everything within me wanting to *fight*.

Cal turns to look at me, just for a moment.

But that moment is all it takes.

The guard uses his distraction as a chance to get the upper hand. He must have noticed Callious limping, because he takes his sword and swipes it across his leg. Cal buckles, trying to hold himself up, stabbing wildly at the man.

The clash of steel rings out one last time. Then, grabbing Cal by the collar, he yanks him closer, spinning Callious around so that he is fully facing me.

Cal's back is to the soldier's chest, and for a second, I fear he is going to place his blade at Callious's throat, making some sort of demand that I will not be able to meet.

But I would try. For him, I would do anything.

I lock onto those green eyes—at the concern they hold for me. At the desperation clawing up within him.

Most of all, the love and regret held there.

His mouth opens in a gasp, breath catching, eyes wide and surprised.

As the Oresteian soldier drives his sword through Cal's back, the tip puncturing his chest, as blood blossoms quicker than I could have imagined.

CHAPTER THIRTY-FOUR
CALLIOUS

His blade is all I can see as I meet it stroke for stroke. The power behind his blows is filled with anger, nearly catching me off guard at how strong this Oresteian man is.

I can't help but think—if Penelope hadn't stepped on that branch, would we have taken the tower already? Would the plan have come to pass?

I can't wonder about those things—I can only do what I can with the reality in which I live. And right now, this fight is all I should focus on. If I can disable this man, if we can continue to the platform without the rest of Oresteia noticing we are here…

I'm glad Pen is staying back during this—her presence would only render me distracted. I fight harder, pushing myself to the edge of my limits, knowing that she's standing behind me. I *can* protect her. I *can* keep Paralia safe.

This soldier is quick—much faster than I could have anticipated, especially considering the gaping wound in his shoulder. My leg is burning, and my stitches are holding on with nothing but will at this point.

Every step threatens to take me down, every swing and violent blow all-consuming. Even so, I hold my ground. I was made for this. I *crave* this. I have to give it my all or I risk losing everything I hold precious.

Like Nelly.

I hear her, just behind the edge of the trees we were hiding in. I can feel the way she hesitates, as if my heart recognizes hers even at a distance. I know she's probably debating how to jump in, how to help me if I falter. But I pray to the sun above that she does not. If she gets involved...

She wouldn't be able to hold her own against him, is all.

No, I *must* finish this fight before it becomes her fight, too. We are so close to ending all of this—to having the life I've dreamed of for so long.

The soldier lunges again, and I step out of the way almost too late, slicing my blade hard across his already injured arm. He cries out as it breaks skin, the cut deep enough to make him stagger and loosen his grip on his sword.

I press the advantage I was just gifted, my chest heaving, every muscle in my body on high alert. The man radiates genuine fury now, his movements sharp and wild. He must not have anything to lose, because if I were him...

I would have conceded. Raised the white flag. Fallen on my knees with my hands up—if it meant I might be spared for *her*.

He's not fighting to win anymore. No, he's fighting to *kill.*

I hear Nel shout. I risk a glance toward her, making sure she's okay. I want to tell her that I'm fine—but there's no time.

Our eyes meet for a brief, perfect second.

She's windswept and determined, her face the perfect picture of someone brave and fierce. But also... terrified.

And in that moment, as I memorize her every feature, pain rips through my injured leg, sharp and hot. The soldier's blade slices across my thigh, and I cry out, dropping hard to one knee as I try to keep myself upright.

My world spins as I slash blindly, my eyes closing tightly of their own volition. I attempt to force him back, creating space between us so I can regain my composure and get back on my feet.

But my leg won't hold me as I struggle to get up. I can't rise.

Our swords meet one more time, and then he's on me.

He grabs me by the sun-forsaken collar and yanks me up with a grunt, spinning me around so I'm facing Pen—so she's *all I can see.*

The tip of his sword is at my back, the sharp prick nearly breaking skin as he holds me tight.

Time slows.

I could find a way to fight this—to come out of it somehow on the other side. But I cannot lie to myself —I will not make it out of this fight alive. The only reason I'm standing right now is because of his strong grip on me.

I angered him too much. I shouldn't have taunted so. I should have ended this long ago. I should have I should have I should have...

What? Changed fate? Even a man in love holds no weight over what has been pre-written.

My mind races, thinking of possibilities. My leg will not hold me, and my sword is lying unreachable in the snow. If I fight him, rendering him angrier, and he kills me *then*, he will advance on Penelope.

She cannot meet his anger or his skills. She might be able to hold him off long enough that someone below notices our plan went wrong, but by the time they get here, it will be too late.

The only way she's winning this fight is if she is just as angry as he is.

And the only thing that would make her feel that way...

My heart drops.

Her eyes lock onto mine—those big, dark eyes I could disappear in if only she would let me. In that moment, I mourn the days we did not get to spend together. The kisses I will not get to lavish upon her. The slow mornings by the sea, the house we won't get to make a home.

She will find a way to move on and live without me, I know. She is so much more than she's ever given herself credit for. Perhaps my memory will be enough to remind her of all that she is when I cannot.

I want to tell her to run, to leave me behind.

But I know she won't.

My father could not protect my mother—he couldn't keep her cries from the pain of childbirth from turning into the anguish of losing her life.

But I can protect Penelope.

I hold her stare as I project words in my mind toward hers.

I love you I love you I love you I love—

Pain explodes in my chest as the blade punches through my back—through ribs and organs and out the other side.

My mouth opens in a gasp, the act taking me by surprise.

Blood drips from my wound onto the dirty snow, but she is all I can see. I try to call out to her, but my voice is rendered useless.

My vision fades black, spots dancing in front of me, but not close enough that I can touch them. The ground is hard, cold. The sword is still in my back, I think, but I cannot be sure.

Sounds ring out as I lose my hearing, a droning buzz pulling me under. There's someone next to me now, their hands cold and tight around my own.

The last thing I hear is half of my heart crying out in agony. My wounded chest pains at that, something in me wanting to make everything right. I command my hand to move, to reach out—so that I might give her peace in knowing that I will be okay.

That *she* will be okay.

But I cannot.

Not before everything goes black.

CHAPTER THIRTY-FIVE

I SEE RED. HOT FURY GROUNDS ME. MY DAGGER IS MY only companion as I shout and cry. There is nothing I can do but watch as the man drops Callious to the ground in triumph—sword and all.

He looks up at me, rabid and victorious, as I lunge. I am a snowstorm, a reckoning, as I slice and stab at every inch of skin I can find on this soldier. I don't think—I just *fight*. The ocean is my guide as I fluidly move, dancing around his firm hands.

Finally, after what feels like days, my dagger finds a soft spot beneath his jaw. I don't feel the kill. I *can't* let myself think about it. I just let it happen—swift and full of vengeance. He falls hard, choking as his last breath leaves his lungs.

My chest heaves. Sweat coats my body as I come back to where I am.

Remembering.

I throw my dagger aside, letting it lie in the cold, hard snow as I wrap my arms around Callious's chest and pull his head onto my legs. Tears fall violently, my sobs stealing air from my chest.

All I can do is scream, rocking back and forth as I beg him to come back to me. His eyes are open a sliver, his chest hardly moving. His hands tighten around mine. Cold. They're so cold. I want to move him, get him to safety, *something*.

I yell for help, but the other Paralian soldiers are all at the bottom of the hill. Only the Captains know we are up here, and by the time they realize our ambush did not go the way they planned, it will be too late.

Cal's face crumples in pain. "You're okay. You're *okay*. Help is coming," I urge.

My hands are slick with his blood—the blood of my best friend. Hot, sticky maroon stains my beige uniform.

"We're supposed to die together, Callious." Tears wet my face, falling onto our joined hands. "You *promised* we'd be together until the end. So this *cannot be the end*."

I'm tempted to remove the blade from him, to ease that piece of his suffering. But wouldn't that make the bleeding worse? There's already so much blood... he's losing it too fast. His usually tan skin is pale, a cold sweat glistening upon it.

His pulse is dimming beneath my fingers. His breath turns shallow and ragged. "No, no, no, no, no, no!"

The mound of cruel, cold earth shakes underneath me. I search for the source of the sound, fear coursing through my body.

Have the soldiers found us? Am I going to die before I can get Callious help?

A thought comes from deep within me. *At least we will die together.*

Blinking through my wave of tears, I see a wide, dark figure racing toward us.

Is that... Agrius?

The black horse comes to a pounding stop in front of me, its rider jumping down at once.

"Come with me," he urges, a gloved hand outstretched.

Mud and speckles of blood cover his white uniform, but he appears unharmed.

The taste of hot salt coats my tongue. "I can't leave him." I try to hold the gasps back, but it's no use. My voice rings out in a blubbery mess.

"He gave you the chance to *live*, Penelope. *Do not waste it.*"

I cry out, looking down at my best friend's still features. Is it just me, or is he no longer breathing? Panic surges, threatening to overtake me—

William places his hands on my shoulders, drawing my attention back up to him. There's urgency in his eyes as he searches mine.

His voice drops an octave. "The rest of Oresteia's soldiers are coming from our Stronghold. They'll be here quicker than Paralia can retreat. *Come with me.*"

He removes his touch, and I nod, numb, recognizing the warning for what it is. He's right—Cal gave me a chance to keep going.

To make things right.

And I will end this war if it's the last thing I do.

The need for revenge burns bright within me. It's kindling for my weary soul.

I'll stay and fight. I don't care how many soldiers Oresteia has moving this way—*I can take them all.*

I look around, searching for where I threw my dagger in my haste to comfort my Nightingale. It's standing upright in the snow, as if someone placed it there purposefully. It's just out of reach, especially with Cal still resting on my legs.

Resting—yes. That's it. He's just… resting.

I grunt as I reach for it. William notices where I'm looking. He walks over to my dagger, plucking it from the ice. Taking a moment to wipe the blood staining it on his own uniform, he hands it to me gently.

After I finagle my dagger back into its sheath, William helps me lift Callious from my lap. We place him lightly on the blood-soaked snow, careful to avoid pushing the sword any further into his body. His face is so cold, his skin so pale.

I hesitate as I stand, my heart refusing to make my legs move. Taking his hands in mine one last time, I place a quick kiss on his palm. His arm is heavy in mine, gravity ripping his fingers from me. I rip my cloak from my body, covering Cal with it, if only to give him a bit of warmth.

An Oresteian horn sounds, alerting all of Paralia to our inevitable doom.

It's time for me to move—to go.

William grabs me with urgency, wrapping his arms around my torso as he all but throws me on top of Agrius. He jumps on quickly behind, pinning me to his chest, as if he read my thoughts.

Screaming in protest, my body convulses and kicks in revolt as we ride down the small hill.

I want to stay! I'm ready to fight!

But another small voice rings out, the real reason for my pain.

I don't want to leave him I don't want to leave him I don't want to leave him!

Those words repeat over and over in my brain, threatening to drown me. I have spent all of my tears. The promise of revenge is no longer within my grasp. My cheeks dry as Agrius rushes us through frigid mountain air.

Without my cloak, my body threatens to shut down. Sleep beckons me—the dull, black void a welcome presence for my grief. Adrenaline has left me dead and alone.

Still, there's a question that I need to ask before I can succumb to the darkness. "Why did you come?" I ask William, my head falling as my eyes droop.

His voice barely registers above the sound of the wind in my ears. "I heard you scream. You needed me."

As we ride away, the battle keeps going.

But I do not.

CHAPTER THIRTY-SIX

IN MY BLEAK STATE, I HARDLY NOTICE THE STORM rolling in.

Snow whips through the peuko trees like it's trying to erase us from the world. I don't know how long I've been slumped on the back of Agrius. Minutes? Hours? Days?

Without my cloak, my body is numb. My nose constantly drips from the frigid air, and my insides feel as though they're being chewed up by my grief.

Callious is dead.

I don't allow myself to say those three words aloud. But within the fortress of my mind, I test them out— seeing if it's a safe space for the admission. My heart cracks in two before the thought fully rolls across my consciousness. My arms tremble as I wrap them around my torso, but not from the cold.

At least, not just the cold.

William keeps one arm steadily wrapped around me, the other guiding Agrius through a violent flurry of white and wind. I want to throw him off this horse so I can steal the beast and force him to carry me *back*.

The urge to scream in William's face is too overwhelming, and I chew on the inside of my cheeks to keep my mouth from opening.

I'm tired. I'm broken.

I don't want to go on anymore.

William murmurs something in my ear, but I don't pay any attention to what he's saying. I just nod, letting him think everything is fine.

Nothing is fine. Nothing at all.

Coming down from a steep mountainscape, we stop in the middle of a grove. The sliver of a clearing is just big enough for Agrius to creep into. Wind howls, loud and clear, and William dismounts, lending me a hand to pull me down from the tall back of his horse.

He's gentle with me, as if he's scared I might shatter.

Maybe I already have. Perhaps I've only ever existed in pieces stitched together by the hands of the person who loved me most.

I give William a quizzical look as he starts taking bags off of Agrius's saddle. "The storm is coming in too fast," he starts. "We can't keep going. We have to pitch camp here for the night."

Opening my mouth to question him, he interrupts me. "You agreed to it. I asked you."

When I nodded.

I clamp my jaw shut, letting him take the bulk of the work needed to pitch his tent. I wander to a thick trunk broken in half, sitting on the cold snow atop it.

Maybe if I lie down for a while, the snow will bury me whole.

William works silently and quickly, hands moving with a sharp efficiency as he raises the tent. Agrius snorts behind us, a dark ghost nearly covered in a white haze.

When the tent is fully up and the bags stashed, William turns to me. "Come inside."

I don't move.

He kneels next to me, snow layering itself in his hair and on his eyelashes. His hand touches my shoulder gently. "Penelope."

Something about the way he says my name breaks through the fog I'm wallowing in. "What about Agrius?"

He looks at his horse. "What about him?"

"We can't leave him out here. He'll freeze!"

William smiles gently. "He's trained for this. He knows how to survive these storms better than I do. I have a thick blanket I'll put over his body." He cocks an eyebrow in my direction. "*After* you are safely inside the tent."

I frown. "He shouldn't be alone."

"Neither should you."

I submit, standing. Not for him, but so that he can make sure Agrius is taken care of.

Inside the small canvas tent, it's quiet. Too quiet. It makes my head loud. It's still cold, but out of the wind at least. William joins me shortly after, unpacking the bags he had on the back of the saddle.

"Do you always travel so heavy?" I ask, teeth chattering.

He grabs a thick cloak from the pile, animal fur lining the inside, and places it around my shoulders. Instantly, I'm thawing. His voice is low as he answers me. "You can never be too prepared here."

Lying out all that he has, he makes a bed with the rest of the furs—just enough material for one.

I shiver.

"Your hands are shaking."

"I'm fine," I lie.

He sits next to me, eyes on the closed tent flap. He peels off his gloves, setting them on my knee. *Take them,* his eyes urge. I relent, removing mine one finger at a time.

Before I can put his on, fingers close around my wrist. "Your hands are bleeding."

I look down, my bare hands revealing red, cracked knuckles.

"I'm fine," I repeat, convincing myself they don't hurt or sting.

He meets my eyes, hand still grasping my bare skin. There's something in his gaze, both unreadable and unbearably kind. I gulp, a tear threatening to shove its way out of my eye. "I have something that would help."

I laugh, the sound empty. "Of course you do."

My heart wants to tell him no, but my body is tired of fighting. So, I let him get up and retrieve whatever it is. I have no energy—only the desperate desire to cease to exist.

Coming back from his pack, he takes my hands and smears a balm across my wounded knuckles. His fingers are warm against mine. I hiss as the balm stings at first, then cools the burn. Peppermint overwhelms my senses, coating the air with its bright smell.

William then wraps the cuts in soft bandages, stretching them so they aren't too tight or too loose.

"Thank you," I whisper, clutching my hands to my chest as I massage the balm into the skin.

He doesn't leave. Instead, he starts rolling up his white sleeve, tending to his own upper arm. The fabric is torn, I notice, the dark color of blood staining the material.

His coat must have hidden the wound.

He struggles as he tries to wrap it, the angle impossible with just one hand.

I shouldn't offer my help. I should just let myself wither away into nothingness.

But I can't.

Shifting to face him, I take the bandages and balm from his hand. "Let me."

He watches me carefully, as if surprised, then nods and extends his arm to me. I cover the gaping wound. The slice is deep, but not deep enough to need stitching.

Wrapping his bicep, I try to move slowly, careful not to tug on the laceration. My cold fingers brush his hot skin, and he exhales, sharp and quick.

Our eyes meet. The stare holds until his blue gaze dips to my lips, brief enough I'm sure I imagined it, and he clears his throat. I look back down, embarrassed.

There's too much silence, not enough distance.

He took you away from Callious. He's not telling you everything.

Oresteia is the enemy.

My brain replays the moment when Callious was impaled, his cold body thrown into the snow as if he meant *nothing.*

The thought cools the blood in my body. My brain is tired. None of this is real.

I need to remember why I'm here, what my mission is.

To take Oresteia down—to figure out once and for all what happened to the Queen's Heart and return it to the Janus Tree. If I fail, Callious's sacrifice was for nothing.

And I will not let that be my reality.

I tear off the bandage, tucking the end into the wrap.

Looking away, I tuck my knees into my chest, resting my chin on them. I hear him get up, rustling around in the bags.

Just as quick, he's standing in front of me, offering me a jug. "Water?" he asks.

I shake my head briskly.

He uncaps it, gulping down the clear liquid. Then, he sets it beside my feet.

"The bed is yours."

I just sigh, pulling my legs closer to my torso, collapsing into myself. The animal fur cloak is warming me just fine—I don't *need* the bed.

Closing my eyes for just a moment, a vision of Callious lying dead in the snow haunts me. Bodies of my friends and family—the rest of Paralia's army—lie beside him in piles.

I shake myself awake, chest heaving, sweat coating

my body. I cannot just sit here and do nothing while the fate of my army is unknown.

But there's no way I'm getting out of here and back home with William watching me.

A plan forms in my head—one that I can't think over too much or I'll talk myself out of it. I rise slowly from where I've been cramped, my dagger in my palm. The wind whistles in the background, a low melody to the havoc I'm about to wreak.

My hand trembles—from the cold, from grief, from rage.

From hesitancy.

Shaking my head, I clear those thoughts. I cannot hesitate. I *won't*. The desire to get back home has to be the *only* thing on my mind.

My heart pounds in my chest as I look at where William sleeps, his head tucked into his chest.

He took me away. He's on Oresteia's side. He could have come sooner—could have intervened before his soldier killed my best friend.

Anger soothes me, its red-hot color a calm embrace.

Silently stalking across the small tent, my dagger is poised and ready. My eyes adjust to the dim light as I look at the soft spot of his abdomen beneath his rib cage.

I don't want to kill him, necessarily. Just… wound him enough that I can take his horse and leave him behind.

Yes, that's the plan.

I match my breathing with the slow rise and fall of his chest. Raising my arm to strike, I crouch.

I'll only have one chance to hit precisely where I need to before he awakens. My dagger will pierce quickly before I run. I'll need to cut the ropes tying Agrius to the tree before hopping on his back...

And hope all of that is enough to render him slow and disabled, so I can make an easy escape.

I steel my nerves, not thinking twice as I slice my blade through the air, the sharp tip aimed for his body.

My hand falls through empty air, my dagger now embedded in the canvas floor.

What?

I spin, only to find William standing behind me. The real William. The quiet song I thought was the wind comes to a stop, and I realize it was his magic all along.

His hands are tucked in his pockets as he assesses me. "Were you trying to kill me?"

My chest heaves, feeling ashamed that I was beaten at my game. "No. Just..." I pause, not wanting to let emotion rule over me. But I can't hold back the flood that is my desperation. "I don't want to be here. I need to go back."

Silence hangs between us as tears threaten to fall. I pluck my dagger from the ground, sheathing it as I stand.

My whole body trembles.

"I hate you," I bite, crying now. I'm not even sure I believe those words, but they feel like the right thing to say.

A sorrow-filled smile graces his lips. "I don't hate you."

Empty laughter bubbles from my chest. "You don't have any reason to hate me."

He cocks an eyebrow, circling me. "I don't?"

"It wasn't *my* soldier that killed *your* best friend." My voice is frantic. I move away from him, pacing in the opposite direction.

"Why do you still want to fight?" he asks.

Grief crashes down on me, sharp and *too much* all at once. "I don't want to fight. I want to *die*. I want to change what happened and save Callious. I want him *back*."

His eyes look at me, full of pity. "I know."

I scream at him, my body finally giving in to the desire to feel rage. It's a choking, guttural sound—one that feels as inhumane as it possibly could.

How dare he be so calm? How dare he look at me with eyes filled with sorrow? He has no reason to be sad!

I throw my dagger down between us. It lands with a dull *thud*.

William steps closer, sidestepping my blade. Still, he does not reach out or touch me.

"You said I needed you," I yell, giving up on keeping any composure. "When you came, you said I needed you. But I don't. I need *him*. And now I don't have him."

My tears come full force now, and I let my head hang in my hands.

A warm body engulfs mine as he wraps his arms around my back, letting me sob into his chest. I have nothing left in me to push him away. His chin rests on top of my head.

We stand in silence, cold creeping back in around us as night overtakes Oresteia.

❊ ❊ ❊

I finally peel myself away from him moments later, my body having no more tears to give.

I fall asleep on the makeshift bed.

But I don't stay asleep for long.

A sound pulls me back—a soft and upbeat humming. It's not quite loud enough to fill the tent, but it tugs at me all the same.

I know that song.

Memories tug at me—ones of a warm, summer day and a new friend running around the Palace with me. Salt dries on my skin as we toss something back and forth, before…

Before his father runs out, furious, grabbing him and whisking him away.

I blink.

No.

It can't be.

I try to ignore the rest of the song, but the deepest parts of my heart recognize it. The notes continue, dipping and rising in perfect cadence.

I open an eye just a sliver, looking at William. He's sitting against the canvas, sharpening his knife, his lips puckered in a low whistle.

I sit, propping myself up on an elbow.

He wrote this song… with me.

All those years ago, in Paralia. The boy who

skipped stones with me into the sea and rolled around in the tall grass. We played catch at the end of the day while our fathers were in a meeting.

Before he was taken away from me.

That scar under his eye—I did that. The stone I threw struck him when his attention was divided, cutting the soft skin underneath.

I knew he looked familiar. But I thought I had never come into contact with Oresteia—we've been in conflict for nearly my whole life.

"We played together," I whisper. "When we were kids."

William's eyes look at me, slowly.

"You started singing when we were on the beach. We wrote that together."

He doesn't deny it. "We called it 'A Summer Day'," he admits. "I've been looking for you. I was... *captivated* by you."

My head spins and my world tilts. I think I've forgotten how to breathe.

Tears threaten to spill again.

"Why didn't you tell me?" I pause, exasperated. "What aren't you telling me, William?"

He looks like he wants to answer me so badly, but he doesn't. He just sits there, silence stretching so tautly between us.

Finally, a whisper of a sentence makes its way to my ears. "I just wanted to know you."

I shake my head. "You don't *get* to know me. You're holding back from me, and I don't know why." He flinches at my words. "You're not who I thought you were. I'm not sure you ever have been."

With that, I plop back onto the blankets, turning so that I'm not facing him. I want to scream or cry. I wish I could beg him to undo everything that went wrong between our families—to explain to me what's *really* going on. But I cannot force him to give me anything he doesn't want to give.

And that's the worst part. Because I don't know what I did to make him not trust me with the secrets he holds.

His breathing steadies as I lie here, his song over. My heart rips open again, over and over.

And this time, when I sleep, I dream of the roaring sea.

CHAPTER THIRTY-SEVEN

Two days later, we're packing up and on our way again. To where, I don't know. William won't talk to me.

Which is fine. I don't want to talk to him, anyway.

It's just... the silence is lonely.

It's the sort of quiet that presses heavily on your chest, trapping you within yourself.

The storm blew over sometime late last night, but William didn't want to pack up and travel in the pitch black. So now we ride in the quiet dawn of the morning, the only sound the crunch of snow beneath Agrius's hooves.

My hands fidget with my cloak, eyes fixed ahead but not really taking anything in. It's all a blur of white and green and gray. My thoughts keep drifting back to Cal—the deep sound of his laughter, how his calloused hand felt in mine.

William brings Agrius to a walk, snow-covered

peuko trees closing in on us. A small path reveals a stone cottage, snow-coated and weathered.

William dismounts and ties Agrius to a short, lone pole. He offers me a hand so I can hop down. I nearly plop into the deep drift of snow under us. He steadies me, making sure I'm balanced before grabbing our things and heading toward the little house.

There's a stiffness in my legs as I follow, stepping over the cottage's threshold. Warmth hits me softly, like a gentle sea breeze. For a moment, I breathe deeply, almost forgetting the turmoil that has brought me to this point.

Almost.

Though I will not admit it out loud, the cottage might be one of the most serene places I've ever been.

Four walls surround everything you might need in a place to rest your head. The worn wooden floors creak under my boots, pieces of ice falling off in clumps as I walk. Grand windows overlook the pristine snowy exterior, brightening up the space.

The main room isn't luxurious, but it feels... enough, somehow. A dark gray couch calls to me, asking me to sink into its leather. A wood-burning heater sits in the corner, where William is adding logs to it.

Someone threw mounds of pale-colored blankets and pillows about haphazardly, as if the cottage itself knows the art of genuine hospitality.

I lay down on the couch while William works, unable to stand on my feet for another second. Curling my lower body up toward my torso, my hands fold into fists under my chin.

My heart wants to cry. But mostly, I just want it all to stop.

As I drift in and out of consciousness, I register William walking over to me, placing a delicate hand on my forehead where my curls stick.

"I need to go to the Stronghold. I'll be back as soon as I can. Eat, Penelope. Sleep."

The door clicks softly behind him as the wind rages on.

Much like the storm inside of me.

The ceiling blurs with tears I refuse to shed as I try to fall asleep.

✿ ✿ ✿

Later that evening, my stomach's rumbling shakes me awake. I don't remember the last time I had something to eat...

Breakfast a few days ago, maybe?

I pull myself off the couch, a blanket somehow around my body. There's a kitchen attached to the living room, where a lantern glows from within, illuminating all the walls its light can touch.

A stove and a basin stand proudly within the small space, with a few baskets and shelves above them to store goods. I find a bag of dehydrated meat, basking in its aroma as I meander around the rest of the cottage.

There's not much else in the main area, just a piano in the corner. A vase full of dried flowers sits on top of its dark wood, a candle with a half-burned wick left beside it. I pick up the glass, solid puddles of wax unmoving as I tilt it toward my nose to breathe in its scent.

It smells like the peuko trees outside—earthy and bright.

I continue to wander as I eat, leaving the candle behind. There's a small wall separating the living room from the cottage's lone bedroom. No door, just open space.

Overtaking the area lies a large bed, a white quilt on top. Someone left the bed unmade, as if they lacked time to finish the chore before leaving. Pillows lean against a massive window along the wall, the bed placed in front of it.

Walking over to the adjacent wall, I run my finger along the spines of worn, rough books sitting on a large bookshelf. I don't recognize any of the titles, but I secretly wish I were in a better headspace so that I might enjoy the words on those pretty pages.

There's a skinny door shut in the corner of the bedroom, most likely a washroom or toilet.

A hot shower sounds like a luxury right now, one that I do not have the energy to partake in.

Walking back to the couch, I finish the bag of jerky, setting it on the cracked leather bench beside the piano.

My heart pangs. I wish I knew how to play an instrument. My parents and the tutors were so busy making sure the *actual heirs* were well-rounded and knowledgeable that my studies fell to the wayside.

I want to lie back down, but the fire lit in the heater captures my attention. What would it be like to be a flame? To burn, day in and day out, at someone else's wishes?

Frowning, I'm about to snuff out the fire in an act of pity when the door creaks open.

William's eyes find mine immediately, and I look away first, busying myself with folding the blanket that was covering me while I slept.

He sets a mug down on the couch, kneeling in front of it, close enough that I can see the exhaustion etched in the lines around his eyes.

"How are you?" he asks gently.

"Fine," I choke, refusing to look at him.

He takes the folded blanket from me. "How does your heart feel?"

That question stumps me. My head droops before I can think twice. "I don't think I have one anymore."

His hand finds my knee, squeezing it once. "I brought you peppermint tea. Did you eat?"

Nodding, I let the herbal tea's scent soothe me before I lift the mug and take a tentative sip.

I hadn't realized how thirsty I was.

Draining the rest of the liquid, the water a perfect temperature, I can't help the small 'ah' that escapes my lips when it's gone.

William laughs a bit, taking the cup from me. "I thought we could talk, if you're up for it?"

I nod again. Words feel too hard to muster right now.

He plops down next to me on the couch, leaving room between us.

"Do you like the cottage?"

"Yes," I begin, testing out the rawness in my voice. "It's cozy. Who lives here?"

"It's mine," he says proudly.

"That's nice that you have something that's just yours." My tone is wistful, a hint of jealousy peeking through. I shift on the couch. "Won't they be looking for you? Your father?" Dread floods my brain. "What if they find me here?"

"There's a tunnel beneath Eremos that connects to our throne room. This used to be the royal family's safe house, before it was all but forgotten. They won't find you."

"Eremos?" I ask, curiosity piquing.

"It means an isolated place. That's what this is to me. I'd rather be here than anywhere else."

He sighs, leaning deeper into the couch. The crackle of the fire makes my head nod as my eyes droop.

"Why did you bring me here?"

William looks at me, the grief in his features unexpectedly matching my own. "None of this was meant to happen. I wanted to give you time to collect yourself; to mourn Callious."

I swallow hard, looking down. A tear escapes from behind the wall I've built. "I wish I could have saved him."

He frowns, clearly unsure of what to say. "Why don't you shower? The water is scalding. It might help clear your head."

I nod, getting up from the couch, my heart in utter agony as I remember his death all over again.

CHAPTER THIRTY-EIGHT

WHEN I COME BACK IN THE FRESH CLOTHES I FOUND IN the bedroom, he's pouring a cup of water. My hair drips all over the old floors, and I apologize for it as I take the cup from him. He shakes his head.

"I feel a little better," I admit after taking a long sip. In truth, I sat on the floor of the shower and let the water wash away my constant flow of tears until I was sure there were none left.

I scrubbed away all traces of blood—mine, Callious's—and watched it intermix with the cinnamon vanilla soap suds and swirl down the drain.

"You're wearing my clothes," he smiles.

Mortified, I look down at my white outfit. It's too big for my body. "I can take them off!"

His cheeks blush at my implication. "Not right now, I mean. Not in front of you. My uniform was covered in mud and Callious's blood, and I couldn't bear wearing it for another second—"

William's hand finds my arm, making me pause. "I know what you were trying to say."

I blush, embarrassed. "Okay," I mumble.

We move to the couch, silently watching the snow fall from behind the windows. "I'm sorry I lied to you," he whispers. "About knowing each other. Before."

I look at his face, the firelight flickering off his cold features. "Why didn't you just tell me?"

He exhales. "That day… it meant a lot to me. Until Selene was brought into our family, I didn't have anyone my age. Getting to meet you—your siblings—it was a bright spot in my life during a very dark time."

His hand rubs the back of his neck, rustling his hair. "My mother died shortly before we graced your shores. My father accused yours of poisoning her. I believe it truly was her magic that took her away, but my father is an angry man. He just wanted someone to blame."

I place my hand on top of his. "I'm so sorry."

Smiling sadly at me, he continues. "That's how the mess between our Kingdoms started. I will admit, I've been curious about you ever since that day we met. I couldn't remember anything other than the fun we had—what your name was, what you looked like. When my father told me he was bringing one of the Frey to Oresteia as collateral while we search for the stone, I put the pieces together when he mentioned your age."

It's as if this conversation has opened a box within William that was begging to be set free. "Then you didn't come. My father was furious, of course, as he is when things don't go to plan. He declared war; started preparing troops. I just wanted to see you—to meet you. I heard a Princess had joined Paralia's army after that first battle, and I thought: surely that's the girl I know. I snuck into your camp, let myself get captured. What I did not expect, though, was for it to be *you* who caught me."

I smile a little. "That was all Callious. It's no surprise he rose in ranks—he's clever."

He smiles at me, blushing a little.

I drop the grin as a question comes to mind. "How did you escape?"

"Did you forget that I have magic?" he asks, joking. "I created an illusion that I wasn't in the tent, which made the guards leave to try and find me. It was then that I made my *actual* escape."

"Why did *you* join the army? Surely your father would rather have his only heir as protected as possible."

He looks down. "I told my father I was just going to make a quick trip to the Gate. But then I saw you again, and I just knew I had to stay. For some reason, something drew me to you. I couldn't stay away."

Meeting my eyes again, he confesses, "He wasn't happy. My father had to send Selene after me as my own personal protection. To him, she's collateral. To me, she's the best General we could have. I promoted her as soon as she entered camp."

"That's kind of her to follow you into war."

His gaze wanders. "It was part of our plan—it's all she's ever wanted."

There's a layer there in his tone that I wish I could pick at, maybe even see the deeper meaning to. But he gets up before I can ask questions.

"I have a few meetings I have to attend over the next couple of days. You'll be safe here. When I'm back for good, we can talk about how to get you home."

The word *home* makes my heart clench, panic creating waves of nausea in my stomach.

My home is dead.

He bids me a quick goodnight, then disappears out the door without another glance back.

I choose the bed to sleep on tonight, the mattress's deep grooves holding me tightly.

Like I wish Callious could.

❊ ❊ ❊

Over the next few days, I rest. Sometimes it feels like I'm making progress—the hole in my heart not quite as big. Other days, I can't get out of bed.

There's plenty of dry goods here for me to eat, but the act of actually *making* something is another thing. The foods here are so much richer and heavier than the ones I'm used to in Paralia.

There are cans of soup with various ingredients, and warming them up in a pot over the stove does not use *too* much energy. Perhaps all that really matters in moments of grief are the small things—focusing on one little thing that you can do at a time.

Snow blows wildly outside the cottage one day as I pace, for some reason feeling like a caged animal. The firelight glints against something on the ground near the heater. I move closer, curiosity peaked.

A little metal object is somehow wedged between the wooden floorboards. Crouching, I reach for it, breath leaving my chest as I pluck it out of a worn groove.

I nearly drop it, my hands shaking as I peer at it as if it will disappear before my eyes.

My gaze searches the room, worried that I'm hallucinating or that all of this is a joke.

It can't be.

But it is. Callious's ring lies in my palm, the old leather cord broken in half and in tatters.

The metal ring is cold in my hand—far too cold. It looks just like it did that day when Cal first showed it to me. I cannot help the tears that fall as I clutch it closer to my chest, reveling in this small piece of him that was gifted to me by the sun above.

I don't know how long I stay there. I'm not sure when I went from standing to kneeling, crouching my body into a small ball as I weep.

Eventually, deep into the night, the tears run dry. I wipe my wet face on my shirt, not caring if I look disheveled.

I run my fingers over the grooves of the inscription, letting those four words wash over me.

Strength, stealth, security, sight.

The Spathe way—something that has been passed down for generations.

Callious was the final Spathe.

Horror floods through me.

Who will tell his father of his fate?

It will need to be me. I'm the one who knows him —I can break the news in the best way possible.

My knees pop as I pick myself up off the floor. I walk back to the couch, plopping down on the leather, as I untie the broken cord from the ring. It's a wonder it didn't separate on its own, but I thank the sun that it didn't.

Thank the sun it ended up right here.

That thought gives me pause. Was Callious... Did he stay in this cottage? Was he here?

I look over the space with fresh eyes, picturing him sleeping facing the door, his mind on me as he traveled far to find me.

A knot forms in my throat.

If only we could go back.

My hands are surprisingly steady as I slip the cold ring on my ring finger. It's far too big for it, so I move it to my index finger instead.

A perfect fit.

My chest feels like it's breaking in two. I wasn't supposed to be the one wearing this ring. And if someday he would have given it to me, it should have been *Callious* gracing it upon my finger.

Not me.

Alone.

CHAPTER THIRTY-NINE

At some point during the long night, I fell asleep on the couch, my hand formed in a fist so that my thumb could touch the ring. My neck has a crick in it as I awaken, William's footsteps soft as if to avoid disturbing me.

"Hi," he whispers.

"Hey," I respond, rubbing sleep out of my eyes. The metal ring is freezing against my cheek.

William leans against the wall, watching me. "New ring?"

He doesn't miss a thing.

"It's Callious's," I choke. "I found it. In front of the heater."

Shock and questions flood his face as he looks toward where I point. "He was here?"

I shrug. "He must have been. When he was... looking for me."

William nods, chewing on his bottom lip. "I thought this place was pretty impossible to find. That makes me nervous that someone from Paralia could enter it and stay without me knowing."

"He was always good at seeing things most people didn't."

William comes to sit next to me, laying his dagger's sheath on the couch. "We need to talk about getting you back. To Paralia."

I shake my head. "I've been ruminating the last few days on what I should do next. I can't go back. Not yet. The jewel is still lost."

He sighs. "I can't ask for your help anymore, Penelope. Maybe if you go back home, we can revisit all of this when you're feeling better."

"I'm feeling fine now," I bite. "I don't want his sacrifice to be in vain. Finding the Queen's Heart gives me a new purpose—do not take that away from me!"

My voice is frantic. Sadness leaks off of him in blue waves.

"Penelope," he begs.

"Please," I plead. "Let me help."

He pauses for a while, thinking. "Do you," he hesitates. "Do you want to say goodbye to him?"

My breath catches. "What do you mean?" I exhale in a whisper.

He fidgets with his fingernails, unsure. I've never seen him this nervous. "My mother died when I was young. Soon after my magic had revealed itself, I started isolating. My father threw me at teachers and tutors, hoping that by getting my musical abilities under control, my magic might follow suit. I was scared of the illusions, honestly. I was just a kid."

I nod along, eyes locked on his jaw as a muscle in it ticks.

"One night... I was lying in bed, crying. My mother used to sing me a song, a lullaby of sorts. In my desperation over missing her, I started to sing it to myself, not thinking about my magic. Just thinking about *her.*" He pauses. "I haven't told my father this. I haven't even told Selene."

I lay a hand on where his fingers pick at themselves. "You can tell me."

He doesn't hesitate. "I conjured an illusion of her, there in my bedroom. It looked just like her, spoke just like her. I cried with her, shouted at her. Told her I wished she was still with us—with *me.*" His voice breaks. "It was as if I could feel her holding me. I was able to say goodbye."

My heart feels exhausted and raw.

"I want nothing more than to give you the chance to say goodbye to the person you love, too."

I breathe in and out, thinking. Would that hinder my healing? Or would it propel me forward? Will he be standing here watching me say goodbye?

My palms sweat, and I wipe them on my thick pants.

Is replacing my last memory of Callious with something that isn't *actually* real the wisest thing?

A vision of the sword sticking through his chest flashes across my brain.

That makes up my mind. I want to see him whole again—feel his touch, witness his smile, hear him laugh.

"Okay," I say.

"Okay?" he asks, tone a little surprised. I nod. "I'm going to play piano. I can only play for a short while—my energy is depleted. I'll have you step outside, the door open, so you can hear it and let my magic seep into your mind. That will also give you some privacy."

I walk outside, leaving the door open just a sliver as I stare up at the night sky. It's a clear night in Oresteia, the stars shining vibrantly above me. I rub my thumb along the ring, letting it spin around the finger as I do.

The piano's notes begin as a soft murmur, rising in sound as William continues to play.

I try to control my breathing, nervous about what is to come. Music pours into my heart like the breaking light of dawn.

The cold air around me thickens, as if the world is waiting with me. Peuko trees sway in the wind, a dusting of snowflakes falling around my face.

The scent of smoke and earth falls away as my surroundings begin to dull. I turn toward the cottage, feeling like a thread is tying me to it, tugging on me.

And when I do, he's there.

He's crouched in the snow, writing something with a gloved finger. His hair is mussed from the wind, dark skin pink from the cold.

I take a step toward him, ice crunching under my feet.

"Callious," I breathe, my world already disoriented at how *real* this feels.

He looks up at me, delight in those green eyes—soft and achingly familiar.

Standing, he assesses me up and down. "Nelly, you look awful."

A laugh erupts out of me, one hiding tears and sorrow. I wipe at my eyes with the sleeve of my shirt. "You don't look much better."

He smiles, wide and radiant, and for a second— one beautiful second—it's as if nothing has changed.

But everything has.

I think the key to this not pulling me down a deep, dark hole is for me to remember that all of this is an illusion. The more real it feels, the less I want to remind myself that it's not.

But I have to.

Strength. I need strength.

Silence folds between us as I speak words that I *need* to utter out loud.

"You're dead," I whisper.

"I wanted to save you." His tone is sincere, and I mull over those words. His eyes catch the ring on my finger, surprised. "You found it."

"You were here?" I ask.

He nods. "When I came to get you back. It must have fallen off while I slept."

"I'm glad it did."

We stand there, just an arm's length away. The music William plays is fading in the background of our conversation, hardly something I notice if I don't focus on it.

"I just wanted to say goodbye," I choke. I cover my mouth with my hand, trying to hold in the sob that forces its way out. "We were supposed to die together, Callious. We were supposed to have a *life* after this war."

He rushes to me, wrapping me up in his warm

embrace. "I know," he says, his chin on the top of my head. "I wanted that too, Pen. So bad."

My hands find his shirt, pulling him in tighter. I breathe him in, all saltwater and gentle sea breeze, reminding me of the places I hold dear. He's solid; warm. I bury my face in the place between his neck and shoulder, letting him wrap his arms around me even tighter.

This is where I belong. Right here, with him.

"I love you," I whisper. "I always have."

He pulls me back, eyes searching mine with fervency. "I would have never let you go, P. But I had to, to keep you alive. Don't waste this. Make me proud like you always do."

"You're everything to me," I whisper.

His expression changes, breaking softly. "Someday you're going to find a new everything." He taps the ring on my thumb. "I'm always with you, Nel."

The music shifts, the tone a final melody. The illusion begins to tug and pull at my vision, Callious's form blurring at the edges.

"I don't want you to go yet." I reach for his face, letting him lean into my hand.

He grabs my fingers tightly, holding them. "You are the tide, Penelope. There's a force within you that is so magnetic, people can't help but be drawn to you. I know I couldn't."

Tears fall freely now, and I let them stain my cold cheeks.

"I love you," I say one last time.

"I love you, Penelope. I'll be waiting for you. I've always been waiting for you."

He kisses my forehead, soft and gentle.

Real enough to utterly destroy me.

And then, he's gone.

I whisper two final words as I look up to the dark sky, the stars blinking as if looking down on me, too.

Surrounded by wind, trees and snow, I let my last admission to him be something that only the earth and night get to witness.

Something just for the two of us.

"Goodbye, Callious."

CHAPTER FORTY

WOOD CREAKS BEHIND ME AS WILLIAM WALKS UP slowly.

"I want to keep fighting," I say, my voice small but sure. "For him, but also for me."

When he doesn't say anything back, I turn to look at him. Deep oranges bleed from his body as pride hits me.

The corners of his eyes turn up in a smile. But it doesn't last, quickly slipping into sorrow. "I'm sorry I couldn't give you more time."

I don't address his apology—I know he did what he could for me. And I'm grateful for it. Which is why I hope he doesn't mind my next request.

A demand, really.

"Take me to your Stronghold."

He blinks, surprised. "Penelope—"

"If the Queen's Heart is anywhere, it has to be there. It's not on Paralia's soil. It can't be. Four eyes are better than two. I can help look while you keep your father busy," I interrupt.

He studies me for a long minute, and I can see the wheels turning in his brain.

Finally, he nods. "We can go in the morning."

I shake my head. "Now."

* * *

I start to pack our few things, heading outside to Agrius, when William stops me.

"We aren't traveling by horseback."

My eyebrow shoots up. "What do you mean?"

He walks into the living room, grabs part of the wooden planks and hoists it up.

A trap door.

I gasp, walking over to peer into the small, square hole. "This has been here the whole time?"

I wonder if Callious found this.

He laughs. "I told you there was a tunnel. I didn't want you sneaking out on me."

I roll my eyes, letting him jump down first so he can help lower me down slowly. The trapdoor shuts above me with a loud *clunk*, startling both of us. We laugh as we separate, the brief moment of fear making us jump together in solidarity.

The tunnel is dark, my eyes hardly adjusting to the dim light. I sneeze, dust blowing around as we walk. I can barely see a foot in front of me, let alone William leading the way.

"You can take my hand if you want to," he says, as

if reading my mind. "I know this tunnel better than anyone."

He reaches back, and I take it lightly, letting our arms extend between our two bodies as we squeeze through the tight space.

"Your fingers are cold," I remark, needing to break the silence.

"Oresteia is cold," he deadpans.

I walk fast, keeping up with his long stride. My eyes start adjusting to the dark walls.

Most of the journey to the Stronghold is frigid and silent. I think William's nervous, but I couldn't feel more ready for this. I try to count my steps, figuring out how long this tunnel is. Eventually, I lose track. As best as I can tell, we're headed north.

"What do I need to know?" I ask. "Before we get there, I mean."

He slows. "We can search the throne room—that's where it's kept normally. The jewel resides within the Oresteian Queen's Crown on a white velvet pillow encased in enchanted glass. It's guarded at all times, but somehow the jewel was removed months ago and replaced with a fake."

"What's the enchantment?" I ask.

"Only someone with the blood of a royal may open it. It's our most sacred heirloom—we've never needed to remove it from the casing."

"How is it that you and Selene can still use magic with it gone? I thought where it sits allows it to funnel into your Stronghold, then into Oresteia?"

"We're using what's left," he responds. "It won't last

forever, but it's enough to allow us to use our magic around the Stronghold and Escaeus."

My brow furrows. "Both you and Selene used magic in Paralia. If the Queen's Heart only funnels magic into your Palace... how is that possible?"

He falters a step, barely catching himself. "Special reserves. It doesn't last long, but it's enough for small amounts of magic."

I tuck that information in the back of my brain, spinning it around and digesting it. Something about it doesn't sit right with me. All of this is too... simple.

"What's Escaeus?"

"It's the mountain you're under. It means 'hidden strength'."

My jaw opens as we come to the end of the tunnel. William pushes on the wall in front of us to open the door, then pokes his head out to check the surroundings.

He motions for me to follow him. The throne room is empty as we enter. There's not even a guard stationed where they supposedly should be.

The tall stone walls loom over us, a chill in the air.

I duck from underneath a tapestry that William holds out of the way for me, reveling in the space.

Our worlds are so... different.

Walking to the center of the room, I spin around slowly, taking it all in. Three thrones sit in the middle, as if they can't help but demand attention.

The arms and backs of each throne are made of twisted silver branches, wound up and around to craft the chair's shape.

Black cushions are plump on the seat, as if rarely used. The biggest throne, presumably Kori's, is on the left when you enter, with the smallest in the middle and a medium-sized one on the right.

Next to what I assume is the Queen's throne, there's a glass casing just as William said there would be. The Queen's Crown lies inside atop white velvet plush. I peer into the clear box, surveying.

The middle jewel is slightly tilted out of place, so unnoticeable that you wouldn't see it if you weren't specifically looking.

William releases the large black flag, coming to stand by me. Silver thread depicts a picture of a large mountain in a beautiful piece of woven creativity.

"What are you thinking?" he asks, hands in his pockets.

"I'm going to look around." I don't give him a chance to rebut or refuse before I'm moving around the vast space. I kneel at each throne, running my fingers along the intertwined branches. I lift the cushions, making sure to place them back exactly where they were before.

I press my hands into the stone floor, crouching so I can place my ear against the cold rock to listen. Pacing, I look for more false doors, hidden compartments, anything.

Nothing.

For some reason, I have this feeling that if the Queen's Heart were in this room, I would know it.

It feels delusional, but my delirious brain can't help but cling to that thought like it's a fact.

Footsteps echo outside the throne room, arriving quickly. Wide-eyed, I look at William, rushing over to him to hide behind his broad figure. There's no time to retreat to the tunnel.

The doors open wide with a *bang*, Kori standing in the threshold, dressed top to bottom in thick, white layers.

Clothes meant for a King.

"What's a lamb doing among wolves?" he bites.

I step out from behind William, fuming. All I can see when I look at Kori is the reason my best friend is dead. I speak without thinking, my tongue too loose after my horrific last few days. "Looking for something that *you* probably just misplaced."

William chuckles a little beside me, amusement on his face when I glance his way.

"You're trespassing onto enemy territory, little girl."

"You wouldn't know trespassing if it hit you in the face."

Kori stomps up to me, towering over my figure as I lean back. "You'll be mindful of how you *speak.*" Spit hits me in the face.

I wipe my cheek, purposefully avoiding eye contact. "Why do you want war so badly, Kori? Is it because, without something to prove, you're nothing?"

William grabs my elbow, propelling me back behind him, holding his hands up to his father in surrender. "She's a little grumpy—didn't sleep well last night."

Kori's eyebrows lift at his son. "Why is she here? Better question—why are *you* here, William?"

I may have done too much damage.

Not giving William a chance to come up with an excuse, I interrupt. "The war between our Kingdoms is ruining us. Our people are dying. But you and my father are doing *nothing* to keep it from happening. You don't even care about the lives lost!"

Kori's stare permeates down to my bones, the frost-filled blue utterly shocking. "You assume all of this is as simple as yes or no. Peace cannot always be the priority."

"But war should *never* be the goal." My voice sharpens, gaining clarity and confidence. "You did this. You started all of this. Pull your armies back—I'll talk to my father and—"

"Your *King* did this," he yells at me, forsaking composure. "*You* did this. Paralia and I came to an agreement, and you did not uphold his end. I gave you a chance to prepare, and I see now that was grace wasted. Forgive me if I choose not to extend the same liberties again."

"You're a selfish ruler—you and my father both."

"Is he still your father?" Kori asks, nonchalantly picking at his fingernails. "You speak loudly for someone with no title."

A guttural sound comes out of my chest, one of rage and frustration. William grabs my waist, pulling me backward away from Kori. I don't need a title to know that the war we are fighting is unnecessary—that the lives lost are ones we will never heal from.

Maybe at the end of the day, the lost jewel—whether truly stolen or not—isn't the real issue here.

Perhaps the real culprit is *ourselves*. Our pride. Our selfishness.

"Get her out, William. Before dawn."

I shake myself from the Prince's grip, turning to stalk out the throne room doors without another word.

Great power play, but I have no idea where I'm going.

I turn the corner, now in a dining room, and hide behind the open threshold to wait for William.

He sighs when he sees me, visibly stressed. "That could have gone better."

I get a bit of a scolding look from him, but I can tell there's a part of him that enjoyed the show. "Sorry if I got you in trouble."

He chuckles as we walk out, through a foyer and outside the Stronghold. "I'm always in trouble, Penelope."

※ ※ ※

William takes us to the Gate, where dawn peeks through hazy clouds. I should be tired, but I can't muster a yawn. The wind has quieted, but my restless soul hasn't.

A guard I recognize greets us as we arrive, taking watch over me as William ties Agrius up somewhere.

We walk through camp, and I notice the abundance of Oresteian soldiers. Bandages cover many, still healing from the last battle.

From our ambush.

I shiver, but not from the cold.

"I'm running point on some sparring lessons. You'll be coming with," he says.

I grumble, shuffling my feet in the grime-coated snow.

A small ring of soldiers silently gathers in the middle of the nearly empty yard. The guard pairs them up, leaving a lone soldier to watch. He's sulking, his broad shoulders turned inward as he eyes the rest of the pairs with envy.

"Why don't you spar with him?" I ask the guard.

He eyes the young boy. Silence.

"I can be his partner," I offer. I don't know why those words came out of my mouth, or where the idea even came from. Maybe something inside me feels like it understands the boy. What it's like to be the one left out.

He just huffs, watching the others warm up. I roll out my neck, coming up to the Oresteian with a little bounce in my step. "Want to spar?"

The boy glares at me, as if offended by the idea of fighting a girl. He scoffs, puffing his chest. "I suppose I wouldn't mind something to boost my ego."

We circle each other. His smirk tells me he's expecting an easy win, but I'm much smaller than he is. I can use that to my advantage.

Our fight begins fast. No weapons allowed, our feet and hands move in a flurry.

He's all lanky arms and legs. The way I move throws him off balance a bit, and I can tell he's confused by not having me pinned already.

The boy's strong, but he throws his entire weight

into each punch and kick. I hardly have to block any of the blows, being able to outmaneuver all of them.

The other duos have stopped to watch, and I hear them calling out, taunting him. The guard tries to control the crowd, but it's no use. They push in, encircling both of us, shouting.

"Send her back home where she belongs!"

"What's Paralia's pet Princess doing on *our* land?"

"He's totally going to get beaten by a girl! What a loser."

The words are like arrows to his pride, wounding him and keeping him from thinking straight. I'm about to grab his wrist, my plan to pin it against his back, when he feints.

He slams his foot into my leg, knocking me off balance.

I hit the ground with an *oomph, and* all the breath whooshes from my lungs.

He pins me down, straddling my hips, hands forcing my shoulders into the snow. I'm about to tap out, let him have this win in front of his friends, when he draws a short knife from his belt.

My eyes pop, frantically looking around for someone who can stop this. I'm surrounded by Oresteian enemies, the circle too tight-knit for anyone to notice what's happening.

He has a wicked gleam in his eye as he brings it above his head, showing all his friends. They cheer, suddenly on his side.

My heart pounds. I can't defend myself with my own dagger, my sheath trapped by his thigh.

He brings his knife down, tip pointed at my throat.

I refuse to close my eyes, ready for death. I can't believe my soft heart brought me to my demise.

This is how it ends for me.

I'm coming, Callious.

Just before the blade hits its mark, he's forcefully pushed aside.

The guard breaks up the circle, shoving the soldier.

"You know the rules," he shouts.

"Haldor, I—"

"Save it for when you answer to the Prince," Haldor roars.

I freeze as they all disperse, Haldor offering me a hand. I wave it off, clutching my stinging cheek as I sit up.

The knife sliced just above my jaw, fresh blood now trickling down my neck and onto the snow.

Haldor points me toward where their physicians work, then stalks off to follow the boy without another word.

❅ ❅ ❅

I stay silent when William finds me in the infirmary tent. They cleaned my wound, and I don't need stitches.

He crouches beside me, hands clenched.

"One of mine did this to you," William says, his voice etched with concern. "What did he look like?"

I look down, ashamed that I was not quick enough to stop the blow; that I could not save myself.

"What did he look like, Penelope?"

I don't answer. If he wants to know badly enough, he can find Haldor. I will not be the one to tattle.

There's urgency in his voice. And perhaps something else… anger?

Couldn't be. It's just a scratch, and I am not his responsibility.

And we are still at war, for sun's sake.

He huffs, his breath warm against my clutched hands sitting in my lap. Abruptly, he stands, rushing out of the tent with intention.

Just minutes later, somewhere else in the camp, screaming begins.

And it does not stop until the morning comes.

※ ※ ※

I sleep through the day in an empty tent. When I awaken, I'm still exhausted, but feeling… lighter. I don't wish to know what William did to the soldier. It's not my place to ask.

Even if what he did was for me.

I tug my cloak around my shoulders, prodding my cheek to see how the cut feels. It throbs, but it doesn't sting quite as badly as before.

I stalk out of camp, looking for a soldier dressed in white. I find him near the peuko trees, sharpening a blade. His breath fogs the air, his hair mused by the harsh wind.

He looks up as he sees me. "How did you sleep?"

"Fine," I reply, avoiding eye contact.

He lays the blade on his knee, and I take a look at

its sharp point, expecting the dagger I've seen him with.

But it's not.

I pause.

I don't know why that catches me off guard the way it does—many people own different types of daggers.

A shining onyx glistens against his white pants. Escaeus stands strongly on the handle, with a detailed silver emblem depicted.

"That's pretty," I remark. "Whose is that?"

"It's mine. I crafted it myself at a shop in Copolis."

I frown. "You have two daggers?"

He tilts his head, confused. "Just this one."

"I've seen you with another one. What happened to it? The one that looks like flames?"

He glances at me, then goes back to sharpening. "That's not mine."

I wait, seeing if he'll give me more information.

"That one's Selene's. She let me borrow it."

He's not necessarily guarded, but he isn't open either. As if there's something he isn't saying.

I study his downcast face, focused on the whetstone and his dagger, carving it in meticulous strokes.

A knot coils deep in my stomach, questions invading my brain.

Selene's dagger. A clear jewel.

Magic in places it's not supposed to be.

I file it all away quietly. Ruminating. Pushing the pieces together... *making* them fit into the puzzle I've created in my brain.

My thumb finds my ring, rubbing it as I think.

Stealth.

Callious was good at that. He was cunning; silent. He fit into the shadows.

A Nightingale.

If he can be that, I can too. I'm going to figure this out.

And his ways will help me.

CHAPTER FORTY-ONE
CALLIOUS

It's dark. Cold.
   Eternity smells dimly of... smoke?
   Images of her dance through my brain.
   In the end, she is all I see.

CHAPTER FORTY-TWO

Why did William hesitate when I asked him about Selene's dagger?

That's the question that replays over and over in my mind as I walk back to camp. If what Mas said is true… they *shouldn't* be able to use magic in Paralia.

And yet, they did.

Multiple times.

"Special reserves," William told me when I asked how.

Frost crunches under my boots, a harsh reminder that this isn't where I'm meant to be.

None of this makes sense.

Truth settles in me like something spoiled. The jewel in the middle of Selene's dagger… it *has* to be the Queen's Heart.

Right?

But why would they take it? Why this ruse? Why not just declare war on us and let it be that? I shake my head. No, they must have found it at some point. But when…

I try to mull that over, but a roar simmers in my blood, low and violent. Every step back toward camp stokes the flame within me.

They've had it this whole time.

They *lied* to me.

I stop in my tracks—my blood suddenly as frozen as ice.

Callious is dead because of their lies.

Talk of unity and kindness tricked us and led us astray. Oresteia allowed war to continue, the battles so outrageous that Paralia would never come out victorious.

They let Callious bleed out in the snow, destined for an unkind and untimely death.

I want to weep, a desperate scream building in my tight chest. I want to take everything they've ever held dear and burn it to the ground.

Breathing in deep, I hold the motion for a few seconds, letting it calm me; releasing all the parts of me that still want to believe that William and Selene had good intentions.

But if they did, then why not tell me the truth all those weeks ago?

I need to bide my time.

There might only be one shot at proving they've betrayed us all, and I need to make sure it hits.

Hard.

I pull Callious's ring off my thumb, rereading the four words.

He could still be alive if I had figured all of this out sooner. If Oresteia wasn't so selfish. If...

I shake my head. I can't think like that. Not when

what I'm about to do requires confidence and precision.

We could have avoided so much of this. But we *didn't*. So, I must take what I have and try to fix this.

Once and for all.

※ ※ ※

I slip into the tent I slept in earlier today, digging into yesterday's pants.

A vial clinks softly as I pull it free from the pocket.

Tarsha's intention might have been to help me rest, but I have something else in mind.

I open the small cork on top, smelling the lavender scent. Drowsiness hits me out of nowhere.

Yes, this will do just fine.

Immediately, I stalk toward the kitchen tent, hoping I can convince Tarsha to let me bake something sweet.

Finding her is easier than I anticipated. She's already stirring something in a large wooden bowl.

"Do you need help?" I ask, reaching to take the bowl from her.

She nods her head toward another one on the table beside us. A smaller bowl with blueberries and a light-colored batter already inside.

Perfect.

I start to stir, careful not to let anything about my facial expressions slip that I'm up to something. We work in silence, and I let the rhythm of it soothe me as the berries bleed into the beige liquid.

We pour the batters into two muffin tins, my flavor

different than hers. I look over at her as I fill the last one, but she's already putting hers into the oven.

With her back turned, I move quickly, uncorking my small vial and dumping the contents into the last muffin. I stir it quickly with my wooden spoon, making sure it's unnoticeable.

The muffins only need a handful of minutes, and as we clean up, I try to keep my eyes on the sedative-filled treat. My heart races, palms sweaty as I wipe down counters and dry the bowls we used.

When the treats finally come out, golden and warm, Tarsha motions for me to take a few. I take two, careful to wrap the sedative one in a cloth napkin as I take a bite of one of hers.

Thanking her, I leave the space, steeling myself for what is to come.

※ ※ ※

William finds me later near the peuko trees. I knew he would come looking for me—he always does. His cloak is unbuttoned, and his hair is wind-tossed. I can't imagine what he would have done today to make him look so... disheveled.

I'm slumped against the rough bark, the tree I'm resting on clear of limbs.

I offer the muffin to him, holding out the cloth.

He sits next to me, taking it, inhaling deeply. "Tarsha's?"

I nod. "I'm sure she sends her love."

We sit next to each other, watching a light flurry of

snow fall around us. The ground is cold beneath me, but my veins are on fire. I can't get my brain to shut off, hyper-aware of every little movement William makes as he finally unwraps the muffin.

Act natural.

I'm too still, too quiet. But if I start moving around and chatting with him, he'll never eat it. I shake off the urge to squirm, holding my tongue.

There's a hum in the air that tickles the back of my neck. Breaking out in a cold sweat, I clear my throat slightly, calming my nerves as he takes his first bite.

After he's scarfed it down, he leans back, sighing. "That was delicious."

I force a smile. "I wish I could claim that I made that one, but all I did was stir the ingredients together."

He taps his bent knee in a consistent pattern, throat exposed as his head hits the bark behind us. "Don't downgrade the part you played."

Smirking a little, he tilts his face so it's facing me. I keep my eyes down, the wind rustling my curls so they're covering my face.

I wait, counting the seconds between the rise and fall of his chest.

Then, just as I'm about to fall asleep myself, his hand falls softly from where it is on his knee.

It hangs limp as I look at the soft features on his face, mouth barely agape, eyes shut.

Regret blooms within me for just a second, but I leave it behind me where all my cares have been shoved aside.

I sit up slowly on my knees, eyes on the sheath tied to his waist. This whole plan was dependent on him bringing it. The covered dagger is lying partially in the snow, forgotten at his side.

I don't take a moment to question why he once again carries the dagger he claims isn't his, solely focused on snatching it without him knowing. Everything is going exactly how I hoped.

Reaching across, I'm careful not to make any unnecessary sounds, chest pounding fervently.

Take the dagger. Run to the Janus Tree. Get back home.

I exhale softly as I come in contact with the dagger, the angle awkward as I pull it gently-

A hand shoots out, wrapping around my wrist. It's as if the fog clears, my eyes seeing what's *real* again.

Wide-eyed, I stare into William's narrowed gaze, unsure how I'm going to talk myself out of this one.

"If you wanted my dagger, Penelope, all you needed to do was ask."

He pulls his dagger out of the sheath, one hand still wrapped around my wrist, throwing it between us.

Onyx metal glints as I search for what I'm missing, but the truth lies right in front of me.

It's not the other dagger.

"William, I—"

He holds up his free hand, stopping me. With the other, he gently removes his grasp from my wrist and plucks the uneaten muffin from the snow beside him. "I could smell the lavender. Quite an overwhelming choice for a blueberry muffin, if I do say so myself."

I mumble, sitting back onto my palms away from him. The snow bites into my uncovered hands. I was so concentrated on getting the dagger and getting out of Oresteia that I forgot my gloves.

"How did you know?" I breathe.

"I could hear the distrust in your voice earlier." His voice breaks. "I wanted to tell you, Penelope. Selene made me swear to secrecy."

Tears well in my eyes, threatening to overflow. "It seems I was right not to trust you. You've been lying to me this *whole time.*"

His gaze grows colder, but not with anger. More like... anguish. "We were telling you the truth about the Heart's connection to the Tree and its claim on our Kingdoms."

I hold up a hand, fury radiating. "When did you find it?"

He hesitates, eyes avoiding my own.

I take a deep breath before I speak. "Don't tell me you stole your own jewel."

William whispers, "I didn't. Selene did."

Anger overtakes every part of me as I stand, but I stay in control enough to refrain from kicking him in the shin. "You've had it this whole time."

He nods, and I break. Selene *wanted* this war between our Kingdoms. She wanted to fight.

She wanted to prove her King wrong.

I shiver. Somehow, Selene stealing the jewel isn't the most hurtful part. Yes, I was strung along. But in some ways, I can understand where she's coming from. She wanted to take control of her own life. And didn't I do the same thing when I chose not to travel to Oresteia? Both of us sentenced the lives of many to death because of our own pride.

But her action took Callious's life. He was going to enlist whether I came with him or not.

It is *that* thought that shatters my heart into unrecognizable pieces.

"You lied to me repeatedly. You let me stand in front of your King, accusing him when it was you two all along. My best friend is *dead* because of *you*!" I scream in his face, tears wetting my cheeks and mouth.

He tries to stand, but I grab hold of his shoulders, pushing him back down onto the ground. His voice shakes as he speaks. "We were going to tell you. But Selene didn't want to tell you yet. She..." He pauses, frantic. "All she's ever wanted was to fight. You know that. And she feared my father would remove her from our army once the jewel was found. She kept pushing back the timeline. And then you and I went to the Tree... And I realized we were in too deep, far too quickly."

"I hope he demotes her," I remark, removing my hands. "If you had just *told* me, all of this could have been avoided. I would have been on your side."

The wind steals his words, my ears hardly catching the quiet sound. "I know."

"I'm going home to relay this to my King. Oresteia will regret this betrayal."

"I regret it now," he bites out quickly.

"That won't bring Callious back. It doesn't change what's already been done."

He doesn't speak as I gather myself, turning toward the north where the Janus Tree awaits. As I'm walking away, I hear him call my name. In a moment of weakness, I face him once more.

"I'm sorry, Penelope."

I straighten my spine, unwilling to let him see how

that affects me so. Even then, tears once again begin to fall, freezing onto my face.

"Me too," I call back. "I'm sorry I ever thought you were anything other than what you truly are."

His head slumps, looking straight at the ground.

And with that, I turn.

My heart is ruined. Not just at his actions, but at the lies built up between us.

How could I ever trust them again?

CHAPTER FORTY-THREE

CALLIOUS'S TENT IS EXACTLY AS HE LEFT IT.

The canvas flap is still tied shut, the fabric stiff. It appears no one's touched it. Being a Captain, he had the space to himself.

So now, there's just a ghost of what was.

I slip inside, bracing myself for what I might find after a long day of travel. I've left my Oresteian layers behind, as well as every part of me that longed for something *better* than the hand I was dealt.

All I want now is to sleep.

The small space smells like him—like saltwater and sweat. His cot is made up neatly, just a bare blanket folded in the middle.

Tears form as I sit on the dusty material, the bed creaking under me. It's too quiet and final. So... wrong.

I grab the blanket, pulling it over my sore body as I lie down on the stiff canvas, ready to succumb to grief once again. But as I unravel the throw, a folded piece of parchment flutters from between the creases, my name scrawled across the front.

My chest gets tight, and I force my lungs to keep breathing as I recognize his penmanship.

Pen.

The sight of my nickname, so simple and short, makes my throat close. With a trembling hand, I grab the note, the paper worn like it's been read repeatedly. I inhale deeply to steady myself as I unfold the paper.

> *Pen,*
> *If you're reading this, then...*
> *Well, we know what that means. Something went wrong. But I pray to the suns above that I'm still there with you, and that this letter is just a way for us to reminisce.*
> *Either way, I needed to write this. Not just for you... But for myself too. There's so much I've never said to you because I never thought there'd be an us. And now that you are mine, I don't want to let another day pass by that I don't tell you how much you mean to me.*
> *I was going to wait for when things calmed down for us. Maybe when the war ended, or when we had time together. But we aren't guaranteed that. I wanted to give you my father's ring—to place it on your finger and publicly declare you as my best friend for all our days.*

My thumb finds the ring, spinning it in circles around my finger.

So here it is, Nelly. Everything I'm thinking.

No one in my life means as much to me as you do. Right now, you're asleep in your tent, and all I can think about are the times you fell asleep on my shoulder. The days we spent lying on the beach. The nights we met up to talk about anything and everything. You have always made sense to me in a way that nothing else did.

As a boy, I believed in heroes. My dad was one of them. Men who fought for those they loved. I wanted to be like them—it's where my aspiration for the army started in the first place.

But then I met you. You changed everything. Suddenly, it wasn't just a dream to fight for who I loved; the person I loved was standing right in front of me. And I couldn't have her, because she was higher than me in so many ways.

But I was willing to be whatever I could be for you if that meant you'd be in my life. I was scared you'd grow up to be like your sisters—a little snotty, if I'm being honest.

Sadness bubbles into laughter at that, tears running down my face as I keep reading.

But you grew up kind, understanding. I still don't know where you got it from. You never said you were better than me, and because of that, you made me better.

I know you don't always see it. In fact, I'm not sure you ever have. You second-guess and you allow yourself to be put in a box by your siblings. It's one reason why I am incredibly proud of you for coming with me.

You made this life your own, Nel. You made the harder choice and chose yourself. You don't need your royal title to be important. You are just by being yourself.

There's always been moments between us... quiet, stolen ones. It was there that I allowed myself to picture what a future might look like. Us, away from your parents. Maybe a small house with just enough space for us to learn new hobbies and run wild like we used to.

I envisioned a peaceful, fulfilled life. With YOU, Penelope. But most of all, I just wanted a chance to stand beside you and make you proud.

Because everything you do makes me proud.

This is the hard part of the letter, I guess. Realizing that if you're reading it, that probably means I'm not there with you. That the future I held onto so tightly slipped through my fingers.

I can't believe I would willingly leave you behind, so I'm sure I had a really good reason for whatever happened. All I've ever wanted was to protect you, even when we were just kids. I hope I did that. I hope I made you proud.

I don't know what's next for you. Maybe my death is fresh. Maybe it's years old. Maybe this letter will sit unopened forever because we went together.

In the end, whatever happens, I need you to promise me that you will not allow anyone to make you cruel. That is one thing that you are not, P. You never will be.

Don't let grief twist the parts of you I love the most.

War makes us into harder people. Battles sharpen us so that we are a weapon ourselves. Be soft, Penelope. Stay true to your heart. It's braver to be kind than it is to take revenge.

Maybe the answer to all of this isn't choosing sides, but being the bridge between them. I think you could be that bridge, Pen.

I've always loved you. Deeply, madly, secretly, proudly. The days we spent together were my favorites, and I know those memories are what flashed before my eyes when it was my time to go.

I am still with you, Nelly. I am always with you. So go be what I've always seen in you. It's always been you and me.

Until the end,

Callious—your Nightingale.

The letter falls into my lap as I break, head folded over into my empty hands. My chest feels locked up, like my heart is trapped and full of something too big to release. Grief mixes with clarity as rage blends into peace.

I let the tears slip slowly from my eyes so I can bring my knees up to my forehead.

He's always seen me, better than anyone else in my life has. I rub my finger across his ring, and the metal catches in the dim light, shining like a new promise.

Security.

This isn't about revenge anymore. This is about the bigger issues between our Kingdoms. This is for everyone who feels as though all hope is lost. It's for everyone who has had someone they love not come home.

I steel myself.

This is for everyone we are still able to save.

✻ ✻ ✻

The trek to the Palace doesn't feel as far in the dead of night. When I arrive, the glow of lights burns from within, as if warning me away.

I swing open the front doors, completely ignoring the guards stationed there who try to steer me away. *No one* will be getting in the way of what I'm about to do.

I meander through the quiet Palace, wondering if it would be best to try my father's office first or go straight to his room. We aren't allowed on that side of the wing without him, so getting through might be a little trickier than I anticipated...

A dark figure moves out of the shadows in my peripheral.

"Nel?"

I recognize my brother at once, but am surprised at the relief on his face. "Carter? What are you doing up?"

He rushes to me, engulfing me in a hug so big it lifts me from the ground. "We all thought you were dead."

I pull away, confused. "Who told you that?"

His dark eyes well with tears. "You've been unaccounted for ever since the last battle. One of your generals came to tell us."

I shake my head, not wanting to get into where I've been with him. "I need to speak with father."

Carter gapes. "He thinks you died, Pen. It'll be like seeing a ghost."

I push past him, walking toward the King's study. "The ghost has things to say."

※ ※ ※

I bounce my crossed leg as I wait behind the large desk, sitting in his cushioned chair. The room is far bigger than what is necessary, but I suppose when you're King, you're always looking for ways to prove yourself better than everyone else.

Which is why I took his seat. If I'm going to be the one waiting on *him*, then I deserve to be comfortable.

I chuckle to myself. Who *am* I? The old me would have *never*.

But I guess I'm not her anymore.

Pictures woven in thick-corded yarn line the wall, showing off scenes of Paralia's stunning landscape. A single candle burns on the desk—the one I lit when I arrived. It casts pale flickers across scrolls of parchment and worn maps.

Strong footsteps sound from the hallway, and I lift my chin as the King enters the room.

"You're alive," he breathes.

I snort, uncrossing my legs to lean my elbows on the table. "You're incredibly observant."

He stays standing, looking down his nose at me. "You'll watch your tone."

Tilting my head, I look him up and down. My heart is beating out of my chest, but I can't let him know that. "No, I don't think I will. Sit."

After a few minutes of staring me down, as if silently ordering me to get up, he concedes.

Interesting.

"We were set up," I begin.

He starts to interrupt, but I hold up a hand. Surprisingly, he quiets. It must be that I disturbed his sleep—perhaps he's too tired to fight me right now.

Good.

"Oresteia's artifact—the Queen's Heart—was in their hands all along. I don't know how much their King knows, but I cannot take him out of the equation altogether. It was stolen by Oresteia's general, Selene.

Their Prince knew and kept it a secret, and went as far as to show me a vision of what will happen to our lands if it were to stay lost."

My father quirks an eyebrow, but does not move another muscle as I continue. "They did not tell me these things. It was only after the most recent battle that I began to put the pieces together. I confronted William, and he gave me what I *believe* was the truth. Still, he let us bleed and fight and *die* all the same."

I can tell he's fuming, the tips of his ears turning an impossible shade of red. Still, I have more to say. "I do not tell you all of these things so we can plan retribution."

Zannan nearly shoots up out of his chair at that, beginning to shout at me. I rise, standing my ground, showcasing confidence that only Callious's memory could give me. He would not back down, so I won't either.

Finally, the King stills in his chair.

"We have been in strife with Oresteia for far too long. *Both* Kingdoms have made mistakes in how we've handled each other. I want to fight for something better —security for our people, a kinder land. We should take a step toward rebuilding what has been broken, so we might come out of it stronger."

The ring on my thumb is heavy, but it still steadies me.

"This is me asking for your help. I don't want to punish them. I just want to end this before it costs us so much more than it already has."

The candle crackles, snuffing out, engulfing the room in darkness.

Silence fills the space between us.

A figure stands in the doorway, tall and broad. My oldest brother's strong voice rings out, so sure in his words. "My King, I'm with Penelope."

Tears form in my eyes at his words, and I cannot help but be thankful they cannot see.

Our father rises, sighing. "Then the future of this Kingdom is on your shoulders, Everett. I will not have any part in this."

I nod, moving out from around the desk to stand next to my brother.

As we leave, King Zannan mumbles to himself, causing me to pause for just a moment.

"I mourned for you," he whispers.

Not turning around, I refuse to let my emotion show. "I did not ask you to."

With that, the King leaves the room.

CHAPTER FORTY-FOUR

DAYS PASS. EARLY ONE MORNING, AS THE SUN HANGS low over the sandy fields, we gather the Kingdoms. I can see the edge of Oresteia's army in the background, huddled around the Isthmus, but I try not to think too much of it.

No. Right now, there's only me and Paralia's army.

Everett called an emergency meeting with everyone who is left fighting, stating the royal family had something to say. That attendance was *required*.

Now I stand before them, knees wobbling while a strained silence extends toward me.

They are battered and bruised, hardly better off than the last time I was here. Somehow, that feels like years ago and yesterday all at the same time.

I step forward, on a pedestal, Everett beside me. My clothes are clean—a pristine uniform was procured for me. I wanted to portray that I am on their side— that I am *with* them.

That I am still one of them.

"My name is Penelope Frey," I say, voice echoing.

The crowd shifts, murmurs rippling. I watch muscles tense, eyes darting back and forth between me and my brother. I know my father watches from the back, flanked by his own guards. I glimpse white nearby—the King and his Prince here with us.

Nerves nearly get to me. But I have to continue.

For Callious. For the life we wanted to have together.

I gulp down the bile that was rising, taking comfort in my brother being on my side.

"As most of you know, I am not here as a daughter of the crown."

I look at their faces, memorizing them, holding them dear to my heart. These are people's loved ones. My chest aches. I wish I could see Callious, or feel his steady presence beside me.

"I am here as one of you. War has cost me *everything*, as I'm sure it has most of you."

Heads nod, and I see tears slip from those closest in proximity to me.

"And for what?" I ask. "Why have we sacrificed everything for this cause? For a rivalry that has been brewing for over ten years?"

My voice booms across the land. Even the ocean's waves remain silent.

"It's time we find a truce between our Kingdoms. There will never be a winner in a war that doesn't need to exist."

I make eye contact with Kori from afar, willing him

to listen earnestly to my words. "Oresteia has turned a blind eye for too long."

Then I match my father's stare. "And Paralia has lost too much."

I wait a beat, letting it sink in. "I'm standing here demanding that we end this. I am not naïve enough to believe that all our issues can be fixed with just a few words from a girl who has nothing to offer. But I *do* know that nothing will change if we do not stop fighting."

Finally, I let myself breathe, my shoulders turning in on themselves as I watch the crowd. Everett shouts from beside me, "I'm with her!"

His voice causes murmurs to spread, some in agreement and others in anguish and anger.

I just watch, hopeful. Kori and my father meet in the back, exchanging words of some sort. I can't read their lips from all the way up here, but maybe if I got closer...

I'm hopping down from the platform when movement to my left catches my eye.

A figure dressed in red steps out of the crowd, slow but certain.

Selene.

A hush spreads across the crowd as she walks closer to me, something in her hands.

The dagger.

Her dagger, with the missing jewel proudly displayed. The Queen's Heart gleams faintly in her palm as if it's alerting me to its presence.

With her head bowed, she kneels before me.

"I took it," she says, voice raspy and loud enough for all to hear. "I've had it all along. I'm so sorry."

A gasp ripples through the Oresteians in the back. Soft curses come from Paralia's side.

"I just wanted to be somewhere I felt like I belonged. I see now that I was selfish. I did not think of the consequences this would reap for our Kingdoms. For *you*, Penelope."

I take the dagger from her outstretched hands, holding it lightly. My fingers shake around the blade. She stands, now facing the crowd. "I believe peace is possible between our two Kingdoms. I'm with her!"

Selene raises a fist in the air, shouting the last three words with fervency. Kori storms forward, grabbing her by the arm. "You must be extremely foolish to commit treason in front of everyone."

She meets his gaze, fire and ice colliding. "If committing treason means this war comes to an end, I would do it again."

His grip tightens. "You are stripped of your title, both as general and royal, and you will be *exiled*—"

William's voice cuts in like a blade as he steps beside Selene, coming out of seemingly nowhere. The sword at his side remains sheathed, but the authority in his tone rings out clearly. "If you cast her out," he begins. "I will go with her. And *you* will be left without an heir."

Kori's jaw clenches, staring daggers into William's very soul.

After a stint of silence, William looks to me. "The Queen's Heart still needs to be returned," he whispers. "Our Kingdoms will never heal until we do."

He raises his voice, shouting clearly to Oresteia. "I'm with her!"

Voices ring out, shouting in response, chanting that they are on my side.

I can't help but grin. For the first time in my life, I feel like I've done something *right*. Like this is exactly where I'm supposed to be.

I only wish Callious could see it. He always saw things in me that I never did.

Placing a hand on the seashell hanging around my neck, I look out across the land. At the faces I long to protect and serve.

Finally, begrudgingly, I meet William's gaze. Anger fizzles out, being replaced with kernels of hope.

He nods to me, and I return the motion.

I can feel the tide shifting.

Maybe we have a chance to change things, after all.

✼ ✼ ✼

A royal meeting is called, advisors and bloodlines alike all huddled within the Paralian throne room.

My siblings mill about, engaging in conversation and gaining as much information as they can.

I spot William and Selene immediately, huddled in the corner, exchanging words.

My stomach flips. I don't want to talk to them, but there are things within me that I cannot leave unsaid.

They turn toward me as I get closer, their eyes full of regret and remorse. The dagger is in its sheath around my waist, and I refuse to remove my hand from it.

"Peace," I begin. "Peace is something we talk about like it's free. But peace between us requires trust, and I don't know if I could depend on either of you ever again."

"I'll earn your trust," she says. "I'll do whatever it takes for the rest of our lives."

I look between the two of them, heart both breaking and mending over and over.

William puts a hand in front of Selene, cutting off whatever she was about to say. "Whether or not you trust us right now is something we can focus on *after* we return the Heart to the Tree."

"Is that all you can think about?" I say, my words cutting sharper than I meant for them to. My eyes find Selene's.

William's gaze is steady, but hers turns downcast. "I never wanted to pull you into the middle of this. I know I've ruined things. If you give me the chance, I will do everything I can to mend what's broken."

"Finish your sentence," I grind, fingers tightening around the hilt of my blade. "It's been broken because of *you*."

"I'm sorry," Selene gasps. "I wanted to be your friend. I still *do*—"

I interrupt her cries. "My *best friend* is dead because of you."

I exhale a quick breath, finally saying out loud what hurt me most since finding out she took the jewel.

Her eyes catch mine, surprisingly unflinching at the bite in my words. "He's not," she whispers.

Silence crashes down on me like a bucket of cold salt water. I lean in, hands and voice shaking. "What did you just say?"

She searches my face, looking for something that I'm not sure she'll find. "Callious is alive."

CHAPTER FORTY-FIVE

WITHIN MOMENTS, I'M IN ORESTEIA ONCE AGAIN. Agrius and Selene's horses carry us far and fast. There's no time to waste.

The path blurs beneath me, trees and shadow stretching like threads of my memory. I try to picture Callious's face, but I can't. My heart pounds, every inch of my body covered in a cold sweat.

Wind bites at my cheek. I try to focus on the journey, but my mind skips back to the day I left him behind. The blood coating the snow, the way the sword pierced his chest...

I nearly run up the stairs once we arrive at Rhea's Place, not bothering to force manners and niceties. I don't *feel* like being nice. In just a few seconds, my whole life will change *again*.

Everything is quieter than I remember. The windows are covered, and Rhea is nowhere to be found. Boots slam against the floor. My stomach wrenches, nausea forcing its way up as I hold on to the wall in an attempt to find relief. Shallow breaths come in, spots darkening my vision.

A hand finds my lower back. Slow, methodical circles repeat, soothing me.

"Do you want to go in alone?" William asks from behind me.

I shake my head, steadying the dizzy spell. He claims he didn't know about Callious. For some reason... I believe him.

Glancing over my shoulder quickly, William's grim face meets my own. His jaw is tight, and there's guilt written all over his features. He opens his mouth to speak, but no words come out.

Which is good. I don't want them. Not right now.

The door creaks open to the sound of labored breathing.

A lantern burns low, casting dim orange light over a pallet on the floor.

Selene walks in first, her shoulders hunched in defeat.

"I thought he'd be dead by now," she mutters.

Her voice lacks its usual sarcasm; tone soft. She doesn't meet my eyes, gaze stuck on Cal.

Callious shifts slightly, groaning on the ground. I survey him from head to toe, frozen in my spot near the door. He's covered in blankets galore, sweat perspiring across his forehead.

My fingers twitch at my side, remembering the sticky heat of his blood when I touched him last. I shouldn't have left him—I should have *known* he was still alive.

I move forward slowly, watching as his shut eyelids continuously pinch together.

He looks so... pale.

But he's alive.

It's almost hard for me to trust it. I listen intently for the sound of humming... but there's nothing. My hand finds my mouth as I hold back a gasping sob.

He's here. He's real.

I watch the rise and fall of his chest, labored but consistent. His mouth is barely open, a wheezing sound coming from his chapped lips.

My chest pounds so violently I'm sure they can hear it.

He's so thin.

Selene strips the blankets, raising his dirty, shredded shirt to press a dark cloth to his stomach. She lifts it to the light, checking the amount of blood staining the towel. Stitches coat his abdomen, shoddy work that will, without a doubt, leave scars.

But it doesn't matter. He's *alive.*

I kneel beside him, taking Selene's towel, the wooden floor cold under my legs.

Dabbing the cold rag on his forehead, I clean up the dirt staining his brow. My fingers shake as I reach toward an unruly brown wave, moving it away from his eyes. His skin is hot to the touch.

His chest hitches at the motion. I move my hand away, quiet. Everything else in the room fades away as I watch, soft murmurs of Selene and William in the background.

Green eyes illuminate in the golden light as he looks at me.

My favorite color surrounds me, warmth flooding as his gaze opens wide.

As if in slow motion, he tries to rise, but my arms are already around his neck as I breathe him in.

Tears coat his skin as I sob into his neck, and he returns the favor. I feel him wince as he gasps for breath, and I make myself back up to give him space.

He puts a hand on the back of my head, fingers tangled in my curls as he brings our foreheads to meet.

I smile through the tears, eyes shut tight, scared all of this is a dream I won't want to wake up from. Again, I take a second to listen. For humming, an instrument playing... anything that might give away that all of this is one of William's illusions.

But it's quiet.

This is *real*. I can't believe it, and yet, the proof is lying right in front of me.

I nuzzle Callious's nose as I whisper, "You came back to me."

"Pen," he begins, our tears intermixing as they fall in his lap. "I never left."

He tries to say more, but I shush him, not wanting to waste precious energy. It's clear he's still hurting and utterly exhausted. Still, he's the most stubborn person I know. He's always been that way. And I've never been able to keep him from doing what he wants to do.

"Every time I thought it was my time... I saw you, Penelope. In the end, you were all I could see. It's like my heart knew I would be with you again—that you were waiting for me on this side."

That breaks me completely, removing all barriers within me in the name of self-preservation. I grab the collar of his shirt gently, pulling him toward me. Salt coats our lips. I kiss him like it's our last.

Behind us, I hear Selene clear her throat. "We'll be outside."

She slips out quickly without a second look.

"Take your time," William says, hesitating in the doorframe. He shifts his stance from leg to leg. "And welcome back to the land of the living, Callious."

With that, it's just us and the glow of firelight. Just my hands pressed against his chest, feeling his pulse beat beneath my palms. The smell of blood and sweat coats the air, but I welcome its earthy scent. To me, right now, this is home.

CHAPTER FORTY-SIX
CALLIOUS

IT'S AS IF HER KISS BRINGS ME BACK TO LIFE.
When I'm with her, there's no end.
This is eternity.

CHAPTER FORTY-SEVEN

CALLIOUS DRIFTS TO SLEEP, BREATHS LOW AND STEADIER than before. His hand never left mine as we talked, unwilling to let each other out of our sights for even a second.

Now, I let him rest, watching the rise and fall of his chest as I remind myself over and over that this is *real*.

Selene slips into the room like a shadow, as if she knew I was ready. She looks… tired. Her eyes are downcast, and there are dark circles underneath. She doesn't speak until I look at her, making sure Cal is in a deep sleep so we don't disturb him.

"I was going to bury him for you," she admits softly, sinking onto the floor against the wall. "His body was stiff, and the blood had slowed. Once the rest of our soldiers showed up and pushed Paralia back, I was rounding up names of those we lost. I recognized him from where you fought side by side."

"You brought him here?" I ask, even though I feel I already know the answer to that.

Selene nods. "I kneeled beside him, my insides torn up at everything my actions had done to both our kingdoms. I grabbed his wrist and felt the faint pulse of life there."

Sighing, she continues. "Everyone else had already left to go back to camp. I panicked. If there was even a slight chance he could survive, could *live*," she hesitates. "I wanted to give that to you. To both of you. I called my horse over, made a makeshift pallet to pull him on it. It was... slow. I asked Rhea to evacuate for a few days so no one would know."

"You didn't tell anyone?"

She shakes her head. "Not even William. I stayed here at first, cleaned him up and gave him water and small sips of broth. I'm sorry for how bad the stitches look... that wasn't something I was taught how to do well."

I tsk at her, joking. "I guess you're not a very good General, then."

Her lips twitch. "I suppose not."

I look back at Callious, at the way his mouth opens slightly to breathe while he sleeps. My heart clenches. "I'm not sure I can leave him again."

"I'll stay behind. His fever broke a few days ago. He's stable even though he's weak. He's a stubborn fighter, Penelope."

I tilt my head at her, assessing what I want to do.

"He would mumble your name in his delirious state, calling out for you. I won't let anything happen to him before we can get him back home."

"Thank you," I whisper.

Floorboards creak behind me. "I think it's time we end this war. Don't you think so, Penelope?"

I turn to look at William, a small smile on his lips. He's nervous. I can just tell.

My eyes fall back to Callious involuntarily, as if he's my magnet. He doesn't stir, and his fingers are still laced with mine. I lean forward to press my lips to his temple, promising silently that I'll be back before he notices I'm gone.

Rising, I roll my neck, shaking off the stress that I've been living with. "Let's go."

☼ ☼ ☼

We ride in silence at first, the trail to the Janus Tree bathed in a soft fog. Mist clings to the peuko needles, curling around Agrius like smoke. I keep my eyes forward, William behind me, unsure of what to say.

He speaks first.

"You're right about me," he says. "I thought I could do everything. Save our Kingdoms, help Selene accomplish her only dream… placate the tension between our lands. But it was too much."

I stare straight ahead, surprised.

His voice remains steady. "I lied to you," he continues. "Multiple times. I made it seem like we were also in the dark about certain things. I used you, and I am so sorry."

"You care about Selene," I speak slowly. "You were looking out for her."

He shifts in his seat. "She's family. My father told

her the only way she'd ever get to fight is if I was called to war first. Stealing the jewel was the only way she could see that happening. And she was right."

William chuckles humorlessly, and I can feel his hair touch the back of my neck as he shakes his head. "I ignored how many people might get hurt in the process."

I nod slowly, letting the weight of his words ground me. "I shouldn't have assumed you had only ill intentions. The time we've spent together has shown me otherwise. But I was hurting. I'm sorry I expected the worst out of you."

We enter the grove soon after. The Tree looms in front of us, like it's been waiting for this moment. The branches and leaves are decaying more than they were last time.

William swings his leg down from Agrius, then helps me hop down. We face each other, and I study the remorse in his face.

"What did you want, before all of this?" I ask, searching his blue gaze. "What do you want *after*?"

He thinks, and the wind quiets as if awaiting his answer. "I want Paralia and Oresteia to coexist. I would like to be your *friend*, Penelope. If you'll have me."

I smile faintly. "I think that can be arranged."

"What about you?" he asks. "What does the girl without a crown weighing her down truly want?"

"Freedom," I answer quickly. "Space. A chance to live a life where I can choose things—who to love, where to go, what kind of person I'd like to be."

He's quiet at first. Then, "Do you think we'll get those things?"

His question pinches my heart. "I don't know. But I know this is a step in the right direction."

We face the Tree. William removes the dagger from where it hangs on Agrius. Together, we approach the worn roots, hard earth packed beneath our feet.

The Queen's Heart pulses faintly from the hilt, casting a slight glow over our faces.

William plucks the jewel from the metal, laying it in my outstretched palm. It's warm in my hand, as if humming with a life of its own.

I touch the bark of the Tree, causing the door to spring forward from the magic within. It's moving slower—sluggish, even. The amber glow doesn't radiate quite as vibrantly as it once did.

Taking a deep breath, I steady my heartbeat, focusing my eyes on a small nook cutout above the Tree. Its shape perfectly matches the size of the gem.

I motion toward it to William, and he nods. Silence overwhelms the grove as William places his hand over mine, guiding it and the jewel forward.

We press the light stone into the carved hollow bark, both of us touching the gem as we hold it there.

Nothing happens at first. We remove our hands slowly, making sure the Queen's Heart stays in place. A sudden wind rushes upward from the base of the Tree, lifting our hair at its ends and twirling strands around themselves.

Light bursts from the trunk, blooming outward in rings of color—emerald, ruby, gold, white. Roots pulse beneath our feet, making us unsteady.

The Tree blooms in front of our eyes, vines twisting all around, leaves turning a remarkable shade of green. They burst from every branch, glowing in a way that's impossible to ignore. I stumble back, nearly falling, breath caught in my throat.

William grabs my arms, holding me upright, using me to keep himself standing as well.

Quiet settles around us as it all stops, a soft humming coming from the bark once more.

Steady breaths rush back into my lungs.

William turns to me, a broad smile on his face. His scar crinkles under his eye. "Thank you. For believing in this, in me."

I hug him, quick and fierce, happiness making me giddy. "Thank you for trusting me."

He removes himself from my grasp, gently squeezing my arms. "Let's go tell our Kingdoms."

A feeling of overwhelming peace, soft and white as snow, falls around us like petals.

The war is over.

CHAPTER FORTY-EIGHT

THE RIDE BACK TO PARALIA'S PALACE IS OVER IN THE blink of an eye.

The air feels lighter, but still just as humid as it always is. I cannot help but look at the landscape differently. The worn-down dirt path, the stones that build up our home.

I used to think the shifting sands of Paralia were unshakable, but the world around me has changed.

I've changed.

My siblings are waiting for me as I walk through the grand front doors, bidding William a quick goodbye as he rejoins his father in the throne room, where talks of a truce must still be at play.

They're clustered together, eyeing me, their postures rounded and tight. I walk to them as if magnetized, and they reach for me collectively the moment I'm within arm's length.

Their words pour out in breathless fragments,

speaking over one another as they have a habit of doing.

"Is it true you walked through a magical Tree?"

"Did you find the lost jewel?"

"What happened in Oresteia? Did you really fight?"

Curiosity brushes against awe, but there seems to be something underneath it, too. Carter's voice rings out above them all. "Why did you leave?"

Worried hands still as voices quiet. They await my answer.

I gulp, palms itching as I wipe the sweat on my light pants.

"I couldn't stay," I respond finally. They push me for more answers, clearly unsatisfied, asking when I'm moving back in and if I'll be taking on larger responsibilities now that I've 'seen the world'.

Shaking my head, I try to push confidence into my voice. "I'm not coming back. Father renounced my title —there's no home for me here anymore."

Leila giggles a bit, eyes looking back and forth between me and everyone else like I'm crazy. "Surely after all you've done for Paralia, our King would welcome you back with open arms."

A chorus of agreement rings out, but I put my hand up to them. "Even if he did, this isn't the life I want to live anymore."

There's a pause. Eva crosses her arms, sneering. "You just get to walk away?"

"Yes," I respond with no hesitation. "And you could too."

I look at Everett, at the way he holds his head up high. He will be an incredible King once it's his time. But there's no need for there to be seven heirs in this Palace.

"You might not see it now, but only *we* can decide who we are and what we do. Being Frey may have shaped us, but our royal title doesn't own us. We have the freedom to choose who we become. I've made my choice. I hope you'll find the courage to make yours."

They don't respond right away, but I watch something slowly soften behind their eyes. Perhaps it's longing, maybe it's envy. Regardless, I have confidence that someday they'll understand what I'm saying.

Without another word, Ana wraps her arms around me, hugging me fiercely. The rest of them join in until we are all huddled together in a tangled web of limbs and tears.

It's the closest I've ever felt to them. A speck of hope blooms in my heart. Maybe after all is said and done, we could be friends.

I think I'd like that.

※ ※ ※

Camp is quieter now. Soldiers have made their way back home, both to previous places and new ones. Callious meets me just beyond the healer's tent entrance, his steps slow but stronger than they were a few days ago when we transferred him here.

He's been working with our physicians on getting

his strength and appetite back. It sounds like the sword that pierced him missed anything vital, and it might have been sheer will alone that brought him through the worst of it.

Cal's shoulder brushes mine as we walk side by side through the heart of camp—past the wounded also being tended to, the Kingdom's banners being lowered, the last of our weapons being counted and cleaned.

There's a strange beauty in the aftermath of something tragic—like the way the sea carves the coast. I know I'm luckier than most, still getting to hold onto the person I love at the end of it all.

"I keep feeling like I'm in a dream I don't want to wake up from," I say.

Callious nods. "I get what you mean. When I was on the brink of dying, everything was… soft. Dark. I don't know how I held on."

I grin, brushing his hand. "But you did."

He smiles back at me, full of love. "And now we get to live. Together."

I glance over Cal's body. At the dirt in his unruly waves, the bandages wrapped around his chest. Most of all, I look into those Neronian-green eyes—at the light that's still held there.

One might think with everything that's happened, that spark might dim. But to me, it feels so much brighter than it was before. He's not broken. If anything, it's made him *more*.

We stop near the Gate, about to make our way down the cliffs beside the Isthmus, when I see a horse swiftly approaching. Travel has opened up between

Paralia and Oresteia, though not *completely* undeterred. Trust is a fickle thing, and healing takes time.

Lots of it.

A white cloak trails the salty breeze as Agrius slows to a stop. There's no crown on William's head, but he's not dressed in a battle uniform either. He's just... *him*.

"I'm glad I found you two," he says, gaze flicking to Callious. "How are you feeling?"

Cal puffs up his chest a little, wincing in the process. I laugh. "Better than I was."

Blue eyes rest on me. "Maybe the news I come bearing will help the healing process go by quicker. I want to offer you something. Both of you."

My breath catches.

He dismounts swiftly, taking Agrius's reins in his hands. "Penelope, you are the bridge between our Kingdoms. None of this," he waves his hand. "Would have been possible without you. I know we still have a road to travel together, but I trust you fully. To be honest, to call us out on things, to *lead*. I'd like to offer you a position as Ambassador to Oresteia. But not just for the politics—for my people. For *our* people."

I blink. "You... what?"

"I need someone who understands both sides. Someone who can remind us what we nearly lost when we inevitably forget." His voice is steady, sure. "You don't have to say yes. But I believe in you and your abilities. You have so much to offer—something so unique within you that I can't help but see."

Cal squeezes my hand. Something swells in my chest as tears gather behind my eyes. I barely register what he says next, but the words land softly at my feet like a flurry of snowflakes.

"We nearly took too much from Paralia. From you," he chokes. "I'd like you to have the Eremos cottage. Both of you. As a gift."

I can't breathe. My mouth gapes at William. "But that's your place. You don't need to give that up."

He gives me a sad smile. "And I didn't need to lie to you either, but I did. Let me make it up to you."

I look at Callious, and he's smiling. Perhaps a little stunned, but more so amazed. We've talked about how I found his ring and how it got there. It seems our world has a funny way of bringing everything full circle.

"Thank you," I manage, my voice catching. "Really, William. Thank you."

He nods, taking a step back as he looks at the waning sky. "I might stay the night before heading back. Is that okay with you?"

"Of course."

With that, he walks away without waiting for an answer.

※ ※ ※

The wind picks up, pulling from the sea like a sigh.

Callious and I sit by a fire, huddled beneath a scratchy blanket.

His thumb brushes the back of my hand. "We've always risen with the sun," he begins. "I can't imagine not living beneath it. It feels... odd."

I tilt my head, contemplating as a silence settles between us.

"Perhaps the stars could have their moment too," I say. "What do you think?"

"I'd follow you anywhere," he responds, squeezing my arm carefully.

"That's not what I mean." I lean into him, breathing in his sea-breeze scent. The ocean breaks against the shore, again and again, as it always has.

He looks down at me, flames bouncing off his scarred face. "I know. But I'd rather ask you this: what do *you* want, Nelly?"

The fire crackles. A lone leaf flutters down from the tree above us. Somewhere far away, the Janus Tree lives. Somewhere far away, a new home awaits. I twirl Callious's ring around my thumb, remembering the four words.

Sight.

Sight to see what's most important. To truly know what matters.

"I want to help rebuild what has remained broken for so long," I finally say. "To be part of something that heals with time, while also living a life that's mine. Maybe more than anything, I long for space to breathe so we can figure out what we want our future to look like. Together."

His hand finds mine, fingers intertwining like they belong there. "Then that's what we'll do."

I rise at dawn, leaving him still asleep in his tent. Climbing down the cliffs to the shore, I sit and watch the sky as the sun emerges. Lavender colors burn into pink blush, the tide low and reflecting.

The sand is cool beneath me, and I think of the girl I used to be—the one who would have never dared stray from the path placed before her.

Oh, how much has changed.

Brushing off my knees, I make my way to a different tent.

I accept William's offer.

The Eremos cottage waits for us, snow turned into slush in some places. Boots crunch on ice as we step through the threshold, the scent of pine and lemon catching my lungs. Vines curl around the outside windows, as if holding the home dear.

This is where our life truly begins.

I place our bags down, both holding enough belongings to get us started. For Callious to heal. To build a routine. To *live*.

Later, when the weather doesn't hold as much of a bite, I write.

I write a letter to the girl I was, and the one I'm yet to become. It's a reflection on all I've learned, and all the hopes I have for the future.

Callious lays his head on my shoulder, slumped from travel. He lets out a soft snore, and I can't help but giggle.

Most of the battles I fought before this were silent ones. Feelings of not being enough, of being underestimated, of regret.

But even though I kept them tucked away in my

heart and mind, others still heard them. The people who care about me most *knew*.

Callious knew.

I have found a sweet sort of freedom in choosing to let love dictate my decisions.

And now, this life is finally ours.

CHAPTER FORTY-NINE

I ONCE BELIEVED THAT TO BE DRAWN TO LIGHT IS TO feel alive.

That to bask in the warmth of the sun is to feel at home.

Until Oresteia.

Before, Paralia had forgone feeling like home. I had longed to experience something new. I begged the sun to hide, so that I might experience the touch of rain on my skin, or the bite of cold air upon my nose.

And yet, the sun did not give in. Day after day, my bright star showed up and asked me to drown in its rays. My only reprieve was the night sky and the coolness that evening brought.

Now here I am, huddled in the warmth of a fire, surrounded by a snowstorm so violent it shakes my windows. I spend my time writing to my siblings about my antics, giving them a glimpse into my life here. Selene and I talk almost daily, taking walks around the city at night with our arms intertwined.

I recharge my soul by sipping on a mug of hot chocolate, lying under a blanket my mother made long ago to symbolize new beginnings.

The sun no longer soaks into my heart and skin, but the memory of its rays will never leave my mind. I still travel back and forth, after all.

I touch the necklaces hanging gently around my neck, the one gifted to me and the one left for me unintentionally.

Here, with Callious, I found a place where my soul can run free without the burden of forsaking change.

Here, in Oresteia, I found home.

EPILOGUE

Watching her live is like seeing the sun rise over the ocean—vibrant, full, steady.

She's constant, like the tide that pulls us in as we swim in frigid waters. When she's near, everything settles—rest to my endless storm. Her brown eyes catch mine with trust, something that only hard-fought battles can earn. Sunlight sticks to her skin like it's meant to be there, gracing Oresteia with its amber glow. Her short, dark curls catch the breeze, wild and free, just like she's learning to be. Her laugh is the familiar sound of waves hitting the shore; one I'll never tire of.

This place—Oresteia—needs her. It's as if it was waiting for her, just like I did.

If she were a story, I would return to her pages forever. If she were a song, it would be the only one to grace my ears.

I remind her every day that I see her—not letting a moment I was gifted go to waste.

And I think she's finally starting to believe me.

MISSED BOOK ONE?

Want more of these characters? Read *The Mountain's Crown* to explore the other side of Penelope's story. Out everywhere now!

ACKNOWLEDGMENTS

On a sunny evening in July, I finished my second full-length novel.

SCREAMS! Oh my gosh, from the first minute I started writing this book, I didn't want to stop. This side of Penelope's story captivated my heart in a way I wasn't prepared for. Somehow, I love this one even more than *The Mountain's Crown* (and I hope you do too!).

Still, writing a book is a daunting task, and I couldn't have done it without the community surrounding me.

To Hunter. This story was always for you. I can't wait to go celebrate with ice cream (many times over).

My ability to write creatively came from Jesus. If you don't know Him, find me. I will happily tell you of all the ways He's saved my life.

To my friends and family, thank you so much for allowing me to talk about this story. Thank you for *reading* this story! I'm so grateful to have people in my corner who are as passionate as I am.

To my beta readers: *I trust you with my life.* You helped me take this story from good to great, and I am so thankful for the time you took out of your busy lives to assist me.

To my arc readers: Your early reviews mean EVERYTHING to me! Every like, comment, share, post, and review does so much for an indie author. Thank you for supporting me in this way.

And speaking of indie authors... To my indie author friends... I love you. From late-night online writing parties, to asking (lots of) questions in the Instagram chat, to reading and reviewing and recommending each other's work. Indie authors make the world go round, and my world wouldn't be complete without you all in it.

I'd also like to shout out The Spark in Mooresville, for the way it's fueled *many* long days of writing, plotting, posting, and everything in between. I'll miss you dearly!

Finally, to my readers. Penelope's story is for *you*. I can't believe you read this book, or even picked it up. Whether you're just now finding me, or you've known me since I was little, or somewhere in between, you are welcome here.

We are all faced with choices, and those choices make us who we are. In the end, who will *you* become? I can't wait to find out.

Reading is both a safe space and home to my heart. I hope you find delight and rest in the words of these pages.

All my love,

Macayla Dawn

ABOUT THE AUTHOR

Macayla Dawn is a reader first and a writer second.

Growing up, she found herself drawn to worlds filled with demigods, fae, mystery and magic. The characters on those pages became more than just words in a book—they became friends. She is passionate about Jesus, grammar, fantasy, creativity, and ice cream.

In her free time, she loves to read (duh!), write, and explore different ways to express her creativity in all she does. She stays active through tennis, pickleball, working out, and walking with her husband and their dog. She loves to soak up the sun and host gatherings of all sorts.

Originally from Southeast Kansas, she now lives her dream life in Indiana.

Be sure to follow her Instagram and TikTok: @authormacayladawn.

Photograph taken by Hunter Redmon.

ALSO BY MACAYLA DAWN

The Mountain's Crown

Echoes of Elynia

www.ingramcontent.com/pod-product-compliance
Lightning Source LLC
Chambersburg PA
CBHW020007120726
47903CB00004B/1169